'Stan Nicholls has managed to continue the momentum in his *Orcs: First Blood* saga without making a false step. This is high fantasy for readers who like their heroes ugly and their wizards weird.' Jon Courtenay Grimwood, *SFX*.

'...the second book bids fair to achieve the same kind of success. Again, Nicholls brilliantly re-invents the Orcs, underdogs of fantasy fiction, and creates a dazzling panoply of wit, invention and violence. The humour is perfectly judged, and it's refreshing to encounter a fantasy writer clearly in possession of a fierce intelligence' Barry Forshaw, LineOne SF site (http://www.lineone.net/)

'Stan Nicholl's *Legion of Thunder* demonstrates a truly coruscating imagination in its outrageous narrative' Books of the Year, *Publishing News*

'Nicholls tells his tale briskly and entertainingly, and doesn't pull any punches when it comes to showing the hard and unglamorous life of military men (and women). It's refreshing to see things from the Orcs' point of view for once, and Nicholls has a different (often amusing) take on each of the elder races'. *Starburst*

D1586127

ORCS
FIRST BLOOD

Legion of Thunder

STAN NICHOLLS

The right of Stan Nicholls to be identified as the author
of this work has been asserted by him in accordance with
the Copyright, Designs and Patents Act 1988.

This edition published in Great Britain in 2000 by
Millennium
An imprint of Victor Gollancz
Orion House, 5 Upper St Martin's Lane,
London WC2H 9EA

To receive information on the Millennium list, e-mail us at:
smy@orionbooks.co.uk

A CIP catalogue record for this book
is available from the British Library

ISBN 1 85798 560 5

Printed in Great Britain by
Clays Ltd, St Ives plc

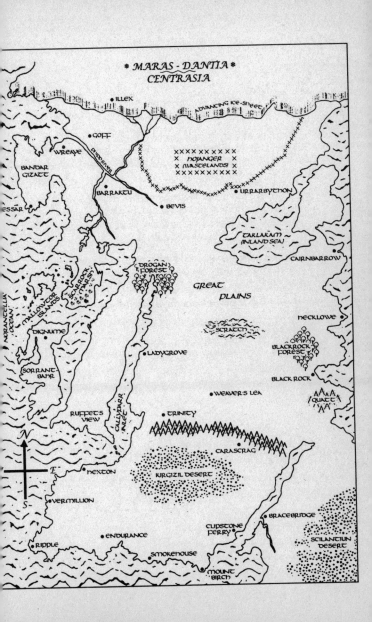

What Has Gone Before

It would be untrue to say that peace reigned unopposed in Maras-Dantia. In a land of manifold elder races, conflict was inevitable. But in general there had always been a measure of tolerance.

That balance was shattered by the coming of a new race. They were called humans and they crossed inhospitable deserts to enter Maras-Dantia from the far south. A trickle at first, growing to a flood as the years passed, the incomers had contempt for the cultures they encountered. They renamed the land Centrasia, and as their numbers increased, so did the destruction they wrought. They dammed rivers, denuded forests, razed villages, tore precious resources from the earth.

Worst of all, they ate Maras-Dantia's magic.

Their rape of the land bled it of essential energies, depleting the magic elder races took for granted. This distorted the climate and threw the seasons into disarray. Summers became autumnal. Winters lengthened, swallowing Spring. An ice field began advancing from the north.

Soon there was war between Maras-Dantians and the humans.

Old rivalries divided the elder races, complicated by the actions of the notoriously opportunistic dwarf population. Many sided with the humans and willingly undertook their dirty work. Others remained loyal to the elder races' cause.

But the humans were disunited themselves, separated into two factions by a religious schism. The Followers of the Manifold Path, commonly termed Manis, observed ancient pagan ways. Their adversaries rallied to the banner of Unity. Known as Unis, they were dedicated to the younger cult of monotheism. Both groups were prone to fanaticism, but the more numerous Unis had the edge in zealotry and no shortage of demagogues.

Of all Maras-Dantia's natives, orcs were the most combative. One of the few elder races not to possess magical powers, they made up for the lack with a ferocious lust for warfare. They were customarily to be found in the eye of the storm.

By orc standards, Stryke was smart. He captained a thirty-strong warband called the Wolverines. Below Stryke were two sergeants, Haskeer and Jup. Haskeer was the most reckless and unpredictable of the group; Jup was the only dwarf, indeed the only member who wasn't an orc, and consequently the object of suspicion. Below the sergeants were corporals Alfray and Coilla. Alfray was the oldest member and a healer, specialising in combat wounds; Coilla was the sole female in the Wolverines, and a brilliant strategist. Below them were twenty-five grunts.

The Wolverines served Queen Jennesta, a wielder of great magical powers who supported the Mani cause. A symbiote resulting from a human and nyadd union, Jennesta's propensity for cruelty, and her sexual voracity, were notorious.

Sent on a secret mission, the Wolverines stormed a Uni settlement to recover a very old, sealed message cylinder. Gaining the artifact, at a high cost in blood, they also seized a large quantity of an hallucinogenic drug. The drug had many names among the elder races but was widely referred to as pellucid. Orcs knew it as the bringer of crystal lightning.

Stryke's mistake was allowing himself and the band to celebrate by sampling it. Awaking the following dawn, they were panic-stricken at the prospect of returning late to Jennesta and facing her wrath. But on their way they were ambushed by kobold bandits, and despite a spirited defence the artifact was taken. Knowing Jennesta would exact a terrible *penalty for their neglect, Stryke saw no option other than pursuing the raiders and trying to retrieve the prize.*

Jennesta ordered General Kysthan, commander of her army, to organise a search for the Wolverines. He despatched a party of crack orc fighters under a captain named Delorran, who had long held a personal grudge against Stryke. Meanwhile Jennesta established contact with her brood sisters, Adpar and Sanara. Separated by distance, they were linked telepathically. But bad blood between the siblings prevented Jennesta discovering if either knew the whereabouts of the Wolverines or the precious artifact.

As he led the search for the kobolds, Stryke began to experience a series of lucid dreams or visions. They showed a world consisting solely of orcs, living in harmony with nature and in control of their own destiny. Orcs who knew nothing of humans or the other elder races. And in this dream place the climate was unaffected.

Stryke feared for his sanity.

Convinced the Wolverines had gone renegade, Delorran decided to extend the deadline he was given to find them. As that went against Jennesta's expressed wishes, it was a hazardous course. But Delorran's vendetta against Stryke drove him to take the risk.

Stryke led his band to Black Rock, the kobolds' homeland. The journey was perilous. They found an orc encampment littered with corpses, struck down by human diseases they had no resistance against. Later, near human settlement Weaver's Lea, the Wolverines were attacked by a Uni mob. Finally reaching Black Rock, the band exacted bloody revenge on the kobolds. They retrieved the artifact and released an aged gremlin prisoner. The gremlin, Mobbs, explained that he had studied arcane languages, and that his captors needed him to decipher the content of the artifact. He believed the cylinder might contain something that had a direct bearing on the origin of the elder races. It was the power of this knowledge the kobolds were after, though whether they were acting for themselves or others was a moot point.

Mobbs believed that what was in the cylinder had some connection with Vermegram and Tentarr Arngrim, two fabled figures from Maras-

Dantia's past. Vermegram was a mighty sorceress, and the nyadd mother of Jennesta, Adpar and Sanara. She was thought to have been slain by Arngrim, whose magical abilities equalled hers. Arngrim himself disappeared.

The passion Mobbs conveyed on the subject brought out a latent spirit of rebellion in the band. Opposed only by Haskeer and a couple of grunts, Stryke successfully argued that the cylinder be opened. It contained an object, fashioned from an unknown material, that consisted of a central sphere with seven tiny radiating spikes of variable length. To the orcs it resembled a stylised star, similar to a hatchling's toy. Mobbs declared it an instrumentality, a totem of great magical power long considered a myth. When united with its four fellows it would reveal a profound truth about the elder races, a truth which the legends implied could set them free. As orcs had known no other life than to serve and die at the behest of others, the prospect of casting off their bondage was appealing. At Stryke's urging, the Wolverines abandoned their allegiance to Jennesta and struck out alone. Their plan was to seek the other stars, reasoning that even a fruitless search was better than the servitude they had known.

Mobbs gave them a clue to the possible location of another instrumentality. His kobold captors spoke of Trinity, a Uni stronghold ruled by fanatical Kimball Hobrow. Stryke and the band travelled that way. Mobbs headed for the free port of Hecklowe, but ran into Delorran and was murdered by him.

Enraged at the lack of progress in finding the artifact, Jennesta had General Kysthan executed, replacing him with a much younger orc officer called Mersadion. The hunt for the Wolverines intensified.

The band fought off an attack by Delorran's group and escaped Jennesta's war dragons. Then Haskeer fell into a life-threatening fever, victim of a human disease. When they reached Trinity it seemed an impregnable stronghold until they discovered that the Unis brought in work parties of dwarves. Jup infiltrated one and got into the redoubt, witnessing first-hand Hobrow's despotism and the brutal antics of the settlement's militia. Establishing that there was an instrumentality in

4

Trinity, Jup also learnt that Hobrow and his cohorts were cultivating virulent plants as part of a plan to exterminate elder races en masse. He managed to torch the arboretum and made off with the star. It took the Wolverines several days to lose a vengeful Hobrow and his posse. Based on information Jup obtained in Trinity, the band made for Scratch, the trolls' forbidding homeland, where they hoped a further star might be located.

Having returned to Jennesta's palace after his unsuccessful hunt, Delorran paid for failure with his life. Impatient with her own minions, Jennesta employed the services of Micah Lekmann, Greever Aulay and Jabez Blaan, ruthless human bounty hunters who specialised in tracking renegade orcs.

Haskeer pulled out of his fever, though his behaviour continued to be erratic. At Scratch, Stryke left him and Coilla in charge of the stars while the rest of the band entered the trolls' underground labyrinth. They were soon attacked by the underworld's denizens, and Stryke and Alfray were separated from the others by a roof fall. Up above, seized by a fit of derangement, Haskeer made off with the stars. Coilla rode after him. Not knowing if Stryke and Alfray were still alive, Jup assumed command and had to choose a course of action in the face of hostility from the grunts.

Tumbled from her horse, unarmed and dazed, Coilla found herself confronted by the bounty hunters.

In the labyrinth, Stryke and Alfray were captured. Tannar, the fearsome troll King, prepared to offer them to his race's dark gods.

And the sacrificial knife he brandished had the third star attached to its hilt.

1

Death moved sinuously through the water.

Grim purpose set her face like stone. She dived deep, impelling herself with powerful strokes from splayed, webbed hands. Her ebony hair flowed free, an inky squid cloud billowing in her wake. Tiny threads of bubbles streamed from her palpitating gills.

She looked back. Her nyadd raiding swarm, massed ranks swimming in formation, was wreathed in an eerie green glow from the phosphorescent brands they carried to light their way. They held jagged-edged coral pikes. Bowed adamantine daggers were sheathed in reed halters criss-crossing their scaly chests.

The murk started to clear, allowing glimpses of the sandy ocean floor, peppered with jutting rocks and swaying foliage. Soon the beginnings of a reef came into view, white and craggy, smothered with purple-tinged fungus. She swept over it, her warriors in tow. They followed the reef's outline, moving fast just above its surface, and this close the corruption was plain to see. Diseased vegetation, and the scarcity of fish, bore witness to the creeping taint. Scraps of dead things floated past, and the unseasonable cold, near freezing the water, was greater at such a depth.

She lifted a hand as they sighted their goal. The troopers let go of the radiant brands, showering the seabed with an emerald cascade. Then they glided in to gather around her.

Ahead of them, where the reef's spine widened, was a stony bluff, riddled with hollows and caves, both natural and artificial. From this distance there was no sign of occupants. She signalled her orders. A dozen warriors separated and made for the enemy cluster, low and stealthy. The rest, with her leading, slowly brought up the rear.

As they neared the redoubt they spotted their first merz, a scattered handful of sentries, ignorant of the approaching advance party. She regarded them with loathing. Their resemblance to humans was only partial, yet she was disgusted by it. To her mind, this, as much as any dispute over territory or food supplies, justified making war. Halting the column, she watched as her scouts moved in.

Two or three warriors targeted each guard. The one closest was male. His bearing was careless, and it seemed he was mindful only of the odd predator rather than the threat of a sneak attack. He drifted, half turning, and confirmed her repugnance.

The merzmale's upper body and head were much like a human's, except for razor thin gills on either side of its torso. Compared to a human, its nose was more broad and flattened, and the eyes were covered with a filmy membrane. There was no hair on the creature's chest or arms. But it did sport a head of rust-coloured locks and a short curly beard.

Below the waist it differed radically from the human form and was closer in appearance to the nyadds. Here the milky flesh gave way to shiny overlapping scales covering a long, slender tail that ended in a large, fan-shaped fin.

The merz was armed with its race's traditional weapon, a spear-length three-pronged trident with arrowhead points.

Two warriors closed in on him. They advanced from the back and side, exploiting the sentry's blind spots, swimming at speed. The merzmale stood little chance. Levelling its barbed pike, the nyadd from the right struck hard, piercing the merz just above his waistline. The shallow blow wasn't fatal, but it served as a painful distraction. As the astonished merz turned to face his attacker, the second nyadd arrived at his back. He held a saw-toothed dagger. Snaking his hand around the enemy's neck, he slashed the merz's throat.

The sentry thrashed wildly for a moment, a crimson cloud billowing from the gaping wound. Then his lifeless body began sinking toward the seabed, trailing red streamers like scarlet ribbons.

Holding back with the main force, she looked on as her forward scouts tackled the rest of the guards.

Similarly taken unawares, a merz was being held by one nyadd as another used a dagger to puncture his chest. A female of the species, a merzmaid, spiralled to the bottom with a spear jutting from between her bare breasts. She fell silently mouthing her pain. Lashing out in panic, a merzmale swiped at a nyadd with his knife, forgetting that jabbing is more effective than slashing movements underwater. He paid for the lapse with a pike thrust to his innards.

Swiftly, brutally, the sentinels were efficiently murdered. When the last was overcome, the killers signed word to her through water tinted with a pink haze.

It was time to deploy the entire swarm. At her direction they advanced, filling their hands with weapons and spreading out. The silence was total. All that moved apart from the nyadd warriors was the guards' floating corpses.

The force had almost reached its goal when there was a flurry of activity at the honeycombed stronghold. Suddenly the edifice disgorged a horde of heavily armed merz. They made a strange sound as they poured out, a high-pitched oscillating wail that served as their language, a noise made more bizarre as it was distorted by travelling through water.

That was something else she hated about them. Now her loathing found a purpose.

At the prow, she led her corps to meet the unorganised defenders. In seconds, invaders and protectors were flowing into each other, the two sides instantly fragmenting into a myriad lethal skirmishes.

Merz magic, like the nyadds' own, was of the descry variety, and most often employed to hunt food or navigate the deep. It had little martial importance. This was a battle to be fought with brawn and skill, blade and spear.

Giving off its keening song, a merzmale swooped in from above bearing a trident. The triple spikes drove deep into the chest of the warrior beside her. Mortally wounded, the nyadd writhed and twisted so much that he tore the trident from the merz's grasp. He sank from view clutching the spear and leaving a red trail.

His main weapon lost, the merzmale drew a knife, a miniature version of the trident, and turned his attention to her. He lashed out. She avoided the blow. The force of the merz's action had its reaction, propelling him to one side and putting him into a half-spin. But he recovered quickly and returned to face her.

She swiftly seized the wrist of his knife hand. Then he saw that her knuckles were wrapped in leather thongs dotted with sharpened metal dowels. He made a desperate grab for her free wrist. Too late. Still holding on to him with one hand, she made a fist of the other and set to pummelling his midriff. At the precise instant she delivered the third punch, she released her grip. The power of the blow impelled him away from her. He looked down at his flowing lacerations, face wreathed in agony, and was swallowed by the chaos.

There were shreds of fishy tissue on her knuckle studs.

A movement at the corner of her vision made her turn. A merzmaid was swimming at her, pointing a trident. With a powerful surge of her muscular tail the nyadd shot upwards, narrowly escaping the charge. Unstoppable, the merzmaid sailed into a knot of the nyadd's followers. They speared and slashed the life from her.

All around, fights raged; one on one, group against group. Everywhere, pairs of antagonists were locked in the outlandish spiral dance, hands clamped to wrists, arms straining to plunge home a dagger. Grievous wounded dyed the water; the dead were elbowed aside.

The nyadd vanguard was fighting on the redoubt itself. Some were battling their way into its entrances. She made to join them.

A merzmale with blazing eyes darted in to block her. He held a toothed blade the length of a broadsword, with a two-handed hilt. To counter the weapon's reach, she produced her own blade; shorter but acute as a scalpel. They circled each other, oblivious to the mêlée on every side.

He lunged forward, intent on running her through. She dodged, batting his blade with her own, hoping to knock it free. He held on to the weapon, quickly rallied and plunged it at her again. A pirouette movement turned her from the blade's path. His outstretched arm was exposed. She struck out at it with a studded knuckle, managing only a glancing blow but still slicing deep into flesh. Her foe was preoccupied enough to let her follow through with the blade. It found his heart. There was an eruption of gore. Pulling loose the blade, she released a gush of ruby-coloured globs. Open mouthed, the merz died.

She kicked away the corpse and returned her attention to the storming of the redoubt.

By now her swarm was all over it. Many had entered to complete the slaughter. In obedience to her orders, the remaining merz were being brutally despatched and the enemy nest cleared. She swam past one of her warriors strangling a thrashing merzmale with a chain while another nyadd stabbed at the victim with a spear.

Few merz remained alive. One or two survivors had fled and were swimming away, but she was content with that. They would spread the word that colonising anywhere near her domain was a bad idea. As she looked on, the young of the merz race were dragged from the redoubt and put to death, according to her instructions. She saw no point in letting trouble brew for the future.

When the deed was done, and she was satisfied that the mission had been accomplished successfully, she ordered the swarm to withdraw.

While heading away, accompanied by her minions, a warrior beside her pointed back to the redoubt. A pack of shony were moving in to feast. These were long and sleek, with skins that glistened silvery blue. Their mouths were impossibly long gashes which in side view parodied a smile. When opened, endless rows of sharp white teeth were exposed. Their eyes were dead.

The creatures didn't unduly bother her. Why should they attack the swarm when they had an abundant supply of ready-butchered meat available?

Maddened with greed, the shony set to downing chunks of bloody flesh in great gulps. They stirred up fusty clouds on the seabed as they thrashed and snapped at each other. Several fought for the same morsel, teeth fastened, tugging at it from opposite sides. More scavengers swept in.

The swarm left the feeding frenzy behind, and in due course began to travel upward, towards a distant ring of light. As they ascended she allowed herself a moment's gratification at the fate of the merz. A little more decisive action and any threat they posed to her sovereignty would be nipped in the bud.

If only the same could be said of other races, especially the human pestilence.

They reached the mouth of a spacious underwater cave, its interior lit by nuggets of the phosphorescent rock. She entered at the head of the swarm. Ignoring the obeisance of the detachment of guards inside, she rose to a large vertical shaft in the cave's ceiling, which was also illuminated. The shaft came to a junction and branched into twin channels, like vast flues. Accompanied by two lieutenants, she swam up into the right-hand passage. The rest of the swarm took the left, to their billet.

Minutes later her party emerged from the water. They surfaced in an immense space flooded almost waist deep; permanently and deliberately so, to meet the needs of an amphibious race requiring constant access to water. The half-submerged structure was part coral, part crumbling rock. Overhead, stalactites had formed. To an untutored eye it might appear a ruin, with a portion of one wall absent and the others covered in slime and patterned with lichen. The smell of rotting vegetation hung in the air. But in nyadd terms it was an antechamber to a palace.

The missing section of wall afforded a view of marshlands, and beyond that the grey ocean, dotted with sinister, craggy islands. An angry sky met the horizon.

Nyadds were perfectly suited to their environment. If a slug had grown to the size of a small horse, developed a carapace like armour and learned to stand upright on a brawny, muscle-lined tail; if it had sprouted back-fins and arms with wickedly clawed hands; if its yellow-green hide dripped with tendrils and it had a head like a reptile, with thrusting jaw, mandible mouth, needle teeth and sunken beady eyes, it would have been something like a nyadd.

But it wouldn't have been like her.

Contrary to the nyadds she ruled, she was not pure bred. Her mixed race origins had given her a unique physiognomy. She was a symbiote, in her case a blend of nyadd and human, though the nyadd strain was primary. Or at least she chose to think it so. Her human ancestery was abhorrent to her, and none who valued their lives would dare remind her of it.

In common with her subjects, she possessed a sturdy tail, and back-fins, though the latter more closely resembled flaps of skin than the hardier, toughened membranes of her subjects. Her upper body and mammary glands, which were bare, combined skin with scales, the scales being much smaller than the nyadd norm and faintly rainbow-hued. Gill slashes patterned both sides of her trunk.

Her head, while unmistakably reptilian in aspect, was where her human heritage was most obvious. As distinct from the pure bred, she had hair. Her face had a faintly bluish tint, but her ears and nose were nearer human than nyadd shape, and her mouth could pass for a woman's.

She had eyes that were much rounder, and lashed, though their vivid green orbs had no comparison.

Only in her nature was she typical nyadd. Of all the sea-dwelling races, theirs was the most obstinate, vindictive and war-like. If anything, she had these traits to a greater degree than her subjects, and perhaps owed that to her human legacy too.

Wading to the breach in the wall, she surveyed the bleak landscape. Aware of her lieutenants hovering near by, antici-pating any need she might express, she sensed how tense they were. She liked tense.

'Our losses were meagre, Queen Adpar,' one of her lieutenants ventured to report. His voice was deep, and had a gritty quality.

'Whatever the number it's a small price to pay,' she replied, pulling off her studded knuckle straps. 'Are our forces ready to occupy the liberated sector?'

'They should be on their way now, ma'am,' the other lackey told her.

'They'd better be,' Adpar retorted, casually tossing the knuckle straps his way. He caught them awkwardly. It wouldn't have gone well with him if he hadn't. 'Not that they'll get much trouble from the merz,' she went on. 'It'd take more than peace-loving vermin to prevail against an enemy like the nyadd.'

'Yes, Majesty,' said the first lieutenant.

'I don't look kindly on those who take what is mine,' she added darkly, and unnecessarily as far as her minions were concerned.

She glanced at a niche carved in one of the coral walls. It housed a fluted stone pedestal obviously intended to display something. But whatever it was had gone.

'Your leadership assures our victory,' the second lieutenant fawned.

Unlike one of her siblings, who cared nothing about what others thought but expected absolute obedience, Adpar demanded both submission *and* praise. 'Of course,' she agreed. 'Merciless supremacy, backed with violence; it runs in my side of the family.'

Her attendants wore looks of incomprehension.

'It's a female thing,' she said.

2

Coilla was in pain.

Her entire body ached. She was on her knees in muddy grass, dazed and winded. Shaking her throbbing head to clear it, she tried to make sense of what had happened.

One minute she was chasing that fool Haskeer. The next, she was thrown from her horse when three humans came out of nowhere.

Humans.

She blinked and focused on the trio standing in front of her. The nearest had a scar running from the middle of his cheek to the corner of his mouth. His pockmarked face wasn't improved by an untidy moustache and a mass of greasy black hair. He looked fit in an unfit sort of way. The one next to him appeared even more dissolute. He was shorter, leaner, slighter. His hair was tawny and a near-transparent goatee clung to his chin. A leather patch covered his right eye, and his leering grin revealed bad teeth. But the last of them was the most striking. He was the biggest by far, easily outweighing the other two combined, but it seemed like all muscle, not flab. His head was shaved, he had a squashed, abused nose and deep-sunk piglet eyes. He was the only one not holding a weapon, and probably didn't need to. All of them gave off the distinctive, faintly unpleasant odour peculiar to their race.

They stared back at her. There was no mistaking their hostility.

The one with the bad skin and oily hair had said something, but she hadn't taken it in. Now he spoke again, addressing his companions, not her.

'I reckon she's one of them Wolverines,' he said. 'Matches the description.'

'Looks like we struck lucky,' the one with the eyepatch decided.

'Don't put a wager on it,' Coilla rumbled.

'Oooh, she's *feisty*,' One-Eye jeered in mock dread.

The big, stupid-looking individual appeared less smug. 'What do we do, Micah?'

'She's but one, and a female at that,' Pox Face told him. 'You ain't afeared of a little lone orc, are you? We've dealt with enough of 'em in the past.'

'Yeah, but the others could be about,' Big and Stupid replied.

Coilla wondered who the hell these characters were. Humans were bad enough at the best of times, but *these* . . . Then she noticed the small, rough, blackened objects hanging from Pox Face's and One-Eye's belts. They were shrunken orcs' heads. That left no doubt about what kind of humans she'd fallen among.

One-Eye was glancing warily into the surrounding trees.

Pox Face scanned the terrain too. 'Reckon we would have seen 'em if they was.' He pinned Coilla with a hard gaze. 'Where's the rest of your band?'

She adopted an air of sham innocence. 'Band? What band?'

'Are they in these parts?' he persisted. 'Or did you leave 'em back in Scratch?'

She kept silent and hoped her face didn't betray anything.

'We know that's where you were heading,' Pox Face said. 'Are the others still there?'

'Fuck off and die,' she suggested sweetly.

He gave her an unpleasant, thin-lipped smile. 'There's hard ways and easy ways of making you talk. Don't much matter to me which you want.'

'Should I start breaking her bones, Micah?' Big and Stupid offered, lumbering closer.

Coilla had been putting an effort into re-gathering her wits and strength. She centred herself, getting ready to act.

'I say we kill her and done with it,' One-Eye offered impatiently.

'Ain't no use to us dead, Greever,' Pox Face retorted.

'We get the bounty on her head, don't we?'

'*Think*, stupid. We want all her band, and so far she's our best chance of finding 'em.' He turned back to her. 'So what you got to tell me?'

'How about eat dung, scum sucker?'

'Wha—?'

She kicked out at him with all her force, the heels of her boots cracking hard against his shins. He yelled and went down.

The other two humans were slow to react. Big and Stupid literally gaped at the speed of her movement. Coilla leapt to her feet, despite the pain in her legs and back, and snatched up her sword.

Before she could use it, One-Eye recovered and piled into her.

The impact knocked the air from her lungs and slammed her to the ground again, but she held on to the blade. They fought for possession, rolling, kicking, punching. Then Big and Stupid and an enraged Pox Face joined in. Coilla took a whack to the jaw. Her sword was dashed from her hand and bounced away. Delivering a roundhouse punch to One-Eye's mouth, she twisted from his grasp. She scrambled away from the scrum.

'Get her!' One-Eye yelled.

'Take her alive!' Pox Face bellowed.

'Like *fuck* you will!' Coilla promised.

Big and Stupid charged in and grabbed one of her thrashing legs. She turned and swung at him, battering his head with her fists, putting all she had into the blows. It did about as much good as spitting to put out Hades. So she slammed the boot of her other foot into his face and pushed. He grunted with the effort of hanging on, her boot sinking deeper into his reddening, fleshy cheek. The boot won. His hold on her leg broken, he staggered backwards and fell awkwardly.

Coilla started to get up. An arm came round her neck and tightened. Gasping for breath, she drove her elbow into Pox Face's stomach, hard. She heard him gasp and did it again. He let go. This time she got as far as standing, and was trying to draw one of the knives holstered in her sleeve when One-Eye, mouth bloodied, crashed into her again. As she went down, the other two returned to the fray.

Still suffering the after-effects of her fall, she knew she was no match for them. But it wasn't in her nature, or that of any orc, to surrender meekly. They fought to pin down her arms. Twisting about to escape this, she found herself in close proximity to the side of One-Eye's head. Specifically, his ear.

Coilla sank her teeth into it. He shrieked. She bit down harder. One-Eye thrashed wildly, but couldn't free himself from the tangle of limbs. She tore at the ear savagely, provoking ever louder agonised howls. Flesh stretched and began parting. There was a salty taste in her mouth. With a final jerk of her head, a chunk of ear ripped off. She spat it out.

One-Eye struggled free and rolled on the ground, clutching the side of his head and wailing.

'Bitch . . . whore . . . freak . . .!'

Suddenly Pox Face was looming over Coilla. His fist came down several times on her craggy temple, knocking her senseless. Big and Stupid clamped her shoulders and finished the job.

'Tie her,' Pox Face ordered.

The big man hauled her to a sitting position and took a length of cord from the pocket of his squalid jerkin. Roughly, her wrists were bound.

Stretched in the dirt, One-Eye was still shouting and cursing.

Pox Face lifted Coilla's sleeve and took away her knives. He commenced patting the rest of her for more weapons.

Behind them, One-Eye moaned loudly and thrashed about some more. *'I'll . . . fucking kill . . . her,'* he bleated.

'Shut up!' One-Eye snapped. He dug into his belt pouch and found a piece of grubby cloth. 'Here.'

The balled cloth landed beside One-Eye. He took it and tried to staunch the blood. 'My ear, Micah,' he grumbled. 'The fucking little monster . . . *My ear!*'

'Ah, stow it,' Pox Face said. 'You never did listen anyway, Greever.'

Big and Stupid boomed with laughter. Pox Face took it up.

'It ain't funny!' One-Eye protested indignantly.

'One eye, one ear,' the vast human cackled, jowls undulating. 'He's got . . . the set!'

The pair of them roared.

'Bastards!' One-Eye exclaimed.

Pox Face looked down at Coilla. His mood changed instantly and completely. 'I reckon that wasn't too friendly, orc.' The tone was pure menace.

'I can be a lot more unfriendly than that,' she promised him.

Big and Stupid sobered. Muttering, One-Eye climbed to his feet and tottered over to them.

Crouching beside her, reeking fetid breath, Pox Face said, 'I'm asking again: are the other Wolverines still in Scratch?'

Coilla just stared at him.

One-Eye kicked her in the side. 'Talk, bitch!'

She took the blow and repaid it with another show of silent defiance.

'Cut it out,' Pox Face told him. But he didn't sound overly concerned about her welfare.

Glowering, One-Eye pressed the cloth to his ear and looked murderous.

'Is it Scratch?' Pox Face repeated to her. 'Well?'

'You really think the three of you could go against the Wolverines and live?'

'*I'm* asking the questions, bitch, and I'm not good at patience.' He pulled a knife from his belt and held it in front of her face. 'Tell me where they are or I start with your eyes.'

A slow pause and some quick thinking occurred. Finally she said, 'Hecklowe.'

'What?'

'She's lying!' One-Eye interjected.

Pox Face looked sceptical too. 'Why Hecklowe? What are they doing there?'

'It's a freeport, isn't it?'

'So?'

'If you have something to sell, it's where you'll get the highest price.' She made it seem that she was giving this out with reluctance.

'Hecklowe's that kind of place, Micah,' Big and Stupid offered.

'I know *that*,' Pox Face retorted testily. He returned his attention to Coilla. 'What have your kind got to sell?'

She baited the hook with a strategic silence.

'It's what you stole from the Queen, ain't it?'

Coilla slowly nodded, desperately hoping they'd buy the lie.

'Seems to me it must be something real precious to go renegade and upset the likes of Jennesta. What is it?'

She realised they didn't know about the instrumentalities, the artifacts she and the band called stars. No way was she going to enlighten them. 'It's a . . . trophy. A relic. Very old.'

'Relic? A valuable of some kind? Treasure?'

'Yes, a treasure.' She meant the word in a way he'd never understand.

'I *knew* it!' There was avarice in his eyes. 'It had to be something big.'

Coilla realised these bounty hunters, which was obviously what they were, could accept that the Wolverines had gone rogue in pursuit of gain. They would never have bought the notion of them acting for an ideal. It fitted their jaundiced view of the world.

'So why ain't you with 'em?' One-Eye butted in, glaring at her suspiciously.

It was the question she was dreading. Whatever she came out with had to be convincing. 'We had some trouble on the trail. Ran into a bunch of Unis and I got parted from the band. I was trying to catch them up when—'

'When you ran into us,' Pox Face interrupted. 'Your bad luck, our good fortune.'

She dared to hope that he at least believed her. But Coilla knew she was taking a risk if they did. They might decide she'd served her purpose, kill her and be on their way. Taking her head with them.

Pox Face stared at her. She braced herself.

'We're going to Hecklowe,' he announced.

'What about her?' asked One-Eye.

'She's coming with us.'

'Why? What do we need her for now?'

'A profit. Hecklowe's just about the best place to strike a deal with slavers. Some pay plenty for an orc bodyguard in times like this. Particularly for an orc from a crack fighting unit.' He jerked his head at the big man. 'Get her horse, Jabeez.'

Jabeez trudged toward her mount, which was grazing a little way off, unconcerned.

One-Eye, still fussing with what was left of his ear, didn't look happy. But he kept his peace.

To Coilla it seemed like a good time for token objections. 'Slavery.' She almost spat the word. 'Another sign of Maras-Dantia's decline. That's something else we owe you humans for.'

'Shut your noise!' Pox Face snapped. 'Get this straight, orc. All you mean to me is the amount you're worth. And you don't need a tongue to ply your trade. Understand?'

Coilla breathed an inward sigh of relief. Greed had rescued her. But all she'd done was bought a little time, both for her and, she hoped, the band.

The band. Shit, what a mess. Where were they? Where was Haskeer? What would become of the stars?

Who was there to help?

For a long, long time he had done nothing but watch. He had contented himself with observing events from afar and trusting fate. But fate couldn't be trusted. Things just got more involved, more unpredictable, and chaos loomed ever larger.

The draining of the magic brought about by the destructive ways of the incomers meant that when he finally decided to act even his powers were too unreliable, too weakened. He had to involve others in the search and that proved a mistake.

Now the instrumentalities were back in the world, back in history, and it was just a matter of time before somebody harnessed their power. Whether it would be used for good or ill was the only question that mattered a damn now.

He couldn't argue to himself any longer that none of it affected this place. Even his own extraordinary domain was threatened. With his abilities diminishing it was all he could do to maintain its existence, notwithstanding that his small elite of acolytes called him Mage and believed he was capable of anything.

It was time to take a more direct hand in what was happening. He had made mistakes and he had to try rectifying them. Some things he could do to help. Others he couldn't.

But he saw what had been, and something of what was to come, and knew he might already be too late.

3

The large, spherical chamber, deep in the underground labyrinth of Scratch, was poorly lit. Such light as there was came from innumerable, faintly glowing crystals embedded in the walls and roof, and from a few discarded torches scattered about the floor. Half a dozen ovals of pitch blackness marked tunnels running off from the cavern. The air was unwholesome.

Above two score trolls were gathered. Theirs was a squat, beefy race, covered in coarse grey fur and of waxen complexion. Incongruously, their heads were crowned with a mass of vivid, rusty orange hair. Their chests were expansive, their limbs overly long, and their eyes had evolved into vast black orbs to cope with subterranean darkness.

For all Stryke and Alfray knew, the chamber was only a small part of the troll kingdom, and these warriors a fraction of its population. But separated from the rest of their band by a rock fall, the Wolverine captain and corporal were destined never to find out. Their hands were bound and they stood with their backs pressed against a sacrificial altar. The trolls arrayed against them were armed with spears, and some had bows.

At their head was Tannar, the troll monarch. He stood taller than any other present. His build was brawnier than all save the orcs. Robes of gold, a silver crown and the long, ornate crook he bore marked his status. But it was what he held aloft in his other hand that mesmerised the captives. He brandished a curved-bladed sacrificial knife, and fixed to its hilt was the very thing the Wolverines had braved Scratch to find.

One of the ancient instrumentalities. A relic the orcs referred to as a star.

The trolls were chanting a guttural dirge. Tannar slowly advanced, intent on murder in the name of his fearful Cimmerian gods. Hardly crediting the bitter irony of their situation, Stryke and Alfray readied themselves for death as the chanting reached a mesmeric pitch.

Eyeing the dagger, Alfray said, 'Some joke fate's played on us, eh?'

'Shame I don't feel like laughing.' Stryke strained at his bonds. They held firm.

Alfray glanced his way. 'It's been good, Stryke. Despite everything.'

'Don't give in, old friend. Even to death. Die like an orc.'

A mildly indignant look passed across Alfray's face. 'There's another way?'

The dagger was close.

There was a flash of light at the mouth of one of the tunnels. What followed seemed to Stryke like an hallucinogenic experience brought on by pellucid. Something shot across the cavern. For a fragment of a second whatever it was left an intensely bright yellow and red trail line.

Then a burning arrow struck the head of one of the trolls standing next to them. Sparks flew as the arrow hit, and the impact knocked the troll to one side. His bushy mane burst into flames as he went down.

Tannar froze. The chanting stopped. A ripple of gasps ran through the chamber. The trolls turned *en masse* to face the tunnel. There was a commotion there. Yells and shrieks rang out.

The rest of the Wolverines were fighting their way in. They were led by Jup, the band's dwarf sergeant, laying into the startled enemy with a broadsword. Orc archers began picking off more targets with fire-tipped arrows. Light was anathema to trolls and the flaming shafts sowed utter confusion in their ranks.

As best he could with hands tied, Stryke took advantage of the distraction. He rushed at the nearest troll and delivered an orc's kiss, a vicious head-butt that buckled the creature's knees and dropped him like a dead weight. Alfray charged an off-guard troll and rapidly kicked him twice in the crotch. The anguished victim collapsed with rolling eyes and twisted mouth.

Tannar had lost interest in his captors and was bellowing orders. His subjects needed directing; their response to the attack was shambolic. The entire chamber housed a furious battle, lit by bursts of illumination from winging arrows and torches the orcs employed as clubs. Screams, wails and the clash of steel echoed from all sides.

A pair of orc grunts, Calthmon and Eldo, battled their way through the tumult to Alfray and Stryke. The prisoners' bonds were slashed and weapons pressed into their eager hands. They immediately turned the blades on anything that moved and wasn't a Wolverine.

Stryke wanted Tannar. To get to him he had to pass through a wall of defenders. He set about the task with a will. The first troll blocking his path thrust a spear at him. Stryke side-stepped, avoiding the lunge by a whisker, and brought his sword down hard on the spear. The blow sliced it in two. A stab to the bewildered spear-carrier's guts put him out of the picture.

The next defender came at Stryke swinging an axe. He

ducked and the cleaver whistled in an arc inches above his head. As the troll pulled back to try again, Stryke bought a second's grace by lashing out at his shin with a boot. The kick connected heavily. Unbalanced, the troll's next swing was wild, and well off its mark. Stryke exploited an opening and slashed at his chest. The blade cut deep. Staggering a few steps and spraying blood, the troll went down.

Stryke moved in on another foe.

Jup was employed carving his way towards Stryke and Alfray. Behind him, grunts were igniting more brands, and the light from them was increasingly affecting the trolls. As they covered their eyes, roaring, the band felled them. But many were still fighting back.

Alfray faced a pair of trolls trying to corral him with levelled spears. He sparred with them, his sword bouncing off the javelins' sharpened metal points. After a moment's to-ing and fro-ing, one opponent overreached himself, his leading arm exposed, and Alfray hacked into it. The troll screamed, let go of his spear and caught the full might of a follow-up slash to the chest.

His maddened companion attacked. Alfray found himself being pushed back as he batted at the menacing spear tip, trying to turn it aside. The troll was too determined for that and pushed on relentlessly. Alfray was close to being pinned to the wall. With the tip jabbing uncomfortably close to his face, he fell into a stoop then pitched to one side, fetching up next to the troll. He instantly aimed a blow at its legs. The blade sliced flesh, not badly but usefully. It sent the troll into a limping retreat, his spear slackly held.

Alfray leapt to his feet and swung his blade at the creature's head. The troll dodged to the left. Twisting to compensate, Alfray's blade turned in flight, so it was the flat, not the edge, that smacked against the troll's cheek. It yelled its pain and came in with crazy eyes and thrashing spear. The reckless move

suited Alfray. He evaded the weapon with ease, spun himself parallel to the troll and sent in a blow. The blade chopped halfway through its neck. A shower of crimson drenched the area.

Alfray expelled a breath from puffed cheeks and thought he was getting too old for this.

Slipping on blood underfoot, Stryke all but collided with the last of Tannar's defenders. This glowering troll had a scimitar. He proceeded to slash with it ferociously, trying to drive the orc away from his monarch. Stryke stood his ground and returned blow for blow. It was stalemate for a moment or two as each fighter parried the other's attacks.

The breakthrough came when Stryke's blade rapped across the troll's knuckles and laid them open. Mouthing a curse, the troll aimed a downward stroke that would have parted Stryke's sword arm from his trunk had it connected. Some deft footwork on Stryke's part made sure it didn't. After that he swerved and took a chance on a swipe to the troll's throat. It paid off.

At last he faced Tannar.

Racked with fury, the king tried braining Stryke with his ornamental crook. The orc was agile enough to avoid that. Tannar threw the unwieldy crook aside and drew a sword, its silvered blade inscribed with swirling runic patterns. He still had the ceremonial dagger, and prepared to work the weapons in unison. Troll and orc squared off.

'What are you waiting for?' Tannar rumbled. 'Taste my steel and wake in Hades, overlander.'

Stryke laughed derisively. 'You talk a good fight, windbag. Now put your blade where your mouth is.'

They circled, each seeking a flaw in the other's guard.

Tannar eyed the combat going on all around. 'You'll pay for this with your life,' he vowed.

'So you said.' Stryke kept his tone insolent.

The goading had its effect. Tannar roared in with a swinge-ing blow. Stryke checked it, the jarring impact he absorbed bearing witness to the strength of his opponent. He sent in a quick counterblow. The king blocked it. Now that their blades had met, the pair flowed into a regular exchange, attacking and defending by turn.

Tannar's style was all power and little subtlety, though that made him no less dangerous a foe. Stryke's technique was not dissimilar, but he had the advantage of much more experience, and was certainly nimbler. He also lacked Tanner's bluster, which showed itself in excessive feigning. Stryke laid on some extra provocation.

'You're soft,' he taunted, swatting aside a pass. 'Lording it over this rabble's spoilt you, Tannar. It's made you mushy as tallow.'

Bellowing, the troll charged at him, knife slashing the air, sword raking. Stryke braced himself and swiped, targeting the point where hilt met blade. He struck true. The sword flew from Tannar's hand, clattering beyond reach. He hung on to the dagger with its precious ornament and brought it to bear. But the shock of losing his sword had turned him leaden-footed. He hadn't a hope of besting Stryke with the knife and every move now was defensive.

The orc crowded him. Tannar began to back off. What he didn't know, but Stryke could see, was that Jup and a couple of grunts had got themselves behind him. Stryke hurried the pace of Tannar's retreat with a torrent of blows.

Jup seized his opportunity. He leapt on to the monarch's back and threw an arm around his neck. With his other hand he pressed a knife to Tannar's jugular. The dwarf's legs were clear of the ground and kicking. One of the grunts moved in and pointed his sword at the king's heart. Tannar thundered his impotent anger. Stryke stepped forward and prised the sacri-ficial dagger from his hand.

One or two trolls saw what was happening. Most were unaware and continued fighting.

'Tell them to stop,' Stryke demanded, 'on pain of your life.'

Tannar said nothing, eyes blazing defiance.

'Stop them or die,' Stryke repeated.

Jup applied pressure with his knife.

Reluctantly, Tannar shouted, 'Throw down your arms!'

Some of the trolls disengaged. Others kept on.

'Drop your weapons!' Tannar barked.

This time, all obeyed. Jup withdrew, but they kept the king well covered.

Stryke placed the ceremonial dagger at Tannar's throat. 'We're leaving. You're coming with us. If anybody gets in our way, you're dead. Tell them.'

The king nodded slowly. 'Do as they say!' he yelled.

'You won't need this stuff,' Stryke said, 'it'll slow us.' He snatched Tannar's crown and threw it to one side.

The impiety brought intakes of breath from many of the watching trolls. Stryke inspired more when he ripped off the king's elaborate robe and abandoned that in the dirt too.

He returned the dagger to Tannar's throat. 'Let's go.'

They began to move across the cavern, a knot of orcs and a dwarf surrounding the towering figure of their hostage. Dazed trolls stood by and let them pass. As the procession made its way to the main tunnel, stepping over enemy corpses, the rest of the band joined it. Several were lightly wounded. It seemed to Stryke that all the fallen were trolls.

At the tunnel mouth he yelled, 'Follow and he dies!'

Hurriedly they backed out of the chamber.

They made as good a pace as they could through the maze of unlit tunnels, their torches throwing huge, grotesque shadows on the walls.

'Nice timing,' Stryke told Jup. '*Tight*, but nice.'

The dwarf smiled.

'How the hell did you get through the roof fall?' Alfray asked.

'We found another way,' Jup said. 'You'll see.'

They became aware of soft sounds behind them. Turning his head to squint into the darkness, Stryke could make out dim, grey shapes in the distance.

'They'll hunt you down,' Tannar promised. 'You'll die before reaching the overland.'

'Then you'll be joining us.' Stryke realised he was practically whispering. To the rest of the band, he ordered, 'Stay together, keep alert. Particularly the rearguard.'

'Don't think they need telling, chief,' Jup said.

A minute or two later they entered the tunnel where the fall took place. Twenty paces ahead it was shut off by weighty boulders and rubble. Before they got to the blockage they came to a crudely cut hole in the wall on their right. The wall was thin, of shale-like material, and another tunnel ran behind it. They began to clamber through. Tannar needed prodding.

'How did this come about, Jup?' Stryke asked.

'Funny what you can do when needs must. This is that dead-end tunnel running from the entrance. Had the band sound the walls with hatchets. We got lucky.'

The new passageway took them to another chamber, not unlike a pit, that lay below the shaft to the surface. There was weak light above. A couple of tense grunts were waiting by a brace of dangling ropes. Peering up the shaft, Stryke saw the heads of two more.

'Move it!' he ordered.

The first band members started to climb. Tannar was stubborn. They lashed a rope around him and hauled him up hand over hand. He cursed all the way. Stryke was the last to leave, the blade of the ceremonial dagger clamped in his teeth.

A small cave housed the shaft. Morning light flooded through its entrance. Stryke and the others came out of it blinking.

Tannar covered his eyes with a hand. 'This is pain to me!' he complained loudly.

'Put this on him,' Alfray suggested, passing over a cloth.

As the king was blindfolded and led off stumbling, Stryke held back and examined the sacrificial dagger. The star was attached to its hilt with a tight winding of twine. He took his own knife, cut through this and discarded the dagger.

The star was recognisable as such but differed from the other two, as they differed from each other. In the light he could see that it was dark blue in colour, whereas the first one they found was yellow, the second green. Like the others it consisted of a round central ball with spikes radiating from it, apparently randomly. It had four spikes; they had seven and five respectively. The same incredibly tough but unknown material had been used to make it.

'Come *on*, Stryke!' Alfray called.

He crammed the star into his belt pouch and jogged after them.

The band headed for their base camp at speed, or at least as fast as they could with Tannar slowing them. They were greeted by Bhose and Nep, and neither grunt tried to disguise his relief.

'We have to get out of here, fast,' Stryke told them all. 'It might be day but I wouldn't put it past them to venture out for him.' He nodded at Tannar.

'Wait, Stryke,' Jup said.

'Wait? What do you mean, wait?'

'I've got to tell you something about Coilla and Haskeer.'

Stryke looked around. 'Where are they?'

'This isn't easy, Captain.'

'Whatever it is, just make it quick!'

'All right, short version. Haskeer went berserk, battered Reafdaw here and made off with the stars.'

'*What?*' Stryke felt as though he'd been poleaxed.

'Coilla went after him,' Jup continued. 'We haven't seen either since.'

'Went . . . went where?'

'North, far as we know.'

'As far as you know?'

'I had to make a decision, Stryke. It was either search for Coilla and Haskeer or try to get you and Alfray out of that warren. We couldn't do both. Rescuing you seemed the best use of resources.'

Stryke was absorbing the news. 'No . . . no, you're right.' His face darkened. 'Haskeer! That stupid, crazy *bastard*!'

'That illness, fever, whatever it was,' Alfray said, 'it had him acting oddly for days.'

'I never should have left him,' Stryke decided. 'That or taken the stars with me.'

'You're being too hard on yourself,' Jup ventured. 'Nobody knew he'd do something so lunatic.'

'I ought to have seen it coming. The way he behaved when I let him look at the stars, it was . . . deranged.'

'There's no point in breast-beating,' Alfray told him. 'What do we *do* about it?'

'We go after them, of course. I want us ready to leave here in two minutes.'

'What about him?' Jup asked, indicating Tannar.

'He stays with us for now. Collateral.'

The grunts broke camp at speed and the horses were readied. Tannar was manhandled on to one and his hands lashed to the pommel on its saddle. The cache of pellucid was divided up among the band members, as it had been before the underground sortie. Alfray found the Wolverines' banner and reclaimed it.

As Stryke moved off at the head of the band his head buzzed with possibilities. All of them bad.

4

Everything seemed so clear to Haskeer now, so obvious. The fog that clouded his mind had lifted and he knew exactly what needed to be done.

Spurring his horse, he entered another valley that would take him further north-east. Or at least he hoped it would. In truth his new clarity didn't extend to all his senses, and he was a little hazy about the precise direction in which Cairnbarrow lay. But he pushed on none the less.

For the hundredth time his hand went instinctively to his belt pouch, where he had the strange objects the warband called stars. Mobbs, the gremlin scholar who had told the Wolverines something about them, said their proper name was instrumentalities. Haskeer preferred stars. It was easier to remember.

He didn't know what the objects were or what they were supposed to do, any more than Stryke and the others did. But although he couldn't understand the stars' purpose, something had happened. Something that made him feel he had a kind of union with them.

They sang to him.

Sang wasn't the right word. It was the nearest he could come up with for what he heard in his head. He might have thought of it as whispering or chanting or the faint sound of an unknown musical instrument, and would have been just as inaccurate. So he settled for singing.

He could hear them doing it now, even while they were in his pouch and out of sight. The things that looked like a hatchling's idea of stars were vocalising at him. Their language, if that's what it was, meant nothing to Haskeer, yet he caught its gist. It told him everything would be all right once he got them to where they belonged. The balance would be restored. Things would go back to being the way they were before the Wolverines went renegade.

All he had to do was take the stars to Jennesta. He expected her to be so grateful she'd pardon the band. Perhaps even reward them. Then Stryke and the other Wolverines would appreciate what he'd had to do, and be grateful.

Leaving the valley, he came to a trail. It seemed to run the way he wanted to go, so he joined it. The track climbed to a rise and he urged his already lathering horse upward to the crest.

When he reached the top he saw a group of riders coming the other way. They were four in number. And they were humans.

They were all dressed in black, and each was more than adequately armed. One of them had the disgusting facial growth their kind called a beard.

Haskeer was too close to avoid being seen, or to turn back without them easily catching him. But in his present mood he didn't care about being seen. His only thought was that it was bad enough them being humans, worse that they were in his path. He wasn't going to tolerate anything that delayed him.

The humans looked taken aback at running into a lone orc in the middle of nowhere. They glanced around suspiciously for sign of others as they galloped towards him. Haskeer kept to the trail and didn't slacken pace. He only stopped when they blocked him, their mounts in a semicircle not much more than a sword's length away.

They took in his weather-beaten, craggy features, the crescent-shaped sergeant's tattoos on his cheeks, the string of snow leopard teeth at his throat.

He stared back, evenly, hard-faced.

The bearded human seemed to be their leader. He said, 'He's one of them all right.' His companions nodded.

'Ugly bastard, ain't he?' a clean-shaven one opined.

They laughed.

Haskeer heard them over the stars' beguiling song. Its urgency couldn't be denied.

'Are there more of your band around, orc?' the bearded one demanded.

'Just me. Now move.'

That set them laughing again.

Another clean-shaven had his say. 'It's you that's moving, back to our master. Dead or alive.'

'Don't think so.'

The bearded rider leaned in to Haskeer. 'You sub-humans are lower than swine when it comes to head work. Try and understand this, stupid. In that saddle or over it, you're coming with us.'

'Stand aside. I'm in a hurry.'

The leader's expression turned flint-like. 'I'm not telling you again.' His hand went to his sword.

'Your horse is better than mine,' Haskeer decided. 'I'll be taking it.'

This time there was a pause before they laughed, and it sounded less assured.

Haskeer gently tugged the reins of his mount, turning it slightly. He slipped his feet from the stirrups. A warm feeling began radiating from the pit of his stomach. He recognised the sign of an imminent frenzy and welcomed it like an old friend.

The bearded human glared. 'I'm going to cut your tongue out, you freak.' He started to draw his sword.

Haskeer leapt at him. He struck square, slamming into the human's chest. Locked together, they plunged from the horse's other side and hit the ground, Haskeer on top. Taking the brunt of the fall, the human was knocked senseless. Haskeer rained punches on him, quickly rendering his face a bloody, pulpy mess.

The other riders were yelling. One jumped down from his mount and rushed in with sword drawn. Haskeer rolled aside from his lifeless victim, scrambling to his feet just as the swordsman launched an attack. Backing off fast from the slashing blade, Haskeer wrenched free his own sword, levelling it to deflect the blows.

As they duelled, the two mounted riders jockeyed to take swipes at him. Dodging their blows, and the careening horses, Haskeer concentrated on the nearest threat. He drove forward, bombarding the human with a relentless series of hefty strikes. Soon he had his opponent in defensive mode, all his energy directed to fending off Haskeer's onslaught.

Ten seconds later Haskeer went into a feint, skirted an ill-judged swing and brought his blade down on the human's forearm. Still gripping the sword, the severed limb portion fell away. His stump pumping blood, the screaming human pitched headlong beneath the hooves of a rearing horse.

While its rider fought to disentangle his mount, Haskeer went for the other horseman. His method was straightforward. Snatching the reins he pulled down with all his strength, as though tugging a bell rope to warn of invasion. The rider was hurled from his saddle and smashed into the earth. Delivering a hearty kick to his head, Haskeer vaulted on to the animal's back. Bringing the horse about, he faced the last opponent.

Spurs biting into his mount's flanks to impel it forward, the black-garbed human met him. Haskeer engaged his whipping sword. They hacked at each other savagely, chopping, bludgeoning, trying to find a way through to flesh, all the while fighting to control their wheeling horses.

At length, Haskeer's stamina proved the greater. His continuous battering found less and less resistance. Then his strikes began to evade the human's guard. One scored, raking the man's arm and bringing a pained cry. Haskeer kept on with new-found vigour, dealing unstoppable passes, hacking like a crazed thing. The human's guard vanished. A well-aimed slash hewed inches deep into chest tissue. He toppled.

Haskeer steadied his new horse and surveyed the corpses. He felt no particular triumph at overcoming the odds; he was more irritated at having been held up. Wiping the gory blade on his sleeve, he returned it to its sheath. Yet again his hand unconsciously went to the belt pouch.

He was reorienting himself, figuring which way to go now, when his attention was caught by movement at the corner of his eye. Looking west, he saw another party of humans, also dressed in black, galloping in his direction. He reckoned there were thirty or forty of them.

Even in his battle-crazed state he knew he couldn't fight a mob of that size single-handed. He urged the horse forward and fled.

The stars filled his mind with their singing.

On a hilltop a quarter of a mile away, another group of humans watched the tiny figure riding across the plains, and a band of their fellows pursuing it.

Foremost of the watchers was a lofty, slender individual, dressed like his Uni companions in head-to-toe black. Unlike them, he wore a tall, round, black hat. The garment was a sign of his authority, though none present would have questioned his leadership whether he wore it or not.

His face was best described as resolute, and showed no hint of ever having been burdened with a smile. Greying whiskers adorned an acute chin, the mouth was a bloodless slit, his eyes were dark and brooding.

Kimball Hobrow's mood, not unusually, was apocalyptic.

'Why do You forsake me, Lord?' he ranted skyward. 'Why let the ungodly, inhuman vermin go unpunished for defying Your servant?'

He turned to his followers, his inner elite known as custodians, and berated them. 'Even the simple task of hunting down the heathen monsters is beyond you! You have the Creator's blessing through me, His worldly disciple, yet still you fail!'

They avoided his gaze, sheepishly.

'Be certain that I can take back what I have bestowed in His exalted name!' he threatened. 'Return what is rightfully the Lord's, and mine! Go forth now and smite the depraved subhumans! Let them feel the wrath!'

His followers ran for their horses.

Down on the plain, the orc renegade and the humans chasing him were almost lost from sight.

Hobrow sank to his knees. 'Lord, why am I cursed with such fools?' he implored.

Mersadion, recently elevated to commander of Queen Jennesta's army, approached a sturdy oak door in the lower depths of the palace at Cairnbarrow. The orc Imperial Guards standing on either side of it stiffened to attention. He acknowledged them with a curt nod.

Reflecting on the fate of his predecessor, and on his own comparative youth, the orc General applied an effort of will to control his nerves as he rapped on the door. He took a morsel of comfort from knowing that obeying a summons from *her* affected everyone this way.

From within, faintly through the solid door, came a response. It sounded melodious and unmistakably feminine. Mersadion entered.

The chamber was of stone with a high vaulted ceiling. There were no windows. Drapes and tapestries decorated the walls, some of the latter depicting scenes and practices he preferred not to dwell upon. At one end of the room stood a small altar, and before it a coffin-shaped marble slab. The purpose of these items of furnishing was something else he elected not to think about.

Jennesta sat at a large table. Scattered about its surface were candles that provided most of the chamber's light. The dim illumination gave her already outré appearance an even more bizarre aspect. There was something almost spectral about her.

Her half-nyadd, half-human origins meant Jennesta's skin had a shimmery green and silver glitter, as though she was covered in tiny scales. A face a mite too flat and broad was framed by ebony hair with a sheen that made it appear wet. She had an overly sharp chin, somewhat aquiline nose and ample mouth. Her striking, uncommonly long-lashed eyes were oblique, and seemed fathomless.

She was beautiful. But it was a kind of beauty observers were unlikely to have known existed until seeing her.

Mersadion stood rigidly just inside the door, not daring to speak. She was preoccupied, poring over ancient-looking tomes and yellowing charts. A massive book with metal clasps lay open beside her. He noticed, as he had more than once before, that her fingers were peculiarly long, an impression added to by lengthy nails.

Without lifting her eyes, she said, 'Be at ease.'

That was something no one managed in her presence. He relaxed a little, but knew better than to overdo it.

An awkward silence stretched as she continued studying. He leaned forward slightly to sneak a look. She noticed and her glance flicked up to him. To his surprise, instead of reacting furiously, as he feared, she smiled indulgently. Naturally that made him feel even warier.

'You are curious, General,' she said. It wasn't a question.

'Ma'am,' he replied hesitantly, mindful of her unpredictability.

'As you have many different weapons in your armoury, so do I. This is one.'

He took in the untidily piled desk. 'Majesty?'

'I grant it doesn't cut or pierce or slash, but its power is as keen as any blade.'

She noticed his blank expression, and added with brittle patience, 'As above, so below, Mersadion. The influence of heavenly bodies on our daily occasions.'

He grasped her meaning. 'Ah, the stars.'

'The stars,' she confirmed. 'More accurately, the Sun, the Moon and other worlds in their relationship to ours.'

He was losing her meaning already, but it was unwise to say so. He remained silent and hoped he looked suitably attentive.

'These,' she went on, tapping one of the charts, 'are a tool in our hunt for the Wolverines.'

'How so, my lady?'

'It isn't easy explaining to . . . lowly intelligences.'

He felt almost relieved at the casual insult. It was more in keeping with her style.

'The position of the celestial spheres resolves both character and coming events,' she explained. 'Character is moulded at the instant of birth according to which spheres are in the sky. The cosmic wheels turn slow and exceeding fine.' She reached for a scroll. 'I had the birth records of the Wolverines' commanders sought out. Naturally the lower ranks are of no consequence. Now I know the natal marks of the five officers, and thus something of their essential natures.'

'Natal marks, Majesty?'

She sighed, and he feared having gone too far. 'You *know* what natal marks are, Mersadion, even if you've never heard them called that before. Or are you going to tell me that the Viper, the Seagoat or the Archer are unknown to you?'

'No. No, of course not, ma'am. Sol signs.'

'As the rabble would have it, yes. But at its heart this discipline is far more profound than the rubbish mouthed by soothsayers in the marketplace. They degrade the art.'

He nodded, judging it wisest to say nothing.

'The . . . *sol signs* of the Wolverine officers give an insight into their personalities,' Jennesta continued, 'and how they might act in certain circumstances.' She weighted the scroll with a couple of candlesticks. 'Pay attention, General. Perhaps you'll learn something.'

'Ma'am.'

'The sergeant Haskeer is ruled by the natal mark Longhorn. That makes him bull-headed, stubborn, impetuous, in extreme situations inclined to savagery. The dwarf sergeant, Jup, is a Balladier. The warrior with a soul. He tends to see the mythic element in events. But he is equally blessed with practicality. The corporal Alfray is ruled by the Spanglefish. That means he can be a dreamer. He has a tendency to live in the past, and is probably conservative. He may possess healing powers. The female orc, Corporal Coilla, is a Basilisk. A spitfire, headstrong, given to reckless bravery. But also a loyal comrade.'

Jennesta paused long enough for Mersadion to venture a prompt. 'And their Captain, Majesty? Stryke?'

'He is in some ways the most interesting of this ragtag band. A Scarab. It rules the divine, the revelation of things hidden, change and the mystical. It also has strong martial properties.' She removed the candlesticks and let the scroll re-roll itself. 'Of course, these are just thumbnail sketches, and all are tempered, strengthened or weakened, depending on many factors.'

'You mentioned coming events, your Highness.'

'Our future paths are mapped out for us. For every action there is a reaction, and this too is pre-ordained.'

'So all is written beforehand?'

'No, not all. The gods have given us the wild card of free will. Though I could wish it were not so in every case,' she added darkly.

Emboldened by her apparent openness, he asked, 'What have your studies revealed of the future, ma'am?'

'Not enough. And to know more I would need the *exact* moment and location of their births in order to cast more accurate charts. Such details are not recorded for mere orcs.'

Mersadion kept to himself his reaction to yet another casually thrown slight.

'The precision of divination,' she said, 'is only found if your aim is on time.'

He looked baffled.

'Don't bother trying to understand. I can't say how the present situation will resolve itself. Not with assurance. But in the matter of the Wolverines I see no let-up in blood and burning, death and war. Their path is fraught with peril. Whatever it is they are trying to achieve, their chances are slim.'

'Will this help us to find them, your Majesty?'

'Perhaps.' She slammed shut the huge book. Dust motes swirled in the candlelight. 'To matters at hand. Has there been any word from the bounty hunters?'

'Not yet, Majesty.'

'I suppose that was too much to hope for. I trust you have more positive news concerning the divisions I ordered made ready for tomorrow's action.'

'Three thousand light infantry, fully armed and provisioned, ma'am. They await your word.'

'Muster them at dawn. I can at least take pleasure in bloodying some Uni noses.'

'Yes, Majesty.'

'All right. Dismissed.'

He bowed and left.

As he walked away from her chamber he began breathing properly again. In his short time serving as the general of Jennesta's army Mersadion had suffered many insults and humiliations at her hands. He had feared for his life on several occasions. But none of that matched the relief he felt at having survived an exhibition of her reasonableness.

5

Stryke got the band away from Scratch as fast as possible. He took them north, reasoning that Haskeer would most likely head in the direction of Cairnbarrow.

At mid-morning they slowed their flight, sufficient distance having been put between them and any trolls that might be in pursuit, even though Stryke was of the opinion that they were very unlikely to follow in daylight. Tannar was no help in verifying this. He refused to do anything but curse.

The Wolverines continued at a more measured pace throughout the day. All the while they searched for sign of Haskeer or Coilla, with scouts sent out ahead and from the left and right flanks. The lengthening shadows brought by dusk made their task near impossible, and there was a palpable atmosphere of despondency in the band.

More than an hour of grim silence was broken when Alfray turned in his saddle and said, 'This is hopeless, Stryke. All we're doing is drifting. We need a plan.'

'And rest,' Jup added. 'None of us has slept for two days now.'

'We've got a plan; we're looking for Coilla and Haskeer,' Stryke told them, his manner surly. 'This is no time to rest.'

Jup and Alfray exchanged mournful looks.

'It's not like you to act without a scheme, Captain,' Alfray responded. 'In a crisis we need a strategy more than ever. You've said that yourself often enough.'

'Then there's him,' Jup reminded them, jerking a thumb at Tannar, riding further back in the column with a grunt on either side. He remained bound and blindfolded.

Alfray nodded. 'Yes, are we going to drag that gargoyle around with us everywhere?'

Stryke glanced back himself and gave a resigned sigh. 'All right, we'll make camp at the first likely place. But we're not stopping long.'

Jup studied the terrain. 'Why not right here?'

Stryke checked for himself. 'It'll do.' He pointed to a dip in the landscape, where an easily defendable knoll had formed. 'There. I want double sentries posted. Tell the grunts to keep down the prattle. No fires.'

Jup relayed the order, minus Stryke's frosty delivery.

They dismounted. Swearing and cursing, the troll king was taken from his horse and lashed to the trunk of a nearby tree, its greenery turning to Autumn colours, months prematurely. The guards fanned out, but stayed close. Stryke, Alfray and Jup came together, and the remainder of the band gathered around them. With a wave of Stryke's hand they sat, many stretching exhausted on the mean sward.

Alfray wasted no time getting to the point. 'What the hell we going to do, Stryke?'

'What *can* we do that we're not doing already? All we have to go on is that Haskeer headed north. Chances are he's making for Cairnbarrow.'

'If he thinks Jennesta's going to show him any mercy, he really is crazy,' Jup said.

'We know *that*,' Alfray retorted. 'But as to him travelling north, I reckon he's too demented to be that predictable. We can't rely on it. He could be riding around in circles out there somewhere.'

'When we find him,' Stryke said, '*if* we find him, I'm going to be in two minds about killing the swine.'

'One mad orc's put us back to square one,' Alfray stated gloomily.

'And Coilla,' Stryke went on. 'Her not coming back's starting to look bad.'

'You're still blaming yourself,' Jup told him. 'You can't keep—'

'Of course I am!' Stryke flared. 'That's what leadership's about, taking responsibility, weighing the odds, foreseeing things.'

Jup snapped his fingers. 'Foreseeing things. *Farsight*, chief. I haven't tried it for a while. It might be worth a go now, yes?'

Stryke shrugged. 'Why not? We've nothing to lose.'

'No promises, mind. You know how low the energy was just about everywhere we've been.'

'Do your best.'

The dwarf moved away from the group, found a piece of ground a little more lush than the average and sat cross-legged. He bowed his head, laid his palms flat on the earth and closed his eyes. The rest of them ignored him. Stryke and Alfray carried on discussing their options.

A few minutes later he was back. They couldn't tell from his neutral expression if he had anything worth telling them.

'Well?' Stryke asked.

'Mixed. The power's definitely waning. But I picked up something. I got a very faint energy pattern I reckon is Haskeer's. Much stronger than that, I felt a female presence, and I figure it's Coilla. Both north of here, her nearer than him.'

'So maybe they aren't together. That's something we didn't know, I suppose.'

Jup's face clouded. 'Might not be good, though. Varying distance isn't the only reason you get one pattern stronger than another. Other things can affect it.'

'Such as?'

'Such as high emotions.'

'You're saying that's why Coilla's coming through stronger? 'Cause her feelings are more fierce?'

'It's a possibility, chief.'

'Good feelings or bad? Can you tell?'

'Could be either. But given what she's doing, I think it's less likely to be good, don't you? If the energy lines weren't so fucked up I might be a bit more certain.'

'Bastard humans, bleeding the magic,' Alfray muttered.

'This just confirms what we thought,' Stryke decided. 'It doesn't change my mind about pushing on northwards.' He turned it over for a moment, then addressed the grunts. 'We're all in this together. I'm for the north and seeking our comrades. Anybody got any better ideas? I mean it. I'll listen.'

Apart from some shuffling and blank faces, there was no response.

'All right,' he said, 'I'll take that as a yes vote. We'll rest a short while before moving. From now on our only priority is finding our comrades, and the stars.'

'Then all you'll find is your deaths!'

They all looked to Tannar, who had been more or less forgotten while they talked.

'That sounds like wishful thinking,' Jup answered.

'It is a prophecy,' the troll king assured him.

'Based on what?' Alfray wanted to know.

'My knowledge of the objects you call stars, which is obviously greater than yours.'

Stryke went to the tree and crouched beside him. Evening was setting in, so he took off the blindfold. Tannar blinked and scowled.

'Let's hear it,' Stryke said.

'Not until I am untied,' the troll demanded with regal arrogance. 'My limbs ache. I'm not used to being treated this way.'

'I'll bet you're not. But maybe we can manage it.'

'Have a care, Stryke,' Alfray cautioned.

'If this warband can't deal with one unarmed tunnel dweller we're in the wrong business.' He drew a knife to cut Tannar's bonds, then stayed his hand. 'Anybody know what kind of magic trolls have?'

Jup did. 'It's two-fold, chief. One part's to do with night vision. Darker it gets, better they see. The other's a sharpened ability to forage food. Rats, fungus, whatever it is they eat. Can't think either would be a threat. Unless he tries snuffling us to death.'

A ripple of laughter went through the band.

'That's what I thought,' Stryke said. He slashed the rope.

Tannar massaged his furry wrists and glared at his captors. 'I'm parched. Give me water.'

'Demands, demands,' Jup mocked, tossing over a canteen.

The troll king downed half the contents, and would have drained it all if Stryke hadn't snatched the bottle away. Tannar coughed, dribbling water.

'So what is it you know?' Stryke asked.

'My race has stories and legends concerning these objects. It seems your kind does not. Perhaps because orcs are rare among the elder races in having no magic. I do not know.'

'What do the legends say?'

'That these . . . stars are very old, and may have been created at the same time Maras-Dantia itself was fashioned from chaos by the gods.'

'Is there proof for this?' Alfray wondered.

'Yours is such a down-to-earth race. How could there be *proof*? It is a matter of faith.'

'Go on,' Stryke prompted. 'What else?'

'Members of many elder races have died and killed for the power the stars represent, as you are now. All that was long ago. Of late, they have disappeared from the ken of most Maras-Dantians. But they remain a part of this land's secret history, as tales handed down within sects and hidden orders.'

'So it's all yarns and moonfluff.'

'You must think it more than that or you wouldn't risk so much to find them.'

'We seek them because they're important to others with sway over us. That makes them useful in our situation.'

'They are so much more than bargaining counters. To see them in so lowly a way is to play with fire when blind.'

'We don't know anything about the stars' power, beyond the hold it has over the beliefs of others.'

'From what I've heard you say, they've changed your lives,' Tannar replied. 'Isn't that power?'

'You mentioned a secret history,' Alfray broke in. 'What did you mean by that?'

'Down through the ages these things you call stars are supposed to have influenced many great Maras-Dantians. They are said to have inspired the making of Azazrels' mighty golden bow, the sublime poetry of Elphame, the fabled Book of Shadows, Kimmen-Ber's celestial harp and much more. You've heard of *those*, no doubt?'

'Yes, even we've heard of those,' Stryke came back gruffly. 'Though in truth we're not much given to poetry, books and fancy music. Ours is more of a . . . practical profession.'

'*How* did the stars bring about these things?' Alfray persisted.

'Revelations, visions, prophetic dreams,' Tannar returned. 'The yielding of a small part of their mystery to those with the knowledge to extract it.'

While Stryke and Alfray were mulling that over, Jup had his own question. 'No one's been able to tell us what the stars *are*; what they do, what they're for. Can you?'

'They're a pathway to the gods.'

'A fine phrase. What does it mean?'

'The schemes of the deities are beyond the grasp of us mortals.'

'Another way of saying you don't know.'

'How did your star come to Scratch?' Stryke wondered.

'A legacy from one of my predecessors, Rasatenan, who gained it for my race long ago.'

'Never heard of him,' Jup commented dismissively.

Tannar scowled. 'He was a mighty hero of trollkind. His exploits are still celebrated by the songsmiths. They tell of how he once caught an arrow in flight, of how he downed fifty enemy single-handed and—'

'You'd do well in an orcs' boasting tourney,' Jup ribbed.

'. . . and of how he took the star from a tribe of dwarfs after defeating them in combat,' Tannar finished deliberately.

Jup coloured. 'I find that hard to believe,' he countered with wounded dignity.

'However you got it,' Stryke intervened, 'what are you trying to say about the stars, Tannar?'

'That they have only ever brought death and destruction unless properly handled.'

'By which you mean fed the blood of sacrifices.'

'You kill too!'

'In warfare. And we lift our swords against other warriors, not the innocent.'

'Sacrifice brings my race prosperity. The gods favour it and protect us.'

'Until now,' Alfray reminded him.

The king didn't try to conceal his displeasure at the gibe. 'And your hands are unsullied by the blood of sacrifice, are they?'

'Never higher lifeforms, Tannar. And mostly we sacrifice to our gods by going into battle. The spirits of those we slay are our offerings.'

'Maybe the fact that you've found more than one star in a short time means the gods favour you too. Or perhaps they're just making you the butt of a jest.'

'Perhaps,' Stryke conceded. 'But why are you telling us all this?'

'So that you'll see how important this artifact is to my race. Return it and release me.'

'Why should we abet you in more slaughter? Forget it, Tannar.'

'I demand that you return it!'

'Demand be damned. We didn't gamble our lives in that hole you call a homeland just to hand the star back. We need it.'

The troll adopted a conspiratorial manner. 'Then consider a trade.'

'What have you got to bargain with that we could possibly want?'

'Another star?'

Stryke, Jup and Alfray traded sceptical glances.

'You expect us to believe you have such a thing?' Stryke said.

'I didn't say I had it. But I might know where one could be found.'

'Where?'

'There's a price.'

'Your freedom and the star back.'

'Of course.'

'How would you expect such a trade to be carried out?'

'I reveal the location and you let me go.'

Stryke pondered that for a moment. 'All right.'

Jup and Alfray made to object. He silenced them with a slash of his hand.

'I have heard that a centaur armourer called Keppatawn possesses a star,' Tannar explained, 'and that it's guarded by his clan in Drogan Forest.'

'Why haven't you trolls tried for it yourselves?'

'We have no insane ambitions to collect them like you. We are content with one.'

'How did this Keppatawn get a star?'

'I don't know. What does it matter?'

'Drogan's a centaur stronghold,' Jup put in, 'and they can be mean about their territory.'

'That isn't my problem,' the king announced loftily. 'Now give me the star and set me free.'

Stryke shook his head. 'We keep the star. And we won't be letting you go just yet.'

The king was infuriated. '*What?* I kept my half of the bargain! You agreed!'

'No. You just thought I did. You're coming with us, at least until we know you're telling the truth.'

'*You* doubt my word? You stinking overlanders, you mercenaries, you . . . *scum!* *You* question *my* word?'

'Yeah, life's unfair, isn't it?'

Tannar began raging incoherently.

'You've had your say,' Stryke told him. He beckoned a grunt. 'Nep. Secure him to that tree again.'

The trooper grabbed the king's arm and started to guide him away. Tannar complained loudly of betrayal, of the indignity of being held captive, of having an inferior lay hands on him. He cast vivid aspersions on the entire band's parentage. Stryke turned his back on the scene to speak further with his officers.

A chorus of yells and expletives burst from the grunts. Tannar bellowed, *'No!'*

Stryke spun around.

Tannar and Nep were facing him, a couple of yards away. The troll had the orc in a neck-lock. He held a knife to the grunt's throat.

'Shit!' Jup exclaimed. 'Nobody searched him!'

'No!' the troll repeated. 'I'll not submit to this violation! I am a *king*!'

Nep stood stiffly, ashen-faced, eyes wide. 'Sorry, Captain,' he mouthed.

'Easy,' Stryke called. 'Be calm, Tannar, and nobody gets hurt.'

The troll tightened his grip and pressed the knife closer to the trooper's jugular. 'To hell with calm! I'm taking the star and my freedom.'

'Let him go. This serves no sane purpose.'

'Do as I say or he dies!'

Nep flinched.

Jup slowly drew his sword. Alfray took up a bow and shaft. All around, the band armed themselves.

'Drop your weapons!' Tannar demanded.

'No way,' Stryke replied. 'Kill our comrade and what do you think happens next?'

'Don't try bluffing, Stryke. You'll not throw away this one's life.'

'We look out for each other, you're right. But that's just part of the orcs' creed. The rest of it is one on one, all on one. If we can't protect, we avenge.'

Alfray notched an arrow and levelled his bow. Several grunts did the same. Nep contorted, trying to make himself less of a target. Tannar grimly hung on to him.

'You can come out of this alive,' Stryke said, 'and see Scratch again. Just throw down the knife.'

'And the star?'

'You've had my answer on that.'

'Then damn your eyes, all of you!'

He made to drag the knife's edge across the grunt's neck. Nep twisted violently, his head instinctively moving forward and down. Alfray loosed his shaft. The arrow skimmed the troll's cheek, gouging flesh, and soared onward. Tannar roared and let go of Nep. The grunt dropped and half ran, half scrambled away, hand to streaming neck.

Two more arrows slammed into Tannar's chest. He staggered under the impact but didn't go down. Slashing the air with his knife and yelling incomprehensibly, he managed to take a few steps in the band's direction.

Tearing his sword from his scabbard, Stryke rushed in and finished the job with a heavy backhand swipe to the king's vitals. Open-mouthed, the troll monarch collapsed.

Stryke nudged him with a boot. There was no doubt.

Alfray was examining Nep's wound. 'You were lucky,' he pronounced, applying a cloth to sop the blood, 'it's superficial. Keep this tight against it.'

He and Jup went over to Stryke. They regarded the body.

'How could he be so *stupid* as to think you'd go for a deal like that?' Jup wondered.

'I don't know. Arrogance? He was used to absolute rule, having everything he said taken as perfect truth. That's bad for any elder racer. Softens the brain.'

'You mean he's talked shit all his life with nobody to gainsay him. Maybe he just couldn't get out of the habit with us.'

'Total power seems to be a kind of insanity in itself.'

'The more I see of rulers, the more I agree with you. Aren't there any *benevolent* dictators left?'

'So now we've added regicide to the list,' Alfray said.

Stryke glanced at him. 'What?'

'Murder of a monarch.'

'It's hardly murder,' Jup suggested. 'More tyranacide, I'd say. That means—'

'I figured what it means,' Stryke informed him.

'Now we've made another set of enemies in the trolls,' the dwarf added.

Stryke sheathed his blade. 'We've made so many another

bunch won't make much difference. Get a hole dug for him, will you?'

Jup nodded. 'Then north?'

'North.'

It was unusual to find a dry spot anywhere in Adpar's realm. Given nyadd physiology, a dearth of water made no more sense than an absence of air. For creatures even more liquid-dependent, like merz, a lack of water inevitably lead to a lack of life. Albeit slowly.

The one place in Adpar's citadel where waterless conditions held sway was the holding area for prisoners, which due to the nature of her rule was rarely occupied for long. Not that she saw that fact as a reason to make it any less unpleasant. Particularly when information was required from the occupants.

Liking to take a hand in such things, she accompanied warders to the cell of two merzmale captives taken after a recent raid. They were spread, chained, upon dusty rock slabs in their arid cells, and had already been given a beating. For the best part of a day moisture had been denied them.

Adpar dismissed the guards and let herself be seen by the prisoners. Their rheumy eyes widened at sight of her, their flaking lips quivered.

'You know what it is we want,' she intoned, her voice soft and bordering the seductive. 'Just tell me where the remaining redoubts are to be found and you can put an end to your suffering.'

Their refusal, croaked from parched throats, was no less than she expected, or in truth hoped for. There had to be a sense of achievement or these visits weren't worth making.

'Bravery can sometimes be misplaced,' she argued reasonably. 'We'll find what we need to know sooner or later whether you help us or not. Why undergo the torment?'

One cursed her, rasping; the other shook his head, painfully slow, dehydrated skin flaking.

Adpar produced the water bottle and turned uncorking it into something like an erotic display. 'Are you sure?' she taunted. She drank, deep and long, allowing the liquid to dribble and gush from either side of her mouth as she did so.

Again they refused to treat with her, though the longing in their eyes grew ever more rapacious.

She took up a fluffy sponge, saturated it and squeezed its contents over her head and body, luxuriating sensuously in the drenching. Silver droplets glistened on her scaly skin.

They ran blackened tongues around barren lips and still refused her.

Adpar soaked the sponge again.

It turned out to be two hours well spent, both in terms of the information they gave up and the pleasure she derived from extracting it.

She made a show of taking the bottle and sponge with her when she left. The despairing expressions they wore added a final *frisson* to her enjoyment.

The guards were waiting outside the cell. 'Let them desiccate,' she said.

6

The band resumed their journey before first light. They veered north-east, still working on the assumption that Haskeer was making for Cairnbarrow. And they clung to the hope that Coilla was somewhere between him and them.

They were on the upper great plains now, an area where cover was less plentiful, so even more care had to be taken. But occasionally they encountered copses and other clusters of trees, and the trail they currently followed wound into a wood. Alive to the possibility of danger, Stryke ordered two advance scouts to be sent forward, and a pair were sent out on either side.

As they entered the trees, Jup said, 'Shouldn't we be thinking about what happens if we haven't found Coilla and Haskeer? By the time we're in sight of Cairnbarrow, I mean. We're hardly going to get a warm reception there, Stryke.'

'I think it'd be *very* warm. But I don't know the answer to your question, Jup. To be honest, I've been starting to fear they might have veered off in a totally different direction.'

Alfray nodded. 'That's in my mind, too. If they have, we could spend our lives looking for them just in these parts. And if they've moved on to somewhere else completely . . .'

'That doesn't bear dwelling on,' Stryke told him.

'Well, we'd better. Unless you plan on us chasing our own tails for ever.'

'Look, Alfray, I don't know any more than you do what we're—'

There was a disturbance at their right. The greenery shook, branches cracked, leaves fell. Smaller trees were pitched aside. Something bulky began crashing its way out of the wood.

Stryke pulled back on his reins. The column halted. Swords were drawn.

A creature emerged. Its grey body resembled that of a horse, but it was bigger even than a war charger, and it walked on clawed feet, not hooves. Powerful muscles rippled beneath its hide. Its neck was elongated like a serpent's, and a woolly black mane ran along the back of it. The head was almost pure griffin, with a feline nose, a yellow, horny beak and upswept fur-trimmed ears.

They saw too that it was young, nowhere near full-grown, and that one of its sinewy wings was broken and hung limp at its side. Which was why, despite its obvious panic, the animal wasn't flying. Notwithstanding its mass it moved with surprising speed.

Crossing their path, the hippogryph whipped its head round to look at them. They caught of glimpse of enormous green eyes. Then it plunged into the trees on the opposite side and was gone.

Several of the orcs' mounts reared and snorted.

'Look at it go!' Jup exclaimed.

'Yes, but *why*?' Alfray cautioned.

A heartbeat later the two right-flank scouts tore out of the woods. They were yelling but the words were unclear. One of them pointed back the way they'd come.

Alfray peered into the trees. 'Stryke, I think—'

Dozens of figures exploded on to the trail. The foremost

were mounted, the second rank on foot. They were humans, every one of them dressed in black and heavily armed.

'Shit,' Jup gasped.

For an eternal second the two sides gaped at each other. Then the spell was broken. Mutual shock evaporated.

Wheeling about, the humans started yelling and moved in to attack.

'We're outnumbered two to one!' Alfray cried.

Stryke raised his sword. 'So let's cut down the odds! *No quarter!*'

The black garbed horsemen charged. Stryke dug his mount's flanks and led the band to meet them. Orcs and humans clashed with a roar and the sound of ringing steel.

Stryke barrelled into the foremost rider. The man flourished a broadsword, slicing the air as he leaned out to engage the orc's blade. Their swords impacted twice before Stryke got under the other's guard and hewed him at the waist. The human pitched to the ground. His empty horse ploughed into the enemy at its rear, adding to the confusion.

The human who took the fallen man's place confirmed Stryke's suspicion of easy victories. This was a much more formidable opponent. He was armed with a double-headed axe, and handled it with practised skill. They exchanged one or two blows. After that, Stryke tried to avoid his blade coming into contact with the axe, lest the heavier weapon snap it.

As they manoeuvred for advantage, Stryke's sword collided with the axe's wooden shank, splintering a notch. It didn't noticeably slow the wielder. But soon the effort of swinging the cumbersome axe did. The man's movements grew leaden, his reactions more prolonged. Not greatly, just enough to give Stryke a precious edge.

The marginal speed advantage allowed Stryke to send in a low pass. It ripped open the human's thigh. He stayed in the saddle, but the pain served to throw him off his balance mentally. His defence went to pieces. Stryke targeted a stroke at his upper chest and it landed true. The human dropped his axe. His hands went to the gushing wound and he doubled over. Bolting, his horse carried him out of range.

A third antagonist instantly filled the void. Stryke commenced fencing again.

Alfray found himself having to deal with a rider on one side and a footsoldier on the other. The human on foot was the greater danger. Alfray took care of him by driving the pointed spar of the Wolverine's banner into his chest. He went down, taking the lance and banner with him. Alfray turned his attention to the horseman. Their swords crossed. On the third strike the human's blade was dashed from his grasp. A length of cold steel to the stomach put an end to him.

Clutching a short spear, another footsoldier tackled Alfray, who rained blows down on him. The spear was sliced in two, and before he could dodge, his skull was cleaved.

Individual fights boiled across and along the trail. A number of humans were trying to get round either side of the band and outflank them. Battling ferociously, the grunts held them back.

Finishing off a mounted human with a sword thrust, Jup didn't notice a footsoldier arriving at his side. The man reached up, seized the dwarf's leg and pulled him from his horse. Jup hit the ground heavily. Looming over him, the human raised his sword to deliver a death blow. Jup gathered his wits just in time to roll from it. Surprised in his dazed state to find he was still clutching his sword, he used it to chop at the human's legs. Hamstrung and screaming, the man collapsed. Jup buried the sword in his ribcage.

Being on foot in such a tumult was unwise. Jup looked around frantically for a horse to mount. That ambition was delayed by a rider singling him out as easy prey. Stretching down from his saddle, the man hacked at him. Jup lifted his sword and began parrying blows. As much by chance as design, he hit lucky and knocked away his foe's blade. Leaping to his feet, Jup slashed upwards with all the force he could muster, inflicting a wound in the human's side. The man fell. Jup took his horse and rejoined the fray.

An arrow whistled past Stryke's shoulder. Its source was one of two human archers further along the trail. Between batting off opponents' advances, he saw the pair of Wolverine forward scouts returning. They galloped up behind the human bowmen and laid about them. Taken unawares, the archers succumbed. Stryke renewed his onslaught.

With a footsoldier attacking from each side of his mount, Alfray had his work cut out. Fending off one then turning to fight the other was exhausting. But they had hold of his horse's trailing reins and left him no option.

Jup hastened in to even the odds. He tackled the human on Alfray's left, chopping his blade deep into the man's shoulder. Alfray himself concentrated on the remaining attacker. He was on the point of besting him when the two left flank scouts, alerted by the uproar, rode in to help. They made short work of the chore.

Stryke parted a human's head from his shoulders with a powerful two-handed swipe. As the lifeless corpse dropped, he looked for his next opponent. But those still alive were retreating. Five or six, on foot and horseback, fled into the woods. Stryke yelled an order and a bunch of grunts rode off after them.

He went to Alfray, who was pulling the banner lance from the dead human's chest.

'How do you figure our casualties?' Stryke asked.

'No fatalities, far as I can tell.' He was panting. 'We were lucky.'

'They weren't fighters. Not full-time anyway.'

Jup joined them. 'Think they were after us, Captain?'

'No. A hunting party, I reckon.'

'I've heard humans hunt for pleasure, not just food.'

'That's *barbaric*,' Alfray said, wiping blood from his face with the back of a sleeve.

'But typical of the race,' Stryke judged.

Grunts were already searching the enemy corpses, taking weapons and anything else useful.

'What do you think they were?' Alfray wondered. 'Unis? Manis?'

Jup went to the nearest body and examined it. 'Unis. Don't the black outfits jog your memory? Kimball Hobrow's guardians. From Trinity.'

'You sure?' Stryke said.

'I saw more of them than you did, and up close. I'm sure.'

Alfray stared at the body. 'I thought we'd shaken off those maniacs.'

'We shouldn't be surprised we haven't,' Stryke replied. 'They're fanatics, and we took their star. Seems nobody's too keen on letting us get away with that.' The grunts despatched after the fleeing humans came back, holding up their bloodied swords in triumph. 'At least there's fewer of them now,' he added.

Jup came away from the body. 'Could they have taken Coilla and Haskeer?'

Stryke shrugged. 'Who knows?'

A grunt ran to them holding a piece of rolled parchment. He handed it to Stryke. 'Found this, sir. Thought it might be important.'

Stryke unrolled it and showed it to Alfray and Jup. Unlike the grunts, they could read, to varying levels of proficiency. Their task was made easier by it being in universal script.

'It's about us!' Jup blurted.

'I think the whole band should hear this,' Stryke decided.

He called them all over, then asked Alfray to read it out.

'This seems to be a copy of a proclamation,' Alfray explained, 'and it bears a likeness of Jennesta's seal. The heart of it reads: "Be it known that by order of . . ." well, by order of Jennesta, that, er, ". . . the orc warband attached to Her Majesty's horde, and known as the Wolverines, are henceforth to be regarded as renegades and outlaws, and are no longer afforded the protection of this realm. Be it further known that a bounty of such precious coin, pellucid or land as may be appropriate will be paid upon production of the heads of the band's officers. To wit . . ." The names of the five officers follow that bit. Let's see. It goes on, "Furthermore, a reward proportionate to their rank shall be paid for the return, dead or alive, of the band's common troopers, answering to the names . . ." Then it lists all the grunts. Even the comrades we've lost. It ends, "Be it known that any harbouring said outlaws . . ." The usual sort of thing.'

He gave the scroll back to Stryke.

A pall of silence had descended over everyone present. Stryke broke it. 'Well, this only bears out what most of us suspected, doesn't it?'

'It's kind of a shock to have it confirmed,' Jup commented dismally.

Alfray indicated the slain guardians. 'Doesn't this mean they were looking for us, Stryke?'

'Yes and no. I think we just blundered into each other this time. Though they must be in these parts because of their master, Hobrow, and the star we took. But plenty *will* be seeking us for the reward.' He sighed. 'So. A moving target is hardest to hit. Let's get on.'

As they rode out of the wood, Jup said, 'Still, look on the bright side. For the first time in my life I'm worth something. Pity it's only if I'm dead.'

Stryke smiled. 'Look.' He pointed. To the west, far off, the hippogryph was making its way across the plain. 'At least he escaped.'

Alfray nodded sagely. 'Yes. Shame he won't live much longer.'

'Thank you very much for that thought,' Jup told him.

They rode for another three or four hours, moving in a great circular sweep as they continued the fruitless search for their fellow band members. To make things worse, they hit a pocket of inclement weather. It was colder. Showers of icy rain and biting squalls came and went unpredictably. The damp, miserable atmosphere did little to lift the Wolverines' morale.

For Stryke it was a time of reflection, and at length he made a decision, though what he settled on went against the grain. He halted the column by a grassy hillock. The advance and outflank guards were called in.

He urged his horse to the crest of the rise, the better to address them all. 'I've decided on a different course of action,' he began without preamble, 'and I reckon we're best starting on it now.'

There was a low-key rumble of anticipation from the ranks.

'We've been running around like headless rocs looking for Haskeer and Coilla,' he went on. 'There's a bounty on us, and there might even be others after the stars. All hands are turned against us now. We have no friends, no allies. It's time to take another tack.'

He scanned their rapt faces. Whatever they expected, it wasn't what he said next. 'We're going to split the band.'

That brought a general outcry.

'*Why*, Stryke?' Jup shouted.

'You said we'd never do that,' Alfray added.

Stryke's raised hands, and the expression on his face killed their racket. '*Hear me!*' he bellowed. 'I don't mean splitting us permanently, just until we do what has to be done.'

'Which is what, chief?' Jup asked.

'Both finding Coilla and Haskeer, and at least checking on the possibility of a star at Drogan.'

Alfray looked far from happy. 'You were against the band splitting before. What's changed?'

'We didn't know about the chance of another star before. Nor did we have proof that we were officially renegades, and all that follows from it. Finding our comrades isn't our only priority now. I can't see another way we can search for our friends *and* a further star without dividing.'

'You're supposing Tannar was telling the truth about there being a star at Drogan. He could have been lying to save his skin.'

More than a few of the band murmured agreement on that point.

Stryke shook his head. 'I think he was telling the truth.'

'You can't know that for sure.'

'You're right, Alfray, I can't. But what have we got to lose in believing him?'

'Everything!'

'If you hadn't noticed, that's what we're already gambling. There's something else. Putting all our eggs in one basket might not be good at this time. With two groups, our enemies have less chance of getting us all. And if each group has one or more stars—'

'*If!*' Jup retorted. 'Remember, we still don't know what the hell the stars do, what they're *for*. It's a gamble on a blind throw.'

'You're right; we're no nearer understanding their purpose than when we started, unless you count the stories Tannar told us. But we *do* know they have a value, if only because Jennesta's after at least one of them. The power we can be certain they have is the power of possession. I still think that if we have them we've got something to bargain with, and that might just get us out of this mess. As I said, what have we got to lose?'

'Isn't what you're saying an argument for *keeping* the band split?' Alfray suggested.

'No, it's not. These are unusual circumstances. We're missing two band members and we have to do our best to find them. Wolverines stick together.'

'You still think of Haskeer as a member of this band? After what he's done?'

'Yes, Stryke,' Jup agreed. 'It looks like treachery. If we do find him, what are we going to do about him?'

'I don't know. Let's find him first, shall we? But even if he has betrayed us, is that any reason not to look for Coilla?'

Alfray sighed. 'You're not going to be moved on this, are you?'

Stryke shook his head.

'So what's your plan?'

'I'll lead half the band in continuing to search for Coilla and Haskeer. You, Alfray, will take the other half to Drogan and make contact with this Keppatawn.'

'What about me?' Jup said. 'Which party do I go with?'

'Mine. Your farsight could be useful in the search.'

The dwarf looked a little rancorous. 'The power's fading, you know that.'

'Even so. We need every bit of help we can get.'

'What kind of welcome can I expect from centaurs?' Alfray wondered.

'We have no argument with them,' Stryke told him.

'We started out having no argument with *most* Maras-Dantians. Look how *that* turned out!'

'Just don't do anything to offend them. You know how proud they can be.'

'They're a warlike race.'

'So are we. That should give some mutual respect.'

'What do you expect me to do once I get there?' Alfray persisted. 'Ask nicely if they've got a star and whether they'd give it to us?'

'Assuming they do have a star, maybe we could parley for it.'

'What with?'

'I should think the pellucid's a good enough trade, wouldn't you?'

'And if it isn't? Or they just decide to take it off us? I'll be leading just half of an already depleted band. The whole band would have a job coping with who knows how many centaurs, and on their home ground.'

'Alfray, I'm not asking you to take them on. All I want is for you to get yourself to Drogan and judge the lie of the land. You don't even have to make contact with them if you think it's too risky. Just wait for the rest of us to get there.'

'When's that going to be?'

'I want to give at least another couple of days to searching. Then there's travelling time. Say five days, maybe six.'

'Where would we rendezvous?'

Stryke thought about it. 'East bank of the Calyparr inlet, where it enters the forest.'

'All right, Stryke, if you really think this is the only way,' Alfray conceded resignedly. 'How do we allot the groups?'

'A straight split of the troopers, which gives each party an even number.' He looked them over. 'Alfray, your group will be made up of Gleadeg, Kestix, Liffin, Nep, Eldo, Zoda, Orbon, Prooq, Noskaa, Vobe and Bhose. Jup and I will take Talag, Reafdaw, Seafe, Toche, Hystykk, Gant, Calthmon, Breggin, Finje and Jad.'

He made a point of including the last three in his group because they voted with Haskeer to not to open the cylinder containing the first star. He had no reason to doubt their loyalty, but thought it best not to have them on Alfray's mission, just in case.

Alfray didn't object to his allocation, and when Stryke gave the grunts themselves an opportunity to protest, none did.

He looked to the sky. 'I want as little delay as possible, but I reckon a couple of hours' rest's in order. Get yourselves ready. They'll be two turns of guards, an hour each. The rest of you get your heads down. Dismissed.'

'I'm going to share out my healing herbs and balms between both groups,' Alfray announced. 'Chances are they'll be needed.' He went off, less than cheerfully.

Jup lingered with Stryke.

Reading his expression, Stryke anticipated his sergeant's thoughts. 'Purely in terms of rank you should be leading the Drogan mission, Jup. But to be blunt, you know there's prejudice against dwarves, maybe even in our ranks. Anything that erodes your authority, inside or outside the band, imperils the mission.'

'Leading the rescue of you and Alfray doesn't count for anything?'

'It counts for a hell of a lot with me and Alfray. That's not the point, and you know it. Anyway, I'd like you with me. We work well together.'

Jup smiled thinly. 'Thanks, chief. Matter of fact, I don't feel that bad about it. When you're one of my kind, you get used to attitudes. Can't argue, either; my race mostly brought it on themselves.'

'All right. Now get yourself some rest.'

'One thing, Stryke; what about the crystal? Should Alfray's group take more of it, given they might have to use it for barter?'

'No, I think we'll keep things as they are. Each band member carrying a ration's the best way of handling it. Still gives Alfray enough should he need to trade. But we make it clear again that nobody dips in without permission.'

'Right, I'll get on that.'

He left Stryke to bed down for a while.

Wrapping himself in a blanket and laying his head on a saddle, Stryke realised how bone tired he was.

As he drifted into sleep he fancied he caught a whiff of pellucid in the air. He put it down to imagination and let the darkness take him.

7

Something large and indistinct loomed over him.

His vision was blurred and he couldn't make out what it was. He blinked several times, focused, and realised it was a tree, lofty and of ample girth. Looking around, he saw that he was in a forest where all the trees were tall and robust, with abundant greenery. Beams of sunlight knifed through the emerald ceiling high above.

There was an almost palpable sense of peace here. Yet it wasn't entirely silent. He was aware of gentle birdsong, and behind that a sound he couldn't identify, like continuous, muted thunder. It wasn't threatening, just totally unfamiliar.

In one direction, where the woodland thinned, brighter light entered. He walked that way. Passing over a bed of crisp fallen leaves, he came to the forest's edge. The roaring, crashing noise was louder. Still he had no notion of what it might be.

Away from the shade of the trees, he was briefly ankle deep in succulent blades of grass. As the ground swept into a mild incline, the grass gave way to an expanse of fine white sand.

Beyond the sand lay a mighty ocean.

It stretched as far ahead as he could see, and to the left and right. It sent white flecked waves rumbling lazily to the shore. Its opulent blue *near matched the perfectly cerulean sky, where chalky, sculptured clouds majestically drifted.*

Stryke was awed by it. He had never seen the like.

He went out across the sand. A pleasantly warm sea breeze caressed his face. The air was perfumed with the quickening bouquet of ozone. Looking back to the treeline, he saw the trail his footprints had left in the sand. He could not say why he found the sight so strangely affecting.

It was then that his eye was caught by something reflecting the sun, perched atop a rocky rise perhaps half a mile along the beach and set a hundred yards back from the shoreline. They were structures of some kind, sharply white. He moved in that direction.

The bluff proved further away than it looked, but was no great hardship to reach. Trudging the hot sand, he passed dunes massed by the industrious wind. Here and there, brilliantly green shoots of tiny plants stabbed through the powdery layer.

As he approached, it was obvious more than one construction sat on top of the black rock. Reaching the seaward face of the cliff, he discovered it was tiered. So he began to climb.

Soon he arrived at what turned out to be a modest plateau. What it housed was ruins: tumbled fluted columns, the remains of buildings, scattered blocks of fashioned stone, a cracked, truncated staircase. It was all surrounded by a crenellated wall, now breached and crumbling. The material used to construct the place had the bleached look of old marble. Mosses and ivy colonised much of its soft dilapidation.

The architecture was unfamiliar to him, its detail and decoration resembling nothing he had seen before. But there were elements that told him what he was looking at was obviously a fortification. Its positioning too, overlooking the ocean and on a high point, confirmed this. It was exactly where he would have put it himself. Anybody with a military slant would have done the same.

Palm shading his brow, he surveyed the view. The wind whipped at his face and clothes.

He stood that way for some time before he noticed movement. A group of riders was coming along the beach from the opposite direction to the way he had. As they got nearer, he could see there were seven of them. Nearer still, it was apparent they were heading for the fortification. A small voice in the back of his mind warned of the possibility of conflict.

Then he saw that they were orcs, and the voice was stilled.

The riders stopped at the foot of the rock pile. As they dismounted, he recognised one of them. It was the female he had encountered here before. Assuming it was here, and wherever 'here' might be.

He let that thought pass over him like a night zephyr.

She led her party in climbing the bluff. Her movements were agile and confident. Reaching the top before the others, she stretched a hand to him. He took it and hoisted her the remaining couple of feet. As with the last time he had her hand in his, he noticed how firm and pleasantly cool it was.

Nimbly springing to him, she smiled. It warmed her strong, open face. She was a mite shorter than Stryke, but the difference was made up by the ornamental headdress she wore, this time a shock of lustrous green and blue feathers. Her physique was fetchingly muscular, her back straight. There was no denying she was a handsome orc indeed.

'Greetings,' she said.

'Well met.'

The other orcs scrambled on to the plateau. Two of them were female. They nodded as they passed him, seemingly friendly and unconcerned with who he might be or why he was there.

'Some of my clansfolk,' she explained.

He watched as they went to stand on another part of the level. They looked out to sea and talked amongst themselves.

Stryke turned back to her. She was staring at him. 'It seems we are drawn together again.'

'Why is that so, do you think?'

Her expression indicated she found the question eccentric. 'Fate. the gods. Who knows? Would you have it otherwise?'

'No! Er, no, I wouldn't.'

She smiled again, a little knowingly he thought, then grew more serious. 'You always look so troubled.'

'Do I?'

'What is it that ails you?'

'It's . . . hard to explain.'

'Try.'

'My land is tormented. Greatly so.'

'Then leave it. Come here.'

'There is too much of importance to hold me in my own place. And how I get here is something over which I seem to have no say.'

'That's hard to understand. You visit with such facility. Can you explain?'

'No. I'm puzzled too, and I have no explanation.'

'Perhaps in time you will. No matter. What can be done to ease your burden?'

'I'm on what could be called a mission which might do that.'

'There is hope then?'

'Might, I say.'

'All that should concern you is doing that which is right and just. Do you think you are?'

He answered without hesitation. 'Yes.'

'And you believe you are being true to yourself in undertaking this mission?'

'I do.'

'Then you have made yourself a promise, and since when did orcs go back on their word?'

'Too often, where I come from.'

She was shocked by that. 'Why?'

'We are forced to.'

'That is sad, and all the more reason not to bend this time.'

'I can't afford to. The lives of comrades are at stake.'

'You'll stand by them. It's the orc way.'

'You make it all seem so simple. But events are not always easy to master.'

'It takes courage, I know, but I can tell that's not something you lack. Whatever this task you have set yourself, you must undertake it to the best of your ability. Else why are we alive?'

It was his turn to smile. 'There is wisdom in your words. I'll reflect on them.'

They felt no discomfort in letting a moment pass in silence.

At length he said, 'What is this place?' He indicated the ruins.

'Nobody knows, except it's very old and orcs lay no claim to it.'

'How can that be? You've already told me that this country of yours is home to no other race but ours.'

'And you've told me that your land is shared with many races. I find that at least as great a mystery.'

'Nothing I see around me accords with my experience,' he confessed.

'I thought I hadn't seen you waiting here before. Is this the first time you've come to greet them?'

'Waiting? And who am I supposed to greet?'

She laughed. It was good-natured. 'You really don't know?'

'I've no idea what you're talking about,' he told her.

Turning, she scanned the ocean. Then she pointed. 'Them.'

He looked and saw the billowing white sails of several ships on the horizon.

'You're so strange,' she added kindly. 'You never cease to make me wonder, Stryke.'

Of course, she knew his name. But he still didn't know hers.

He was about to ask when a black maw opened and swallowed him.

He woke up haunted by her face, and sweating despite the cold.

After the brightness he had experienced, it took a few seconds for him to adjust to the watery daylight that was becoming the norm in this world. He checked himself. What was he doing thinking in terms of 'this world'? What other world was there, apart from the one he'd created for himself in his dreams? If dreams they were. Whatever he called them, they were becoming more vivid. They made him doubt his sanity. And at a time like this the last thing he needed was his mind playing tricks on him.

Nevertheless, though he didn't understand the dream, it had somehow stiffened his resolve. He felt absurdly optimistic about the decision he'd made, never mind the many fresh obstacles it threw in their path.

His reverie was broken by a shadow falling across him. It was Jup's.

'Chief, you don't look too good. You all right?'

Stryke gathered his wits. 'I'm fine, Sergeant.' He got up. 'Is everything ready?'

'More or less.'

Alfray had mustered his half of the band and was supervising the loading of their horses. Stryke and Jup went towards him.

As they walked, Stryke asked, 'Did anybody use crystal last night?'

'Not that I know of. And nobody would without permission. Why?'

'Oh . . . no reason.'

Jup gave him an odd look, but before he could say anything they were with Alfray.

He was tightening his horse's saddle straps. Giving the leather stay a final jerk, he said, 'Well, that's it. We're all set.'

'Remember what I said,' Stryke reminded him. 'Don't make contact with the centaurs unless you're sure there's no danger.'

'I'll remember.'

'Got everything you need?'

'I reckon so. We'll be looking out for you at Calyparr.'

'Six days at most.'

Stryke stretched his arm and they shook warrior fashion, clasping each other's wrist. 'Fare well, Alfray.'

'And you, Stryke.' He nodded at the dwarf. 'Jup.'

'Good luck, Alfray.'

The band's standard jutted from the ground next to Alfray's horse. 'I'm used to having this in my charge,' he said. 'Do you mind, Stryke?'

' 'Course not. Take it.'

Alfray mounted and pulled free the banner's spar. He raised it and his troopers took to their horses.

Stryke, Jup and the remaining grunts watched in silence as the small column headed west.

'So where to?' Jup wanted to know.

'We'll cover the ground eastward of here,' Stryke decided. 'Get 'em mounted.'

Jup organised things while Stryke got on to his own horse. He was still disoriented by the lucidity of his dream, and took several deep breaths to centre himself.

He looked to his reduced band and dwelt again on the resolve the dream had given him. Still sure he was taking the right course, he nevertheless couldn't shake off the feeling that they might never see Alfray and the others again.

Jup brought his horse to Stryke's side. 'All ready.'

'Very good, Sergeant. Let's see what we can do about finding Haskeer and Coilla, shall we?'

They made Coilla walk, tied to the end of a rope attached to the pommel on Aulay's saddle. Her own mount was led by Blaan. Lekmann rode in front, setting a brisk pace.

She had learned their names by listening to their conversations. Something else she'd come to understand was that none of them had any regard for her wellbeing, beyond an occasional drink of water, grudgingly offered. Even this was only to protect what they saw as an investment they intended realising in Hecklowe.

The trio occasionally exchanged words, sometimes as whispers so she couldn't hear. They gave her sidelong glances. Aulay shot her murderous looks.

Coilla was fit and used to marching, but the speed they maintained was a punishment. So when they came across a stream and Lekmann, the pock-faced, greasy-haired leader, ordered camp struck, it was all she could do to contain her relief. She slumped to the ground, breath short, limbs aching.

The weaselly Aulay, whose ear she'd taken a chunk out of, secured her horse. What she didn't see was him giving Lekmann a conspiratorial wink from his one good eye. Then he tied her, in a sitting position, to a tree trunk. That done, the trio settled down.

'How much longer to Hecklowe?' Aulay asked Lekmann.

'Couple of days, I reckon.'

'Can't be too soon for me.'

'Yeah, I'm bored, Micah,' piped up the big, stupid one called Blaan.

Aulay, fingering his grubbily bandaged ear, pointed a thumb at Coilla. 'Maybe we should have some fun with her.' Drawing a knife, he brought it back in a throwing position. 'A little target practice would pass the time.' He got a bead on her.

Blaan laughed inanely.

'Leave it be,' Lekmann growled.

Aulay ignored him. 'Catch this, bitch!' he yelled and threw the knife. Coilla stiffened. The blade buried itself in the earth just beyond her feet.

'*Cut it out!*' Lekmann bellowed. 'We won't get a good price for damaged goods.' He tossed his canteen at Aulay. 'Fetch us some water.'

Grumbling, Aulay added his own canteen, collected Blaan's and went to the stream.

Lekmann stretched out, his hat over his eyes. Blaan laid his head on a rolled blanket, facing away from Coilla.

She watched them. Her eyes flicked to the knife, which they seemed to have forgotten. It looked to be just within reach. She carefully eased a foot in its direction.

Aulay returned with the canteens. She froze and lowered her head, pretending slumber.

The one-eyed human stared at her. 'Just our luck to be stuck out here with a female and she ain't human,' he complained.

Lekmann sniggered. 'Surprised you don't try her anyway. Or are you fussy these days?'

Aulay pulled a disgusted face. 'I'd rather do it with a pig.'

Coilla opened her eyes. 'That makes two of us,' she assured him.

'Well, fuck you,' he retorted.

'I'm not a pig, remember?'

'Valuable or not, I've got a mind to come over there and give you a kicking.'

'Untie me first and we'll make a match of it. I'd enjoy doing some damage to whatever you've got between those scrawny legs.'

'Big talk! With *what*, bitch?'

'With these.' She flashed her teeth at him. 'You know how sharp they are.'

Aulay boiled, a hand to the remains of his ear.

Lekmann grinned.

'How do we know she ain't lying about her band going to Hecklowe?' Aulay said.

'Don't start that again, Greever,' Lekmann replied wearily. He turned to Coilla. 'You aren't lying, are you, sweetheart? You wouldn't dare.'

She held her peace, contenting herself with an acid look.

Digging into a jerkin pocket, Lekmann brought out a pair of bone dice. 'Let's all calm down and kill an hour with these, shall we?' He rattled the dice in his fist.

Aulay drifted over. Blaan joined them. Soon they were engrossed in a noisy game and lost interest in Coilla.

She concentrated on the knife. Slowly, with one eye always on the boisterous trio, she stretched her foot towards it.

Eventually her toe touched the blade. Further straining and wriggling got her foot around the knife. She pulled back. It fell, fortunately her way. With some ungainly, stealthy acrobatics, she managed to get it near enough to reach.

A rope had been run around her, fastening her arms to her sides, but there was just enough give to allow her fingers to reach the weapon. Very carefully, she got the knife into her palm and, her hand at an awkward, painful angle, finally placed its cutting edge against the rope.

The bounty hunters were still playing, their backs to her.

She moved the knife on the rope, working it up and down as quickly as she dared. Shreds of hemp frayed. Applying pressure by flexing her muscles against the bond helped speed the process.

Then the last threads parted and she was free.

With imperceptible, almost glacial deliberation, she un-wound the rope. The humans carried on throwing dice and yelling at each other, completely oblivious of her. She moved, ever so cautiously, towards her horse which was also on their blind side.

Crouching low and clutching the knife, she reached the mount. Her worry now was that the animal might snort or make some other sound to alert them. She patted it gingerly and whispered softly to keep it docile. Slipping a foot into the stirrup, she reached for the saddle to pull herself up.

The saddle came away, sending her sprawling. Her knife flew out of her hand. Shying, the horse bucked.

Roars of laughter broke out. She looked over and saw the bounty hunters doubled up with barbarous mirth. Lekmann, sword drawn, came to her and kicked the knife out of reach.

It was then that she noticed the saddle straps had been undone.

'You've gotta make your own entertainment out here on the plains,' Lekmann hooted.

'Her *face!*' Aulay mocked.

Blaan was holding his massive belly and rocking. Tears ran down his ample cheeks.

Suddenly something caught his attention and he stopped. He stared and said, 'Hey, look.'

A rider was approaching on a pure white stallion.

8

As the rider drew nearer they saw he was human.

'Who the hell's *that*?' Lekmann said. The other two shrugged, blank-faced. Lekmann knelt and bound Coilla's hands behind her back.

The bounty hunters armed themselves and watched as the horseman approached at a steady pace. Soon he was close enough for them to make out clearly.

Even seated it was obvious he was tall and straight-backed, but wiry rather than muscular. His auburn hair reached his shoulders, and he had a neatly trimmed beard. He wore a chestnut jerkin, lightly embroidered with silver thread. Below that were brown leather breeches tucked into high black boots. A swept-back dark blue cloak completed the outfit. Apparently he wasn't carrying a weapon.

He pulled on the reins of his white stallion and stopped in front of them. Without asking, he dismounted. His movements were easy and assured, and he was smiling.

'Who are you?' Lekmann demanded. 'What do you want?'

The stranger's eyes flicked to Coilla, then back to Lekmann. The smile didn't waver. 'My name's Serapheim,' he replied in a sonorous, unhurried tone, 'and all I want is water.' He nodded at the spring.

His age was indeterminate. Blue eyed, with a slightly hawk nose and a well-shaped mouth, his face was handsome in a nondescript sort of way. Yet there was something about him that had presence, and a command transcending looks.

Lekmann glanced at Blaan and Aulay. 'Keep your eyes peeled for more.'

'I'm alone,' he told them.

'These are troubled times, Serapheim, or whatever you call yourself,' Lekmann said. 'Wandering about with less than a small army's asking for trouble.'

'You are.'

'There's three of us, and that's enough. We know how to look after ourselves.'

'I don't doubt it. But I offer none a threat and no one threatens me. Anyway, aren't you four?' He looked to Coilla.

'She's just with us,' Aulay explained. 'She ain't one *of* us.'

The man made no reply. His expression stayed non-committal.

'Seen any more of her kind in these parts?' Lekmann asked.

'No.'

Coilla studied the newly arrived human and reckoned his eyes spoke of more shrewdness than he was letting on. But she saw no realistic chance of him helping her in any way.

The stranger's horse walked to the stream, dipped its head and began drinking. They let it be.

'Like I said, in these dark days a lone man takes a risk approaching strangers,' Lekmann repeated pointedly.

'I didn't see you until the last minute,' Serapheim admitted.

'Going round with your eyes shut ain't wise either.'

'I'm often in a dream. Living in my head.'

'That's a good way of losing it,' Aulay commented.

'You with the Unis or the Manis?' Blaan put in bluntly.

'Neither,' Serapheim replied. 'You?'

'Same,' Lekmann said.

'That's a relief. I'm tired of walking on eggs. A stray word in the wrong company can be a problem these days.'

Coilla wondered what he thought he was in now.

'You're godless, then?' Aulay asked.

'I didn't say that.'

'Figured you had to have faith in some higher power not to carry a blade.' It was a comment designed to mock.

'I don't need one in my trade.'

'Which is what?' Lekmann said.

Serapheim gave a little flourish of his cloak and bowed his head theatrically. 'I'm a roving bard. A storyteller. A word-smith.'

Aulay's groan summed up the low opinion they all had of that particular occupation.

Coilla was even more convinced this wasn't someone likely to aid her.

'And how do you gallants make *your* way in the world?'

'We supply freelance martial services,' Lekmann replied grandly.

'With a little vermin control on the side,' Aulay added. He gave Coilla a cold glance.

Serapheim nodded, the smile fixed, but said nothing.

Lekmann grinned. 'With wars and strife and all it has to be a bad time in your line.'

'On the contrary, uncertain times suit me.' He noted their doubtful expressions. 'When things look black, folk want to forget their everyday worries.'

'If business is good, you must be doing well,' Aulay suggested slyly.

Coilla thought this stranger was either a fool or too trusting for his own good.

'The riches I have can't be weighed or counted like gold.'

That puzzled Blaan. 'How so?'

'Can you put a value on the sun, the moon, the stars? On the wind in your face, the sound of birdsong? This water?'

'The honeyed words of a . . . *poet*,' Lekmann responded disdainfully. 'If Maras–Dantia makes up your riches you're hoarding shoddy goods.'

'There's some truth in that,' Serapheim allowed. 'Things are not as they were, and getting worse.'

Aulay applied some sarcasm. 'You saying you eat the sun and stars? Dine on the wind? Sounds a poor return for your wares.'

Blaan smirked inanely.

'In exchange for my yarns folk give me food, drink, shelter. The occasional coin. Maybe even a story of their own. Perhaps you have a story to pass on?'

'Of course not,' Lekmann snorted derisively. 'The sort of stories we have would be of little interest to you, word-forger.'

'I wouldn't be so sure. All men's stories have a value.'

'You ain't heard ours. Where you heading?'

'Nowhere in particular.'

'And you've come from nowhere in particular too, have you?'

'Hecklowe.'

'That's where we're going!' Blaan exclaimed.

'*Shut your mouth!*' Lekmann snapped. He directed a bogus smile at Serapheim. 'How, er, how are things in Hecklowe these days?'

'Like the rest of the land – chaotic, less tolerant than it was. It's turning into a haven for felons. Place was crawling with footpads, slavers and the like.'

It seemed to Coilla that the stranger placed more than a little emphasis on the word slavers, but she couldn't be sure.

'You don't say,' Lekmann returned, feigning disinterest.

'The Council and the Watchers try to keep things under control, but the magic's as unpredictable there as anywhere else. That makes it hard for them.'

'Guess it must.'

Serapheim turned to Coilla. 'What does your elder race friend here think about visiting such a notorious place?'

'Having a choice would be a good start,' she told him.

'She ain't got nothing to say on the subject!' Lekmann quickly interrupted. 'Anyway, she's an orc and she can take care of herself.'

'Believe it,' Coilla muttered.

The storyteller took in the trio's harsh expressions. 'I'll just get some of that water and be on my way.'

'You'll have to pay for it,' Lekmann decided.

'I didn't know anyone owned the stream.'

'Today we do. Possession's nine tenths and all that.'

'As I said, I've nothing to give.'

'You're a teller of tales, tell us one. If we like it, you get to join your horse and drink.'

'And if you don't?'

Lekmann shrugged.

'Well, stories are my currency. Why not?'

'Suppose you'll give us something meant to frighten idiots,' Aulay grumbled. 'Like some tale sung by fairies about trolls eating babies, or the doings of the fearsome Sluagh. You word weavers are all the same.'

'No, that's not what I had in mind.'

'What then?'

'You mentioned the Unis earlier. Thought I might give you one of their little fables.'

'Oh, no, not some religious trash.'

'Yes and no. Want to hear it or not?'

'Go ahead,' Lekmann sighed. 'I hope you're not too thirsty, though.'

'Like most people you probably think of the Unis as narrow-minded, unbending fanatics.'

'Sure as hell we do.'

'And you'd be right about most of them. They do have a woeful number of zealots in their ranks. But not every one of them is like that. A few can bend a bit. Even see the funny side of their creed.'

'That I find hard to believe.'

'It's true. They're just plain folk, like you and me, apart from the hold their faith has on them. And it comes out in stories they sometimes tell. Stories they're careful to tell in secret, mind. These stories pass around and some of them come to me.'

'You gonna get on with it?'

'Do you know what the Unis believe? Roughly, I mean?'

'Some.'

'Then maybe you know that their holy books say their lone God started the human race by creating one man, Ademnius, and one woman, Evelaine.'

Aulay sneered suggestively. 'One wouldn't be enough for me.'

'We know this stuff,' said Lekmann impatiently. 'We ain't ignorant.'

Serapheim ignored them. 'The Unis believe that in those first days God spoke directly to Ademnius, to explain what He was doing and what His hopes were for the life He'd made. So one day God came to Ademnius and said, "I have two pieces of good news and one piece of bad news for you. Which would you like to hear first?" "I'll have the good news first, please, Lord," Ademnius replied. "Well," God told him, "the first piece of good news is that I've created a wonderful organ for you called the brain. It will enable you to learn and reason and do all sorts of clever things." "Thank you, Lord," said Ademnius. "The second piece of good news," God told him, "is that I've created another organ for you called the penis." '

The bounty hunters smirked. Aulay nudged Blaan's well-padded ribs with his elbow.

' "This will give you pleasure, and give Evelaine pleasure," '
Serapheim continued, ' "and it will let you make children to
live in this glorious world I've fashioned for you." "That
sounds wonderful," Ademnius said. "And what's the bad
news?" "You can't use them both at the same time," God
replied.'

There was a moment's silence while the payoff soaked in,
then the bounty hunters roared with crude laughter. Though
Coilla thought it quite possible that Blaan didn't get it.

'Not so much a story as a short jest, I grant you,' Serapheim
said. 'But I'm glad it met with your approval.'

'It was all right,' Lekmann agreed. 'And kind of true, I guess.'

'Of course, as I said, it is customary to offer a coin or some
other small token of appreciation.'

The trio sobered instantly.

Lekmann's face contorted with anger. 'Now you've gone
and spoilt it.'

'We was thinking more in terms of *you* paying *us*,' Aulay
said.

'As I told you, I have nothing.'

Blaan grinned nastily. 'You'll have less than that when we've
done with you.'

Aulay did some stocktaking. 'You got a horse, a fine pair of
boots, that fancy cloak. Maybe a purse, despite what you say.'

' 'Sides, you know too much about our business,' Lekmann
finished.

Notwithstanding the menacing atmosphere, Coilla was
convinced that the storyteller wasn't fazed. Though it must
have been as obvious to him as it was to her that these men
were capable of murder just for the hell of it.

Her attention was drawn by something moving on the plain.
For a moment, hope kindled. But then she identified what she
was looking at and realised it wasn't deliverance. Far from it.

Serapheim hadn't noticed. Neither had the bounty hunters.

They were set on enacting a violent scene. Lekmann had his sword raised and was moving in on the storyteller. The other two were following his lead.

'We've got company,' she said.

They stopped, looked at her, followed her gaze.

A large group of riders had come into sight, well ahead of them. They were moving slowly from east to south-west, on a course that would bring them close, if not actually to the stream.

Aulay cupped a hand to his forehead. 'What are they, Micah?'

'Humans. Dressed in black, far as I can see. Know what I reckon? They're those Hobrow's men. Them . . . whatever they call themselves.'

'Custodians.'

'Right, right. Fuck this, we're out of here. Get the orc, Greever. Jabeez, the horses.'

Blaan didn't move. He stood open-mouthed, staring at the riders. 'You reckon they ain't got no sense of humour, Micah?'

'No, I don't! Get the horses!'

'Hey! The stranger.'

Serapheim was riding away, due west.

'Forget him. We got more pressing business.'

'Good thing we didn't do for him, Micah,' Blaan opined. 'It's bad luck to kill crazy people.'

'Superstitious *dolt*! Move your fucking self!'

They bundled Coilla on to her horse and took off at speed.

9

'*Look at it!*' Jennesta shrieked. 'Look at the scale of your *failure*!'

Mersadion stared at the parchment wall map and trembled. It was littered with markers: red for the queen's forces, blue for the Uni opposition. They were roughly equal in number. That wasn't good enough.

'We've suffered no *losses* as such,' he offered timorously.

'If we had I would have fed you your own liver by now! Where are the *gains*?'

'The war is complex, ma'am. We're fighting on so many fronts—'

'I need no lectures on our situation, General! What I want is results!'

'I can assure—'

'This is bad enough,' she sailed on, 'but it's as nothing compared to the lack of progress in finding that wretched warband! Do you have news of them?'

'Well, I—'

'You do not. Have we heard from Lekmann's bounty hunters?'

'They—'

'No, you haven't.'

Mersadion didn't dare remind her that bringing in the human bounty hunters had been her idea. He had quickly learned that Jennesta took credit for victories but saddled others with the blame for defeats.

'I had hopes of you doing better than Kysthan, your *late* predecessor,' she added pointedly. 'I trust you're not going to disappoint me.'

'Majesty—'

'Be warned that as of now your performance is under even closer scrutiny.'

'I—'

This time he was interrupted by a light rap at the door.

'Enter!' Jennesta commanded.

One of her elf servants came in and bowed. The androgynous creature had a build so delicate its limbs looked fit to snap. Its complexion was almost translucent, and the fragility of its face was emphasised by golden hair and lashes. The eyes were fairest blue, the nose winsome.

The elf pouted and lisped, 'Your Mistress of Dragons, my lady.'

'Another incompetent,' Jennesta seethed. 'Send her in.'

As a brownie, the hybrid progeny of a goblin and elf union, the dragon dam bore some resemblance to the servant. But she was more robust, and tall even by the norm of her lanky race. In keeping with tradition, she was dressed entirely in the reddish-brown colours of an autumnal woodland. Her only concessions to adornment were narrow gold bands at her wrists and neck.

She acknowledged Jennesta's superior station with the tiniest bow of her head.

As usual in her dealings with underlings, the queen squandered no breath on niceties. 'I confess to being less than happy with your efforts of late, Glozellan,' she informed her.

'Ma'am?' There was a piping quality to the brownie's voice,

and a calm remoteness characteristic of her kind. Jennesta had been known to find it irritating.

'In the matter of the Wolverines,' she emphasised with menacing deliberateness.

'My handlers have followed your orders to the letter, Majesty,' Glozellan replied, an expression of self-esteem on her face that many would have equated with haughtiness. It was another trait of her proud race, and even more infuriating to the queen.

'But you have not found them,' she said.

'Your pardon, ma'am, but we did engage with the band on the battlefield near Weaver's Lea,' the dragon mistress reminded her.

'And let them escape! Hardly an engagement! Unless you think merely spotting the renegades counts as such.'

'No, Majesty. In fact they were pursued and narrowly avoided our attack.'

'There's a difference?'

'The uncertain nature of dragons means they are always unpredictable to some extent, ma'am.'

'A bad artisan always blames her tools.'

'I accept responsibility for my actions and those of my subordinates.'

'That's as well. For in my service a responsibility shirked leads directly to consequences. And they aren't of an especially pleasant nature.'

'I only make the point that dragons can be an erratic weapon, Majesty. They have notoriously obstinate wills.'

'Then perhaps I should find a dam more capable of bending them.'

Glozellan said nothing.

'I thought I'd made my wishes clear,' Jennesta went on, 'but it seems I need to repeat myself. This is for your ears too, General.' Mersadion stiffened. 'Do not delude yourselves that there is any cause more vital than locating and returning to me the artifact stolen by the Wolverines.'

'It might help, Majesty,' Glozellan said, 'if we knew what this artifact was, and why—'

The sound of a weighty slap echoed off the stone walls. Glozellan's head whipped to one side under the impact. She staggered and raised a hand to her reddening cheek. A thin dribble of blood snaked from the corner of her mouth.

'Mark *that* on account,' Jennesta told her, eyes blazing. 'You've asked before about the item I seek, and I repeat what I said then: it is none of your concern. They'll be more and worse if you persist with insubordination.'

Glozellan returned her gaze with a silent, lofty stare.

'*All* available resources will be devoted to the search,' the queen declared. 'And if you two don't give me what I want, I'll be looking for a new General and a new Mistress of Dragons. You might dwell on the form your . . . *retirement* would take. Now get out.'

When they'd gone, Jennesta vowed to herself that she would be having a much more direct hand in things from now on. But she put that aside for the time being. There was something else on her mind. Something that greatly displeased her.

Using another, less obvious door, she left the strategy room and descended a narrow, winding staircase. Footfalls reverberating, she trod subterranean passages to her private quarters in the bowels of the palace. Orc guards came to attention by the door as she swept in.

Others were busy inside the spacious chamber, lugging buckets to a large, shallow wooden tub reinforced with metal hasps. They finished the chore while she stood impatiently watching. Once they were dismissed she settled by the tub and rippled her fingers through its tepid contents.

The blood seemed adequate for her needs, but she was vexed to discover that a few small pieces of flesh had been left in it. When advocating this particular fluid as a medium, the ancients had been quite clear on it being as pure as possible. She made a mental note to remind the guards about the need for filtering, and to have a thrashing administered to underline the point.

As the blood's surface was already thickening, she undertook the necessary incantations and entreaties. The glutinous ruby broth hardened further and took on a burnished look. At length a small area palpitated, swirled sluggishly and formed the semblance of a face.

'*You choose the damnedest moments, Jennesta,*' the likeness complained. '*This is* not *a good time.*'

'You lied to me, Adpar.'

'*About what?*'

'About that which was taken from me.'

'*Oh, no, not that doleful subject again.*'

'Did you or did you not tell me that you knew nothing about the artifact I've been seeking?'

'*What you've been looking for I have no knowledge of. End of conversation.*'

'No, hold. I have ways, Adpar. Ways, and eyes looking out for me. And what I now know fits only with my artifact.' She grew thoughtful. 'Either that or . . .'

'*I feel one of your bizarre fancies coming on, dear.*'

'It's another, isn't it? You have *another*!'

'*I'm sure I don't know what—*'

'You deceitful bitch! You've been hoarding one in secret!'

'*I'm not saying I did or I didn't.*'

'That's as good as an admission coming from you.'

'*Look, Jennesta, it is possible that I had something not dissimilar to what you're looking for, but that's history now. It was stolen.*'

'Just like mine. How convenient. You don't expect me to believe that?'

'*I don't give a damn whether you believe it or not! Instead of persecuting me about your obsessions you should be concentrating on finding the thieves. If anybody's playing with fire, they are!'*

'Then you *do* know the object's significance! The significance of all of them!'

'I just know it has to be something extreme for you to get so worked up about it.'

A small eruption disturbed the dark red, coagulated skin. Another face formed and a new voice was added. *'She's right, Jennesta.'*

Adpar and Jennesta groaned simultaneously.

'Stay out of this, prodnose!' Adpar snapped.

'Why can we never have a conversation without you butting in, Sanara?' Jennesta grumbled.

'You know why, sister; the bond is too close.'

'More's the pity,' muttered Adpar.

'This is no time for the usual petty squabbling,' Sanara cautioned. *'The reality is that a group of orcs have at least one of the instrumentalities. How can they possibly understand their awesome power?'*

'What do you mean, at least one?' Jennesta said.

'Do you know for certain they haven't? Events are moving apace. We are entering a period when all things are possible.'

'I've got it under control.'

'Really?' Sanara commented sceptically.

'Don't mind me,' Adpar sniffed, *'I've only got my own war to fight. I've plenty of time to sit here listening to you two swapping riddles.'*

'Perhaps you don't know what I'm talking about, Adpar, but Jennesta does. What she needs to understand is that the power should be harnessed for good, not evil, lest complete destruction be brought down on all of us.'

'Oh, *please*,' Jennesta hissed sarcastically, 'not Sanara the martyr again.'

'Think of me what you will, I'm used to it. Just don't underestimate what's about to be unleashed now the game's afoot.'

'To hell with the pair of you!' Jennesta exclaimed, petulantly slashing her hand through the layer of crusty blood. The images disintegrated.

She sat there for some time going over everything in her mind, and it was indicative of her character that she gave no credence to Sanara having a valid point, or giving Adpar the benefit of the doubt. Rather she resolved that the time was near to do something about at least one of her troublesome siblings.

Mostly she burned at the thought of all the trouble the Wolverines had brought down on her. And of the punishment she would exact for it.

Haskeer was still not sure if he was travelling in the right direction. He wasn't even entirely aware of his surroundings, and he was indifferent to the worsening northern climate.

All that was real to him was the singing in his head. It drove him mercilessly, impelling him further and faster on a bearing which, if he thought about it at all, he trusted would take him to Cairnbarrow.

The trail he followed dipped into a wooded valley. He galloped on without hesitation, gaze fixed straight ahead.

About halfway through, at the valley's lowest point, water had settled and formed an expanse of mud. The path was narrower too, bringing the growth on either side nearer, which despite the wintry conditions was still quite dense. He had to slow to a canter, much to his irritation.

As he picked his way through the bog, he heard a soughing noise on the right. Then a creaking swish. He turned and caught a glimpse of something speeding towards him. There was no time to react. The object struck him with a tremendous crack and he toppled from the horse.

Lying dazed in the mud, he looked up and saw what had hit him. It was a length of tree trunk, still swinging, suspended by stout ropes to a strong overhead branch. Someone in cover had launched it at him like a ram.

Aching, badly winded, he was only thinking of getting up when rough hands were laid on him. He had an impression of black garbed humans. They set to punching and kicking him. Unable to fight back, the best he could do was cover his face with his hands.

They hauled him to his feet and took his weapons. The pouch was ripped from his belt. His hands were bound behind his back.

Through the agony, Haskeer focused on a figure that had appeared in front of him.

'Are you sure he's secure?' Kimball Hobrow asked.

'He's secure,' a custodian confirmed.

Another henchman passed Haskeer's pouch to the preacher. He looked inside and his face lit with joy. Or it might have been avarice.

Thrusting in his hand he brought out the stars and gleefully held them aloft. 'The relic, and another to match! It was more than I dared hope. The Lord is with us this day.' He threw up his arms. 'Thank you, Lord, for returning what is ours! And for delivering this creature to us, the instruments of Your justice!'

Hobrow scowled at the orc. 'You will be punished for your wrongs, savage, in the name of the Supreme Being.'

Haskeer's head was clearing a little. The singing had faded and been replaced by this ranting human lunatic. He couldn't move or get his hands free. But there was one thing he could do.

He spat in Hobrow's face.

The preacher leapt back as though scalded, his expression horrified. He began rubbing at his face with the back of his sleeve and muttering, 'Unclean, unclean.'

When he was through, he asked again, 'Are you sure he's well bound?'

His followers assured him. Hobrow came forward, balled his fist and delivered several blows to Haskeer's stomach, yelling, 'You will pay for your disrespect to a servant of the Lord!'

Haskeer had taken worse. A lot worse. The punches were quite feeble, in fact. But the custodians, probably realising how ineffective their leader's efforts were, also started laying into him.

Over the beating he heard Hobrow shout, 'Remember the lost hunting party! There could be more of his kind around! We must leave here!'

Barely conscious, Haskeer was dragged away.

Alfray and his half of the Wolverines journeyed in the direction of Calyparr Inlet for most of the day without incident.

He had used his authority to confer a temporary field promotion on Kestix, one of the band's more able grunts. In effect, this meant Kestix acted as a kind of honorary second-in-command. It also meant Alfray had somebody to pass the time with on a nearly equal basis.

As they rode westward, through the yellowing grasslands of the plains, he sounded out Kestix about the mood in the ranks.

'Concerned, of course, sir,' the trooper replied. 'Or perhaps worried would be a better word.'

'You're not alone in that.'

'Things have changed so much and so fast, Corporal. It's like we've been swept along with no time to think.'

'Everything's changing,' Alfray agreed. 'Maras-Dantia's changing. Maybe it's finished. Because of the humans.'

'Since the humans came, yes. They've upset it all, the bastards.'

'But take heart. We could make a difference yet, if we carry out our captain's plan successfully.'

'Begging your pardon, Corporal, but what does that mean?'

'Eh?'

'Well, we all know it's important for us to find these star things, only . . . *why*?'

Alfray was nonplussed. 'What are you getting at, trooper?'

'We still don't know what they do, what they're for. Do we, Corporal?'

'That's true. But apart from any . . . let's say any magical power they might command, we do know they have another kind of power. Others want them. In the case of our late mistress, Jennesta, powerful others. Maybe that gives us an edge.'

Alfray turned to check the column while Kestix digested that. When he righted himself, there was another question.

'If you don't mind me asking, how do you see our mission to Drogan, Corporal? Do we go straight in and try to grab the star?'

'No. We get as near to this Keppatawn's village as possible and observe. If things don't look too hostile, we might see about parleying. But basically we watch and wait for the rest of the band to turn up.'

Hesitantly, Kestix asked, 'You think they will?'

Alfray found that mildly shocking. 'Don't be defeatist, trooper,' he replied, a bit sternly. 'We have to believe we'll rejoin with Stryke's party.'

'I meant no disrespect to the captain,' the grunt quickly affirmed. 'It's just that things don't seem in our control any more.'

'I know. But trust Stryke.' He fleetingly wondered if that was good advice. Not that he didn't think Stryke was to be trusted. It was just that he couldn't shake off the nagging feeling that their commander might have bitten off more than he could chew.

His reverie was cut through by shouts from the column, and Kestix yelling, 'Corporal! Look, sir!'

Alfray gazed ahead and saw a convoy of four wagons, drawn

by oxen, coming round a bend ahead. The trail the orcs and the wagons were on ran through a low gully with sloping sides. One party or the other would have to give way. It wasn't yet possible to make out the wagons' occupants.

Several thoughts ran through Alfray's mind. The first was that if his band turned around it was bound to attract attention. Not to mention that it wasn't in the nature of orcs to run. His other thought was that if whatever was in the wagons proved hostile, they were unlikely to number many more than his company. He didn't see that as insuperable odds.

'Chances are these are just beings going peacefully about their business,' he told Kestix.

'What if they're Unis?'

'If they're any kind of humans, we'll kill 'em,' Alfray informed him matter-of-factly.

As the two groups drew nearer, the orcs identified the race in the wagons.

'Gnomes,' Alfray said.

'Could be worse, sir. They fight like baby rabbits.'

'Yes, and they tend to keep themselves to themselves.'

'They're only ever a problem if anybody takes an interest in their hoards. And I seem to remember their magic has to do with finding underground gold seams, so that shouldn't be a problem.'

'If there's any talking to be done, leave it to me.' Alfray turned and barked an order to the column. 'Maintain order in ranks. No weapons to be drawn unless necessary. Let's just take this easy, shall we?'

'Do you think they'd know about the band having a price on its head?' Kestix wondered.

'Maybe. But as you said, they're not usually fighters. Unless bad manners and foul breath count as weapons.'

The lead wagon was now a short stone's lob from the head of Alfray's column. There were two gnomes on the riding board.

A couple more stood behind them, in the wagon proper. Whatever load the wagon carried was covered by a white tarpaulin.

Alfray threw up a hand and halted the column. The wagons stopped. For a moment, the two groups stared at each other.

Some held that gnomes looked like dwarves with deformities. They were small in stature and disproportionately muscular. They had big hands, big feet and big noses. They sported white beards and bushy white eyebrows. Their clothing was no-nonsense coarse jerkins and trews in uninspiring colours. Some had cowls, others soft caps with hanging bobs.

All gnomes appeared incredibly old, even when new-born. All had made an art of scowling.

After a moment's silence, the driver of the lead wagon announced testily, 'Well, *I* ain't moving!'

Further back, stony-faced wagoneers stood to watch.

'Why should we clear the road?' Alfray said.

'Hoard? *Hoard?*' the driver fog-horned. 'We ain't got no hoard!'

'Just our luck to get one hard of hearing,' Alfray grumbled. 'Not *hoard*,' he enunciated slow, loud and clear, '*road*!'

'What about it?'

'Are you going to shift?' Alfray shouted.

The gnome thought about it. 'Nope.'

Alfray decided to take a more conversational, less disputatious tack. 'Where you from?' he asked.

'Ain't saying,' the gnome replied sourly.

'Where you heading?'

'None of your business.'

'Then can you say if the way to Drogan is clear? Of any humans, that is.'

'Might be. Might not. What's it worth?'

Alfray remembered that gnomes were notorious for knowing the price of everything but the value of nothing. Good road courtesy, for instance.

He gave in. At his order, the column urged their horses up the sides of the gully and let the gnomes through.

As the lead wagon passed, its poker-faced driver mumbled, 'This place is getting too damn crowded for my liking.'

Watching them rumble away, Alfray tried jesting about the incident. 'Well, we made short shrift of them,' he stated ironically.

'That we did,' Kestix said. 'Er . . . Corporal?'

'Yes, Private?'

'Where exactly do shrifts come from?'

Alfray sighed. 'Let's get on, shall we?'

10

Coilla had never spent so much time in the company of humans before. In fact most of her previous experience had to do with killing them.

But being with the bounty hunters for several days made her more aware than ever of their otherworldliness. She had always viewed them as strange, alien creatures, as rapacious interlopers with insatiable appetites for destruction. Now she saw the nuances that underlined the differences between them and the elder races. The way they looked, the way their minds worked, the way they smelt; in so many ways humans were *weird*.

She put the thought aside as they reached the crest of a hill overlooking Hecklowe.

It was dusk, and lights were beginning to dot the freeport. Distance and elevation made it possible to see that the place hadn't so much been planned as simply had happened. As befitted a town where all races met on an equal footing, Hecklowe consisted of a jumble of structures in every conceivable architectural style. Tall buildings, squat buildings, towers, domes, arches and spires cut the skyline. They were made from wood and stone, brick and wattle, thatch and slate. Beyond the town's far edge the grey sea could just be made out in the fading light. Masts of taller ships poked up over the rooftops.

Even from so far away a faint din could be heard.

Lekmann stared down at the port. 'It's a while since I been here, but nothing's changed, I reckon. Hecklowe's permanent neutral ground. Don't matter how much you hate a race, in there it's a truce. No brawling, no fights. No settling of scores in a lethal way.'

'They kill you for that, don't they?' Blaan said.

'If they catch you.'

'Don't they search for weapons on the way in?' Aulay asked.

'Nah. They leave it to you to give 'em up. Searching ain't practical no more since Hecklowe became such a popular place. But if you're fighting in there, it's summary execution by the Watchers. Not that they're as lively as they used to be. They can still do for you, though, so be careful of 'em.'

Coilla spoke out. 'The Watchers don't work properly because your kind's bleeding the magic.'

'Magic,' Lekmann sneered. 'You sub-humans and your fucking magic. Know what I think? I think it's all horse shit.'

'You're surrounded by it. You just can't see it.'

'That's enough!'

'If we find them orcs there's gonna be fighting, ain't there?' Blaan said.

'I'm thinking we're just going to stay on their tails until they come out, then move. If we have to face 'em inside, well, we're used to slipping a blade into somebody's ribs on the quiet.'

'That sounds like your style,' Coilla remarked.

'I told you to shut your face.'

Aulay was unconvinced. 'This ain't much of a plan, Micah.'

'We work with what we got, Greever. Can you think of another way?'

'No.'

'No, you can't. Be like Jabeez here, and leave the thinking chores to me. All right?'

'Right, Micah.'

Lekmann turned to Coilla. 'As for you, you'll behave down there and hold your tongue. 'Les' you want to lose it. Got that?'

She gave him an icy stare.

'Micah,' Blaan said.

Lekmann sighed. *'Yes?'*

'Hecklowe's where all the races can go, right?'

'That's right.'

'So there could be orcs there.'

'I'm banking on it, Jabeez. That's why we're here, remember?' His synthetic patience was wearing thin.

'So if we see orcs, how do we know if they're the ones we're looking for?'

Aulay grinned, displaying rotting teeth. 'He's got a point, Micah.'

Lekmann obviously hadn't thought that aspect through. Finally he jabbed a thumb at Coilla. 'She'll point them out for us.'

'Like hell I will.'

He leered menacingly at her. 'We'll see about that.'

'So what do we do about weapons?' Aulay said.

'We'll hand in our swords at the gates, but keep a little something in reserve.'

He took a knife from his belt and slipped it into his boot. Blaan and Aulay did the same, only Aulay hid two knives – a dagger in one boot, a thrower in the other.

'When we get down there you'll say nothing,' Lekmann repeated to Coilla. 'You ain't our prisoner, you're just with us. Got it?'

'You know I'm going to kill you for this, don't you?' she replied evenly.

He tried to laugh that off. But he'd looked into her eyes and his performance was unconvincing. 'Let's go,' he said, spurring his horse.

They rode down to Hecklowe.

Near the gates, Aulay cut Coilla's bonds and whispered to her, 'Try to run and you get a blade in your arse.'

There was a small multiracial crowd at the gates, on foot and mounted, and a queue moving past a checkpoint where weapons were being handed in. The bounty hunters and Coilla got in line, and reached the checkpoint before they saw their first Watchers.

They were bipedal, but that was about as much resemblance as they had to flesh and blood creatures. Their bodies were solidly built and seemed to consist of a variety of metals. The arms, legs and barrel chests looked something like iron. Bands of burnished copper ran around their wrists and ankles. Another, wider band girdled their waists, and it could have been beaten gold. Where there were joints, at elbows, knees and fingers, silver rivets glistened.

Their heads were fashioned from a substance akin to steel and were almost completely round. They had large red gems for some kind of eyes, punched hole 'noses' and a slot of a mouth with sharpened metal teeth. On either side of their heads depressed openings acted as ears.

They were of uniform height, standing taller than any of the bounty hunters, and despite the nature of their bodies they moved with surprising suppleness. Yet they did not entirely mimic the motions of an organic lifeform, being given to occasional ungainliness and a tendency to lumber.

Their appearance could only be described as startling.

The humans placed their weapons in a Watcher's out-stretched arms and it moved off with them to a fortified gatehouse.

'Homunculi,' Coilla mouthed. 'Created by sorcery.'

Aulay and Blaan exchanged awed glances. Lekmann tried to look casual.

Another Watcher arrived and dropped three wooden tags into Lekmann's palm by way of receipts. Then it waved them into the town.

Lekmann passed out the tags as they walked. 'See, told you it was no problem getting a few blades in.'

Stuffing his tag into a pocket, Aulay commented, 'I thought they might have been a bit more thorough.'

'I reckon the so-called Council of Magicians running this place is losing its grip. But if they ain't competent that's good news for us.'

They made their way into the bustling streets, leading their horses and carefully keeping Coilla boxed in. Aulay saw to it that he covered her back, the better to deliver his threat.

Hecklowe swarmed with elder races. Gremlins, pixies and dwarves talked, argued, bargained and occasionally laughed together. Little groups of kobolds weaved through the crowd, chattering among themselves in their own unintelligible language. A line of stern-faced gnomes, pickaxes over shoulders, went purposefully about their business. Trolls wearing hoods as protection against the light were led by hired elf guides. Centaurs clopped along the cobbled roads, proudly aloof in the throng. There were even a few humans, though it was noticeable that they were less often to be seen mixing with other races.

'What now, Micah?' Aulay asked.

'We find an inn and work out our strategy.'

Blaan beamed. 'Ale, good!'

'This ain't no time to be getting all unnecessary, Jabeez,' Lekmann warned him. 'We need clear heads for what has to be done. Got it?'

The man mountain sulked.

'But let's get these horses stabled first,' Lekmann suggested. To Coilla he added, 'Don't get no smart ideas.'

They worked their way further into the port's teeming thoroughfares. They passed stalls and handcarts brimming with sweetmeats, fish, breads, cheeses, fruit and vegetables. Costermongers sang out the quality of their trays of wares. Merchants pulled stubborn asses laden with bolts of cloth and sacks of spices. Wandering musicians, street performers and vociferous beggars added to the cacophony.

On corners, brazen succubi and incubi whores touted for customers with appetites jaded enough to brave the dangers of going with them. The smell of pellucid sweetened the air. It mingled with incense wafting from the open doors of a myriad temples dedicated to every known pantheon of gods. Through it all Watchers patrolled, paths miraculously clearing for them in the chaos.

The bounty hunters found a stable run by a gremlin, and for a few coins housed their mounts. They continued on foot, Aulay still close to Coilla.

At one point she thought she glimpsed a couple of orcs, crossing a distant intersection. But a Kirgizil dragon and its mean-faced kobold rider blocked her view and she couldn't be sure.

Aulay, she noticed, was fidgeting with his eye-patch. He obviously hadn't seen what she had, but for a moment she wondered if there might not be something in his 'orc sense' after all.

She knew there was no reason orcs shouldn't be here, although they were less likely because most of the orc nation was under arms, fighting others' causes. As was their lot. If there were any they could be deserters, which wasn't un-known, or on official business. That might mean they were searching for the renegade Wolverines. The other possibility, of course, was that the two she glimpsed *were* Wolverines. It was too fleeting for her to tell. She decided to be positive and allow herself some small hope.

'This'll do,' Lekmann decided.

He pointed to an inn. A coarsely painted wooden sign hung over the door. It read: *The Werebeast and Broadsword.*

The place was jammed with boisterous drinkers.

'Get in there and find us somewhere to sit, Jabeez,' Lekmann instructed.

Blaan scanned the interior, then used his mass to barge through the press, the other three in his wake. With the innate instinct of a bully, he zeroed in on a group of pixies and turfed them out.

As soon as the bounty hunters and Coilla sat, an elf serving wench arrived. Lekmann opened his mouth to order. She plonked four pewter tankards of mead down on the table, reciting, 'Take it or leave it.'

Blaan contemptuously tossed her some coins. She scooped them up and left.

The three humans' heads came together for a hushed, conspiratorial discourse. Coilla leaned back in her chair with folded arms.

'The way I see it, we've got a small problem,' Lekmann whispered. 'The ideal thing would be to get rid of this bitch first and be done with watching her. But if she's sold we won't have her to pick out the other orcs.'

'I told you,' Coilla said, 'I'm not doing that.'

Lekmann bared his teeth and hissed, 'We'll *make* you.'

'How?'

'Leave it to me, Micah,' Aulay offered. 'I'll get her to do it.'

'Eat shit, one-eye,' she responded.

Aulay seethed.

'Look, let's assume this crazy freak *ain't* gonna help us,' Lekmann argued. 'Which case it might be best if we split up. Me and Jabeez will look for somebody to buy her. You, Greever, can start searching for orcs.'

'Then what?'

'We meet back here in a couple of hours and pool stories.'

'Fine by me,' Aulay said, glaring at Coilla. 'I'll be glad to see the back of it.'

She took a deep draught of her ale and wiped the back of a hand across her mouth. 'Couldn't put it better myself.' She slammed her tankard down on Aulay's hand. Hard. There was a loud crack. His face convulsed and he let out an agonised yell.

He stared at his little finger. His face was ashen, his eyes watered. *'She . . . broke . . . it . . .'* he whined through trembling lips. Fury twisting his face, he reached for a boot with his other hand. *'I'm gonna . . . kill you . . .'* he promised.

'Shut up, Greever!' Lekmann snapped. 'There's beings watching! You ain't doing nothing to her, she's valuable.'

'But she broke my little . . .'

'Stop being such a baby. Here.' He tossed over a rag. 'Wrap this round it and close your trap.'

Coilla treated them all to a warm smile. 'Well, let's get me sold, shall we?' she purred sweetly.

'It's more of them, isn't it?' Stryke said.

'No doubt of it,' Jup confirmed. 'Same as at Trinity, and that hunting party.'

They were concealed in a thicket, stretched flat and looking down at a camp in a hollow. It was occupied by a party of humans. The rest of the band had been ordered to stay back, out of sight, and from their position Stryke and Jup couldn't see them.

The black-garbed humans undertaking various chores below were all males and numbered around twenty. They were conspicuously and heavily armed. A makeshift corral had been built for their horses, and near the centre of the camp a covered wagon was parked.

'*Shit*, that's all we need,' Stryke sighed. 'Hobrow's custodians.'

'Well, we knew they were likely to be somewhere in the area. We couldn't expect them to give up trying to get back the star we took.'

'We could do without it, though. There's enough to worry about.'

'Do you reckon they might have Coilla or Haskeer?'

'Who knows? Do you think your farsight might help?'

'It hasn't aided us much so far. But I'll give it a try.'

He gouged a hole in the earth with his fingers and wormed a hand into it. Then he concentrated, eyes closed. Stryke held his peace and continued studying the camp.

Eventually Jup opened his eyes and let out a long breath.

'Well?'

'I picked up a faint orc presence, but I'd say it wasn't as close as down there. It's not too far away, though.'

'Is that all?'

'Just about. Couldn't tell if it was male or female. Nor the direction. If those bastard humans weren't so keen on eating our magic—'

'Look.'

Down in the camp, a figure was climbing from the back of the covered wagon. It was a human female. She was of an age where childhood had been left behind but womanhood had yet to blossom. The lingering puppy fat of youth, along with honey-coloured hair and china blue eyes should have made her comely. But she wore a sullen, ill-tempered scowl and her mouth was mean.

'Oh, no,' Jup groaned.

'What?'

'Mercy Hobrow. The preacher's daughter I told you about.'

She moved around the camp with a cavalier gait, yelling at the custodians. They jumped to obey her.

'She's not much more than a hatchling,' Stryke said. 'Yet she's obviously issuing orders.'

'Tyrants are often distrustful. They'd prefer to use a member of their family than rely on outsiders. And it looks like he's groomed his spawn well.'

'Yes, but leaving a . . . *child* in command?'

'Humans are all fucking mad, Stryke, you know that.'

Now the girl was laying about the custodians with a swish.

'Have those men no pride?' Stryke wondered.

'No doubt fear of her father is the stronger emotion. But you're right about the error of giving her authority; they haven't even put out any guards.'

Stryke whispered, 'Don't speak too soon.'

Jup made to say something. Stryke clamped a hand over his mouth and moved the dwarf's head to face to their right. Two custodians were walking slowly toward their hiding place, swords drawn. Stryke removed his hand.

'They haven't seen us,' Jup said.

'No. But if they carry on this way they will, or they'll see the band.'

'We've got to take them out.'

'Right, and without alerting the others. Feel like being bait?'

Jup smiled wryly. 'Do I have a choice?'

Stryke glanced at the approaching sentries. 'Just give me enough time to get in position.' He snaked into the bushes, moving in the direction of the nearing sentries.

Jup counted to fifty in his head. Then he stood up and stepped out into the path of the sentries.

They froze, surprise on their faces.

He moved their way, hands well out from his sides, clear of his weapons. He added to their confusion by smiling.

One of the custodians barked, 'Stay where you are!'

Jup kept coming and kept smiling.

The sentries raised their swords. Behind them, Stryke quietly emerged from the undergrowth, a dagger in his hand.

The custodian bellowed again. 'Identify yourself!'

'I'm a *dwarf*,' Jup replied.

Stryke piled into them from the rear. Jup ran forward, drawing his own knife.

The four of them went down in a scrum of twisting limbs and flying fists. A few seconds of struggling sorted them into two separate fights. But the custodian's swords were second best at close quarters. Armed with knives, Jup and Stryke had the advantage.

Jup's kill was quick. He saw the way clear to his opponent's heart and took it. One blow was enough.

Stryke had more of a task. In the clash he lost his knife. Then his rival managed to get himself on top. He clutched his sword two-handed and made to bring it down like a dagger to Stryke's chest. Stryke had hold of his forearms and pushed back. The stalemate was broken when he somehow found the strength to topple the human. A brief tussle for the sword was won by Stryke. He planted it in the custodian's guts.

'Quick, let's get their bodies out of sight,' Stryke ordered.

They were pulling the corpses into the undergrowth when three more sentries appeared from the opposite direction.

Jup swiftly whipped up his knife and lobbed it at one of them. The human took it in the midriff and hit the ground. His companions charged.

Orc and dwarf met them with drawn swords and they paired off to fence.

Aware of drawing attention from the camp, Stryke tried to end his foe as fast as possible. He went at the human furiously, pouring blows on him, and ducked and weaved to find an opening. The sheer force of his assault reduced the man's defence to tatters. With a hefty swing, Stryke cleaved his neck.

Adopting similar tactics, Jup's style was unsubtle frenzy. The custodian he faced parried the first half dozen blows then flagged. Backing off, he started shouting. Jup moved in quickly and whacked him in the mouth with the flat of his blade. That put a stop to both the yelling and the human's guard. A follow-through to his stomach settled the issue.

Stryke padded to the bushes and peered down at the camp. His fear that the shouts might have been heard proved unfounded. With Jup's help, the bodies were concealed.

'What happens when they don't report back?' the dwarf panted.

'Let's not be here to find out.'

'So where to?'

'The only direction we haven't tried – due west.'

'That takes us dangerously near to Cairnbarrow.'

'I know. Got a better plan?'

Jup slowly shook his head.

'Then let's do it.'

It was half a day of hard riding before Jup said it. 'Stryke, this is useless. There's just too much land to cover.'

'We don't give up on our comrades. We're orcs.'

'Well, not *all* of us,' the dwarf reminded him, 'but I'll take being included as a compliment.'

His captain gave a tired smile. 'You're a Wolverine. I tend to forget your race.'

'It might be better for Maras-Dantia if more of us had such a poor memory in that respect.'

'Perhaps. But like I said, one thing we can't forget is members of our band, whoever they are, whatever they've done.'

'I'm not saying we should abandon them, for the gods' sake. It just seems so futile going about it this way.'

'You've come up with another plan?'

'You know I haven't.'

'Then whinging serves little purpose.' It was said harshly. Stryke moderated his tone when adding, 'We'll keep looking.'

'What about Cairnbarrow? We're getting nearer all the time.'

'And we'll get closer yet before I think of giving up.'

A pall of silence fell over them as they continued their westward trek.

Eventually they saw a rider galloping toward them from the direction they were heading.

Jup identified him. 'It's Seafe.'

Stryke halted the column.

Seafe arrived, pulling hard on the reins of his lathering horse. 'Forward scout reporting, sir!'

Stryke nodded.

'We've found him, Captain! Sergeant Haskeer!'

'*What?* Where?'

'Mile or two north. But he's not alone.'

'Don't tell me. Hobrow's men.'

'Yes, sir.'

'How many of them?' Jup said.

'Hard to tell, Sergeant. Twenty, thirty.'

'And Hobrow himself?' Stryke asked.

'He's there.'

'Any sign of Coilla?'

'Not that we could see. I left Talag keeping an eye on them.'

'All right. Well done, Seafe.' He turned and waved in the band. 'Seems we've found Sergeant Haskeer,' he relayed. 'But he's being held by Hobrow's Unis. Seafe's going to lead us there. Be ready, and approach with stealth. Let's go, Seafe.'

In due course they came to a ridge beyond which, Seafe explained, the terrain swept into a dip.

'I reckon it'd be better to dismount here and lead the horses, sir,' he suggested.

Stryke agreed and issued the order. They climbed quietly to an arrow's shot away from the top of the rise.

'Guards?' Stryke said.

'A few,' Seafe confirmed.

'That's our first priority, then.' What went through Stryke's mind was how much harder it was operating with half a band. He summoned Hystykk, Calthmon, Gant and Finje. 'Find the sentries and deal with them,' he ordered. 'Then get yourselves back here.'

As they moved off, Jup said, 'Think four's enough?'

'I hope so. It's all we can spare.' He collared a trooper. 'Stay here with the horses, Reafdaw. When the others have finished with the guards, send them up.'

'We'll be at the foot of that,' Seafe told Reafdaw, pointing to a particularly tall, gaunt tree that could just be seen above the rise. Reafdaw nodded.

Seafe led Stryke, Jup, Toche and Jad up the rise. A pitiably small crew, Stryke reflected.

They reached the crest and found themselves looking down into a lightly wooded area. Keeping low they got to Talag, stretched out beneath the tall tree. He signed for them to focus on a gap in the greenery.

Through it, they saw a clearing where trees were dotted much more sparsely. A temporary camp had been set up, with two dozen or more custodians moving about it. To one side stood a horseless buggy. Its shafts rested on a couple of downed tree trunks.

'Where's Haskeer?' Stryke whispered.

'Yonder,' Talag replied, indicating an area to the left where trees blinded the view.

They stayed in position for a good ten minutes, waiting for something significant to happen below. Then the other orcs returned. Gant gave the thumbs-up sign.

'Sure you got them all?' Stryke said.

'We covered the whole circuit, sir. If there were others, they were well hidden.'

'Well, they won't be missed for long. Anything we do has to be soon. Are you sure you saw Haskeer down there, Seafe?'

'I'm sure, chief. Couldn't mistake his ugly puss.' Hurriedly he added, 'No offence, sir.'

Stryke smiled thinly. 'That's all right, trooper. I think we know what you mean.'

More empty time passed. They were starting to get jumpy when there was a commotion below. Some kind of movement could be seen through the trees. The orcs tensed.

Kimball Hobrow appeared, straight-backed, striding purposefully. He was shouting, but they couldn't make out the words. Following him was a jeering mob of his black-costumed custodians.

They were frog-marching Haskeer.

His hands were tied behind his back and he staggered more than walked. Even from a distance it was obvious he'd been ill treated.

They took him to the middle of the clearing, by a high tree. A horse was brought over. The crowd hoisted him on to it.

Jup was puzzled. 'They're not going to let him go, surely?'

Stryke shook his head. 'No way.'

One of the humans produced a noosed rope and slipped it over Haskeer's head. The rope was secured around his neck and the other end tossed over a projecting bough. Eager hands pulled it taut.

'If we leave it another minute,' Jup whispered, 'we'll be watching a lynching.'

11

Stryke watched as the braying mob prepared for Haskeer's hanging.

'I wouldn't have your job at a time like this, chief,' Jup told him.

Down below, Hobrow climbed on to his buggy and stood on the seat. He raised his arms. The mob fell silent. 'The Supreme Creator has seen fit to return our holy relic!' he boomed. 'More than that, He has gifted us another!'

'They've got the stars,' Stryke said.

'And in His boundless wisdom, the Lord has also delivered to our justice one of the ungodly creatures who stole our birth-right!' Hobrow pointed an accusing finger at Haskeer. 'And today we have the sacred task of putting the sub-human to death!'

'Fuck that!' Stryke exclaimed. 'If anybody's going to kill Haskeer, it's me.' As Hobrow ranted on, he beckoned over one of the grunts. 'You're the best archer we've got, Breggin. Could you hit that rope from here?'

Breggin squinted and studied the target. He sucked a finger and held it up. His tongue poked from the corner of his mouth as he concentrated. Frowning, he considered the wind speed, angle of trajectory and force required to loose the shaft.

'No,' he said.

'. . . as we shall smite all our enemies with the aid of the Lord God Almighty, and . . .'

Stryke took another tack. 'All right, Breggin. Take Seafe, Gant and Calthmon and get Reafdaw up here with the horses. *On the double!*'

The grunt scurried off.

'We're going in?' Jup asked.

'We've no choice.' He nodded toward the clearing. 'Assuming they don't kill Haskeer first.'

'If they're waiting for that windbag to stop talking we might have time yet.'

'. . . to His everlasting glory! Behold the Lord's bounty!' Hobrow produced a small hessian sack and brought the stars out of it. He held them aloft and his followers roared.

Jup and Stryke looked at each other.

'. . . He moves in mysterious ways, brethren, His wonders to perform! Praise Him, and send this creature's soul straight to perdition!'

Haskeer seemed only vaguely aware of what was going on.

Stryke glanced around. 'They'd better hurry with those horses.'

Hobrow sliced his arm downward. Haskeer's horse was struck on the flank with a whip. It bolted.

The grunts returned at a run, leading the horses.

Haskeer was suspended, feet kicking.

'Mount up!' Stryke barked. 'I'm going for Haskeer. Jup, you'll back me. The rest of you, kill some Unis!'

He rode full pelt through the trees with the band following.

They ducked forks and swishing branches as they rushed down the incline. They weaved around tree trunks. They goaded their mounts to greater speed.

Then exploded into the clearing.

The custodians outnumbered them perhaps three to one.

But the orcs were mounted and had the element of surprise. They charged into the mob and laid about them. Shocked by the unexpected attack, the humans' response was a shambles.

Haskeer squirmed and twisted on the end of the rope. Stryke fought desperately to get to him, Jup lashing out wildly at his side.

A howling wedge of humans came between their horses and separated them. Jup's spooked mount turned in the flow and fetched up at a right angle in a sea of hostile blades. Cutting at them like a scythe against wheat, he fought desperately to right himself.

Stryke stayed on course but met just as much resistance. He ploughed into them with the horse, kicked out with his boots, pummelled their swords with his blade. A custodian leapt up and grabbed his belt, and tried pulling him from the saddle. Stryke cracked his skull and sent him flying back into the throng.

Above the clamour, Hobrow could be heard screaming curses and loudly invoking the name of his god.

Battling on, Stryke caught sight of two of the grunts ploughing into the back of the mob surrounding him. The diversion drew away enough custodians to give him a fighting chance of reaching Haskeer. Only a pair of humans barred his way. He despatched the first with a downward swipe that hewed his throat. The second he hacked in the face. He fell, hands to the flowing gash.

Finally getting to Haskeer, Stryke found he'd stopped struggling and was hanging limply. It looked as if it was too late.

Suddenly Jup arrived. He manoeuvred his horse beneath Haskeer's dangling feet and seized his legs. 'Hurry, Stryke!' he yelled.

Stryke stood in his stirrups and slashed through the rope. Jup gasped as he took the orc's apparently dead weight. Between them, awkwardly and very nearly unsuccessfully, Jup and Stryke got Haskeer over the dwarf's horse.

'Get him clear!' Stryke hollered.

Jup nodded and started to move off. A custodian blocked his way, waving his arms in an attempt to panic the horse. Jup rode him down. Then he headed for the treeline, taking a serpentine route in the hope of avoiding scattered humans.

Members of the band were embroiled in actions all over the clearing. Stryke looked towards the buggy. A couple of custodians stood there, trying to protect Hobrow. He was still shouting orders and hurling oaths. The sack was clutched in his hand.

Stryke decided to go for it.

He spurred his horse, but got only a short way before three custodians blocked his path. Stryke had enough speed up that he simply galloped by the first, who slashed at him ineffectually as he passed. The other two, further along, were more artful. They rushed in at him from either side. One directed an axe blow at Stryke's leg. It narrowly missed. The other leapt, intending to unhorse him. He was still in the air when Stryke's thrusting elbow met him on the bridge of his nose. The man spiralled away. Stryke resumed the dash.

In the greater mêlée, Seafe was pulled from his horse. He stood his ground against three or four encroaching custodians. Then Calthmon bowled into them and managed to haul Seafe on to his own mount.

Hobrow saw Stryke approaching and cowered, shouting for his pair of defenders to protect him. Almost immediately one of them was cut down by a passing orc. Stryke thundered in and buried his blade in the other's skull. But the victim went down with the embedded sword and it was lost.

Stryke wheeled about to face Hobrow. By now the preacher was gibbering. Stryke whipped his reins around one of the buggy's shafts and jumped, rocking the carriage as he landed. Unable to escape, Hobrow pressed himself into the seat and squirmed. Stryke grabbed a handful of his coat, pulled him to his feet and commenced battering him. His hat flew off, his face bloodied, but he held on to the sack.

A gang of custodians was running their way. Stryke increased the lathering and prised free the sack. Hobrow went down. He was still alive, much to Stryke's regret. But there was no time to rectify that now. He hastily remounted and pulled away as the first wave of would-be rescuers swept in.

Breggin and Gant had managed to loose the humans' horses and stampeded them. Several custodians tried to stem the bolting animals and were horribly trampled. The horses ran on to spread further chaos.

Stuffing the sack into his jerkin, Stryke bawled the order to retreat.

The Wolverines disengaged and began to move out. Where they could, they struck down the enemy as they left.

Into the trees and climbing the slope, Stryke spotted Jup ahead. He caught up with him. Haskeer was semi-conscious, his head rolling from side to side, and breathing shallowly. They came out of the trees and made the crest of the rise, the remainder of the band close behind. Stryke quickly checked. All were present.

Several loose custodians' horses also emerged from the dip and ran off in different directions.

'That should keep 'em busy!' Jup shouted.

'Look!' a grunt yelled.

From the south, another group of black-garbed humans was riding hard their way. At the rear was a covered wagon.

'Mercy's group,' Stryke said.

Some of them made for the rise. Others started after the Wolverines.

Stryke spurred his mount and led the band across the plain.

Evening wasn't far off. A chill wind blew in from the great northern ice field. It grew even colder.

Alfray's half of the Wolverines was making good progress in its journey to Drogan. Good enough that when they came to a tributary that flowed inland from the Calyparr Inlet before taking a great loop back, he decided to make early camp on its bank. He reasoned they could start out again before first light.

When the band petitioned for a ration of pellucid, he reasoned further that it would do no harm. They deserved it. But just a little; they were still a fighting unit and, after all, the crystal was meant for bartering.

A cob or two of the drug was imbibed. Then Alfray and Kestix fell into what passed, in orc terms, for a philosophical discussion.

'I'm just a simple soldier, Corporal,' the grunt said, 'but it seems to me that no one could ask for better gods than ours. What need is there for others?'

'Ah, how much easier things would be if everybody agreed with us,' Alfray replied, not entirely seriously.

Kestix saw no irony. Voice a little slurred and eyes glassy from the crystal, he pressed the issue. 'I mean, when you've got the Square, what more could you want?'

'It's always seemed enough for me,' Alfray agreed. 'Which one of the Tetrad do you favour most?'

'Favour most?' Kestix looked as though no one had ever asked him the question before. 'Well, the way I look at it, there's not much to choose between them.' He thought for a moment. 'Maybe Aik. Everybody likes the god of wine, don't they?'

'What about Zeenoth?'

'The goddess of fornication?' Kestix smirked like a hatchling. 'She's worthy of glorifying, know what I mean?' He gave Alfray a lewd wink.

'And Neaphetar?'

'He'd have to be the one, wouldn't he? God of war and all that. He's the name on *my* lips when we go in for a fight. Boss orc, Neaphetar.'

'You don't think him cruel?'

'Oh, he's cruel, yeah. But just.' He stared vacantly at Alfray for a second, then asked, 'Who's your favourite, Corp?'

'Wystendel, I think. The god of comradeship. I enjoy combat. *'Course* I do, I'm an orc. But sometimes I think the camaraderie of a good band's the best of our lot.'

'Anyway, I reckon the Square's got it right. Fighting, fucking, feasting. Rude and rowdy. That's how gods *should* be.'

A grunt passed him a pipe. He sucked on it, his cheeks hollowing as the smoke went down. Pungent vapour billowed from the bowl. Kestix handed the cob to Alfray.

'What I don't understand,' the grunt went on, 'is this gassion, er, passion . . . this passion for a single pod. Shit! *God*. For a single god.'

'It does seem a strange notion,' Alfray allowed. 'But then humans aren't short of crazed ideas.'

'Yeah, I mean, how can *one* god handle everything all by himself? That's a team effort, surely?'

The pipe had Alfray comfort conscious. It set him ruminating. 'You know, before the humans came, races used to be a damn sight more tolerant of each other's beliefs,' he slurred. 'Now everybody's trying to ram their religion down your throat.'

Kestix nodded sagely. 'The incomers have a lot to answer for. They've caused such ructions.'

'Still, you've made me think that we haven't paid enough attention to our gods lately. Reckon I'll sacrifice to 'em soon as I get the chance.'

They slipped into silence, each lost in his own kaleidoscopic mind theatre. The rest of the band slumped too, though there was a measure of horseplay and chuckling.

An indefinite amount of time passed. Then Kestix sat up. 'Corporal.'

'Hmmm?'

'What do you think that is?'

Creamy mist was rising from the rivulet. Through it, from the direction of the inlet, a vessel approached.

Alfray roused the band. Somewhat unsteadily, and grumbling, they lurched to their feet and armed themselves.

The tendrils of smog parted.

A barge glided majestically towards them. Low in the water, it was wide, its sides almost touching the banks. There was a spacious deck cabin astern. A carved figurehead in the likeness of a dove stood at the prow. The craft's single canvas sail rippled and crackled in the evening breeze.

When the barge was near enough for its crew to be seen, a groan went up from the band.

'Oh, no,' Kestix sighed. 'Just what we need.'

'At least they're not life-threatening,' Alfray reminded him.

'Bloody aggravating, though, sir.'

'No need to kill unless you have to,' Alfray told the grunts. 'The only magic they've got is for moving themselves about, so that's no real threat. Hang on to anything of value.'

He thought of simply ordering a speedy retreat. But that meant leaving behind possessions to be looted, and chances were that those on the barge would only follow them until their notorious curiosity was satisfied. Which could amount to being dogged for days. Better to get it over with and weather the squall.

'Perhaps they'll just go by,' Kestix said, more in hope than expectation.

'I don't think that's in their nature, trooper.'

'But we're *orcs*. Don't they know it's *dangerous* tangling with us?'

'Probably not; they aren't very bright. But remember it won't go on for ever. We can wait it out.'

The barge's sail dropped. An anchor splashed.

Then a couple of dozen diminutive figures rose from the deck like balloons and headed for the orcs. It wasn't so much flying as directional floating. They pointed themselves the way they wanted to go, languidly flapped their stumpy little arms, and slowly glided.

They looked a bit like human or dwarf babies. Alfray knew they weren't. Some of them were probably older than he was, and all of them were well versed in thieving ways. But he reckoned it was their resemblance to young helpless lifeforms that prevented many more of them being slaughtered by irate travellers.

The imps had large heads and big, round eyes that would have been appealing but for their wicked glints. They were pink-skinned and hairless, save for short, wispy down on their heads. Their sex was undefined. They wore tanned hide loincloths not unlike shiny black diapers, ringed with cloth pouches. Imps did not bear arms.

As they floated, they babbled. High-pitched, unintelligible, annoying.

A cluster of the creatures arrived overhead. Then they swooped, and suddenly they weren't so indolent.

They descended on the band's heads, shoulders and arms. Tenaciously clinging to the orcs' clothes, their prying fingers scrabbled to filch anything they could find in pocket and pouches. They tried prising away weapons and trophy neck-laces. Petite hands snatched grunts' helmets.

Alfray grabbed and shook one of the miniature pilferers to disengage it from his jerkin. It was surprisingly hard work. When he got it loose he shoved it away forcefully. The imp sailed off, spinning on its axis.

More and more of them disgorged from the barge and collected over the band like winsome vultures. As an orc disentangled himself from one imp another dropped and took its place.

Swatting at an assailant with the back of his hand, Alfray yelled, 'How do they get this many on a damn little boat like that?'

Kestix would have answered, except one of the creatures was tweaking his nose in its tiny fist. Its other hand was delving into the grunt's belt pouch. With an effort, Kestix pulled the imp off and flung it from him. It coasted into a hovering knot of its fellows, scattering them like slow motion skittles.

As Alfray peeled away an imp hugging his chest, a grunt hopped past with one clutching his leg. He was kicking furiously in an attempt to shake it free.

But every so often evidence of Maras-Dantia's failing magic was apparent when an imp plummeted and landed hard on the ground. Bouts of frantic arm-waving were needed to get them unsteadily aloft again. Alfray figured this happened because the imps passed over weakened lines of energy that broke the spell. Unfortunately it didn't down enough of them.

Still they rained down, anchoring themselves on any un-occupied parts of their victims. Orcs booted them aside, elbowed them, ripped them from clothes and threw them clear. Alfray saw a grunt holding an imp by an arm and leg. He spun around several times and let go. Thumb planted in its mouth, the imp shot towards the barge in a great arc.

Alfray started to worry that the grunts would lose patience and start killing the pests. 'Get rope!' he bellowed, batting an imp from his face. *'Rope!'*

It was an order easier issued than obeyed. Bent double, a couple of grunts made for the horses, hands over their heads to fend off dive-bombing imps. With difficulty, they managed to retrieve a length of rope.

'Take ends and spread out with it!' Alfray shouted. As they battled to do that he drew his sword. 'Present weapons! Use the flats to round them up!'

An awkward struggle ensued, with grunts doing their best to shed imps and corral them together. It took a lot of bottom-whacking and bullying, but after about ten frustrating minutes most of the bleating creatures were bunched. Some rose above the cluster, but there was nothing to be done about them.

Alfray barked an order. The grunts with the rope encircled the mass of imps with it. A couple of tugs and a hastily tied knot secured the bond.

Under Alfray's direction the band hauled the living load back to the barge. The rope was tied to the mast and the anchor brought up. They raised the sail. It caught the wind and billowed. With a helping push from all hands, the craft moved off, gathering speed.

Struggling ineffectually, the restrained imps squealed as the barge was swallowed by mist. A handful of stragglers flew after it.

Alfray expelled a breath as he watched it go. He ran the back of a hand across his forehead. 'I hope Stryke's having a better time of it,' he said.

Hobrow's men didn't pursue Stryke's group for long, so at the earliest opportunity he halted the band.

Haskeer was helped down from Jup's horse and his bonds cut. He was conscious but largely insensible. They sat him down and gave him water, which he had trouble swallowing. His neck bore vivid rope burns.

'I wish Alfray was here,' Stryke said as he examined Haskeer's injuries. 'He's taken quite a battering, but I'd say there's no major damage.'

'Except maybe to his brain,' Jup returned. 'Don't forget why he's in this state in the first place.'

'I haven't.' He slapped Haskeer's cheeks several times. 'Haskeer!'

That brought him round a bit, but not enough. Stryke took the water canteen and poured its contents over Haskeer's head. The liquid streamed down his face. His eyes opened. He mumbled something they couldn't understand.

Stryke slapped him some more. 'Haskeer! *Haskeer!*'

'Hmm? Wha——?'

'It's me. Stryke. Can you hear me?'

Haskeer responded weakly. 'Stryke?'

'What the hell you been playing at, Sergeant?'

'Playing . . . ?'

Stryke shook him, not far short of violently. 'Come on! Snap out of it!'

Haskeer succeeded in focusing. 'Captain . . . what . . . what's happening?' He seemed totally bewildered.

'What's happening is that you're a fairy's breath away from a charge of desertion. Not to mention trying to kill other band members.'

'*Kill* . . . ? Stryke, I swear——'

'Forget swearing, just explain yourself.'

'Who am I supposed to have tried killing?'

'Coilla and Reafdaw.'

Angrily, Haskeer snapped, 'What do you think I am, a . . . a . . . *human*?'

'You did it, Haskeer. I want to know why.'

'I . . . I can't . . . I don't *remember*.' He looked around, still dazed. Jup and the grunts were staring at him. 'Where are we?'

'Never mind. Are you saying you don't know what's been going on? That you're not responsible?'

Haskeer slowly shook his head.

'All right. What *do* you remember?' Stryke persisted. 'What was the last thing?'

Haskeer set to thinking. It was obviously an effort. Eventually he said, 'The battlefield. We went through it. Then . . . dragons. Dragons chasing us. Fire.'

'That's all?'

'The singing . . .'

'Singing? What do you mean?'

'There was . . . not singing exactly. A sort of music and words, but not singing.'

Stryke and Jup exchanged glances. Jup raised his eyebrows meaningfully.

'This sound, whatever it was . . .' He gave up. 'I don't know. Only other thing I remember was being sick. I felt bad.'

'That's something you never let on about,' Jup said, his tone accusing.

At one time Haskeer would have lashed out at the dwarf for a comment like that, for less, but now he just stared at him.

'Alfray thought you'd picked up a human disease from that orc encampment we torched,' Stryke told him. 'But I don't think that was enough in itself to explain your behaviour.'

'*What* behaviour, Stryke? You still haven't told me what I'm supposed to have done.'

'We were at Scratch. You attacked Reafdaw and Coilla, and made off with these.' He reached into the sack taken from Hobrow and showed him the pair of stars.

Haskeer glazed over at the sight of them. He whispered, 'Take them away, Stryke.' Then yelled, *'Take 'em away!'*

Puzzled, Stryke put them in his belt pouch, where he already had the star from Scratch.

'Take it easy,' Jup told Haskeer, near gently.

There was a sheen of sweat on Haskeer's forehead. He was breathing heavily.

'Coilla took off after you,' Stryke continued. 'We don't know where she is. Do you know what happened to her?'

'I told you, I don't know anything.' He put his face in his hands.

Just before he did, Stryke thought he looked frightened.

He and Jup moved away from him. Stryke nodded to a couple of the grunts. They went to keep an eye on Haskeer.

'What do you think, chief?'

'I don't know. He seems to be saying he had some kind of blackout. Maybe he's telling the truth, maybe not.'

'I reckon he is.'

'Why?'

'Nobody knows better than me what a bastard Haskeer is. But he isn't a deserter and, I don't know, call it my sixth sense, but something tells me that what happened was . . . beyond his control.'

'Given the history you two have, I'm surprised to hear you say that.'

'It's what I think. Not giving him the benefit of the doubt's answering injustice with injustice far as I can see.'

'Even if what you say is true, and he was under the influence of the fever or whatever, how do we know it won't happen again? How can we trust him?'

'Think on this, Stryke. If you decide he can't be trusted, where does that leave us? What do we do? Abandon him? Cut his throat? Is that the way you want to run this band?'

'I need to think on it. And I have to decide what to do about Coilla.'

'Don't delay, Captain. You know how short time is.' He pulled his jerkin closer against a wind that had grown piercing. 'The weather doesn't seem of a mind to be helpful either.'

As he spoke, a scattering of snowflakes mixed with the wind.

'Snow,' Stryke said. 'In this season. The world's broken, Jup.'

'Ah, and it might be beyond fixing, Captain.'

12

Jennesta spelt it out. 'I'm offering you an alliance, Adpar. Help me find the artifacts and I'll share their power with you.'

The face on the surface of the congealed blood was impassive.

'It's only a matter of time before Sanara butts in on this,' Jennesta added impatiently. 'So will you *say* something?'

'She doesn't always. Or doesn't choose to take part. Anyway, to hell with Sanara; I don't mind saying this in front of her. No.'

'Why?'

'I have more than enough to deal with here. And unlike you, my dear, I have no ambitions to build a bigger empire.'

'The *biggest*, Adpar! Big enough for both of us! Power enough for both!'

'I have a feeling that sharing, even with your beloved sister, would prove something you couldn't manage for long.'

'Then what about the gods?'

'What about them?'

'Plumbing the mysteries of the instrumentalities could restore our gods, the true gods, and see off this absurd lone deity the humans have brought.'

'The gods are real enough here; they need no restoring.'

'Fool! The taint will reach even you sooner or later, if it hasn't already.'

'Frankly, Jennesta, the notion just doesn't appeal. I don't trust you. Anyway, are you capable of . . . "plumbing the mysteries"?' It was meant insultingly.

'So you're going for them yourself, is that it?'

'Don't judge everybody by your own standards.'

'You don't know what you're turning your snooty nose up at!'

'At least it's my nose, and not indentured to anybody else.'

Jennesta fought to keep her temper in check. 'All right. If you're not interested in joining me and you say you make no claim on the instrumentalities for yourself, why not trade me the one you have? I'd pay substantially for it.'

'I don't have one! How many more times? It's gone!'

'You let somebody take something from you? I find that hard to believe.'

'The thief was punished. He was lucky to escape with his life.'

'You didn't even kill this convenient robber?' Jennesta mocked. 'You're going soft, sister.'

'Your stupidity I'm used to, Jennesta. What I can't stand is how boring you can be.'

'If you ignore my offer you'll regret it.'

'Will I? And who's going to make me? You? You could never best me when we were youngsters, Jennesta, and you can't do it now.'

Jennesta seethed. 'This is your last chance, Adpar. I won't ask again.'

'If you want me so much you must need me. I take pleasure from that. But I don't take kindly to ultimatums, whoever issues them. I'll do nothing to hinder you, and nothing to help either. Now leave me alone.'

This time it was Adpar who terminated the conversation.

Jennesta sat in deep thought for several minutes. She came out of it with resolve.

Dragging aside a heavy, ornate chair and pulling back several rugs, she revealed the flagstone floor. From a cabinet in a darkened corner she selected a particular grimoire, and on her way back to the cleared space plucked a curved dagger from the altar. These she deposited on the chair.

Having lit more candles, Jennesta skimmed handfuls of clotted gore from the tub. On hands and knees, she used it to mark out a large mullet on the floor, carefully ensuring that there were no breaks in the circle or its five pointed stars. That done, she took up the book and knife, and moved to the circle's centre.

She peeled back the sleeve of her gown and with a swift, deep slash of the blade cut into her arm. Her lighter blood dripped and mingled with the darker red of the pentagram. It intensified the link with her sibling.

Then she turned to the book and began something she should have done long ago.

Adpar enjoyed thwarting her sister. It was one of life's more sublime pleasures. But now she had a routine chore to attend to, though in its way it was no less gratifying.

She left the slime-encrusted viewing pool and waded from her private retreat to the larger chamber beyond. A lieutenant awaited her, along with a guard detail and two disgraced members of her swarm.

'The prisoners, Majesty,' the lieutenant hissed in peculiarly nyadd fashion.

She looked over the accused. They hung their scaly heads.

Without preamble, Adpar outlined the charge. 'You two have brought shame on the imperial swarm. That means shame on *me*. You were lax in carrying out your orders in the recent raid, and were seen by a superior officer to let several merz escape with their lives. Do you have anything to say in your defence?'

They didn't.

'Very well,' she went on, 'I take your silence as admission of dereliction. It should be well known that I'll not have weaklings in the ranks. We are fighting to keep our place in this world, and that leaves no room for idlers or cowards. Therefore the only possible verdict is guilty.' A believer in the power of theatrics, she paused for effect. 'And the penalty is death.'

She beckoned the lieutenant. He came forward holding a basin-sized brown and white shell containing two coral daggers. A pair of guards followed him carrying deep, wide-mouthed earthenware pots.

'In accordance with tradition, and as a courtesy to your martial status, you are allowed a choice,' Adpar told the condemned. She pointed to the knives. 'Carry out the sentence with your own hand and you will die with a measure of honour.' Her gaze flicked to the containers. 'Or you have the right to place your fate in the hands of the gods. If they will it, you could keep your life.'

Turning to the first prisoner, she commanded, 'Choose.'

The nyadd tensely weighed his options. Finally he uttered, 'The gods, Majesty.'

'So be it.'

At her signal, several more guards moved in and held him firm. One of the pots was brought to her. She stared into it, one hand poised completely still above the opening. She stood that way for what seemed an eternity. Then suddenly her hand darted into the jar and she pulled something from the water.

It was a fish. She held it by the tail between two fingers and her thumb as it writhed and struggled in the air. The fish was about as long as a nyadd's hand and its girth equal to three arrows bound together. Its scales and stubby fins were silvery blue. Whiskers grew from either side of its mouth.

Handling it with care, Adpar tapped the fish's side and quickly withdrew her finger. Dozens of tiny quivering spikes shot out from its body.

'I envy the dowelfish,' she stated. 'It has no predators. Its spikes are not only sharp, they pump a lethal venom that kills with excruciating pain. The fish gives its own life but always takes its enemy's.' She dipped the animal back into the pot, immersing it in water but keeping hold of it. 'Prepare him,' she ordered.

The guards forced the prisoner to his knees. A length of thread was passed to Adpar and she looped it around the dowelfish's back fin. Using the thread, she slowly pulled the fish from its pot again. Calmed by the water, it had retracted its spikes.

'Offer yourself to the gods' mercy,' Adpar told the prisoner. 'If they favour you three times, you'll be spared.'

The accused's head was roughly pushed upwards and his mouth prised open to its fullest extent. He was held in position. Adpar approached, holding out the dangling fish. Very slowly, she lowered it into the nyadd's gaping mouth. He stayed absolutely motionless. The scene was not unlike the displays put on by sword-swallowers in marketplaces all over Maras-Dantia. Except that was a trick.

Everybody watched in silence as the fish disappeared from sight. Adpar paused for a second before continuing to play out the thread, guiding its load down the nyadd's gullet. At length she stopped. Then the process was reversed and she began winding the thread around a finger as she reeled the fish up. It emerged from the nyadd's mouth wriggling feebly.

The prisoner let out a shuddering breath.

'It seems the gods have smiled on you once,' Adpar declared.

The fish was immersed in its jar once more and brought back for the second time. Again it was lowered at a leisurely pace, again she paused before its journey down the throat, again she wound the thread. In due course the dowelfish came out of the mouth without causing harm.

Shaking and gasping, the accused looked near collapse.

'Our gods are benign today,' Adpar said. 'So far.'

A last return to the water and the apparently pacified fish was ready for the third trial. Adpar went through exactly the same routine. The point was reached where she stayed her hand before lowering the fish into the nyadd's craw. She began unwinding the twine.

The thread trembled. A shudder ran through the prisoner. Eyes wide, he took to retching, and struggled against the guards. The thread snapped. Adpar stood back and motioned for the guards to release him. They let go and involuntarily his mouth snapped shut.

Then he started screaming.

Hands clawing at his throat and chest, he rolled and contorted. Spasms wracked his body, green bile erupted from his mouth. He shrieked and contorted.

The death throes lasted an unconscionable amount of time. They were terrible to witness.

When silence returned and the prisoner was still, Adpar spoke. 'The gods' will has been done. They have called him to them. It is fitting.'

She turned to the second quaking prisoner. The other pot and the knives were offered. Without a word he took a knife. The carapace at his throat meant the jagged blade had to be forcefully applied several times. At length a crison spray marked his success.

At a wave of Adpar's hand the guard detail set to removing the bodies.

'We are fortunate that our culture is ruled by divine justice and compassion,' she proclaimed. 'Other realms are less benevolently governed. Why, I myself have a sister who would have *gloated* over a scene like this.'

The snowfall was heavier, the sky black.

Much as he wanted to push on, Stryke had to concede that travel was impossible. He ordered the column to halt. There being no natural shelter, the band built a fire, which fought the snow and wind to burn. They huddled round it miserably, swathed in horse blankets.

Jup had used some of Alfray's salves to treat Haskeer's wounds. Now Haskeer sat in silence, staring at the meagre flames. Nobody else felt much like talking either.

The hours passed and the blizzard was constant. Despite the weather, some of the band managed to drowse.

Then something loomed out of the snow.

It was a tall figure mounted on a handsome white horse. As it drew closer they saw the figure was human.

The band leapt up and went for their weapons.

Now they could make out that the human male was wrapped in a dark blue cloak. He had shoulder-length hair and was bearded. His age was hard to reckon.

'There might be more of them!' Stryke yelled. 'Stand ready!'

'I'm alone and unarmed,' the human called out, his voice calm. 'And with your leave I'll dismount.'

Stryke glanced about, but saw nothing else moving in the snow. 'All right,' he agreed. 'Do it slowly.'

The stranger dismounted. He held out his hands to show he had no blade. Stryke ordered Talag and Finje to search him. That done, they brought him forward. Reafdaw took charge of his horse, winding its reins around a withered tree stump. The eyes of the band flicked in turn from the surrounding whited-out terrain to this tall, unruffled human who had arrived in their midst.

'Who are you, human?' Stryke demanded. 'What do you want?'

'I am Serapheim. I saw your fire. All I want is warmth.'

'It's dangerous riding into a camp uninvited these days. How do you know we won't kill you?'

'I trust in the chivalry of orcs.' He glanced at Jup. 'And of those they ally with.'

'What are you, Mani or Uni?' the dwarf said.

'Not all humans are either.'

'Huh!' Jup exclaimed sceptically.

'It's true. I carry no baggage of gods. May I?' He stretched his hands to the fire. But Stryke noticed that despite the bitter cold this stranger did not look discomforted; his teeth didn't chatter, his disgustingly pale skin showed no tinge of blue.

'How do we know you're not part of some trap?' Stryke asked.

'I can't blame you for thinking that. The perceptions my race have of yours are just as distrustful. But then, many humans are like mushrooms.'

They gave him puzzled looks. Stryke thought he might be a simpleton. Or mad.

'Mushrooms?' he said.

'Yes. They live in the dark and are force-fed shit.'

A ripple of laughter came from the band.

'Well put,' Jup told the stranger in guarded good humour. 'But who are you that you should be travelling a war-torn land alone and unarmed?'

'I'm a storyteller.'

'A story's all we need right now,' Stryke commented cynically.

'Then I'll tell you one. Though I fear it's short on plot and could end as a tragedy.' There was something about the way he said it that held them. 'Could it be that you're seeking one of your own kind?' the human added.

'What if we are?'

'A female member of your band?'

'What do you know of that?' Stryke rumbled darkly.

'A little. Enough to aid you perhaps.'

'Go on.'

'Your comrade's been captured by bounty hunters of my race.'

'How do you know this? Are you one of them?'

'Do I *look* like a mercenary? No, my friend, I'm not one of them. I've just seen them with her.'

'Where? And how many of them?'

'Three. Not far from here. But they would have moved on by now.'

'How does this help us?'

'I know where they've gone. Hecklowe.'

Stryke eyed him suspiciously. 'Why should we believe you?'

'That's your choice. But why would I lie?'

'For a dark purpose of your own, maybe. We've learnt the hard way to doubt anything a human says.'

'As I said, you can't be blamed for that. On this occasion a human is telling you the truth.'

Stryke stared at him. He couldn't read his face. 'I need to think,' he said. He detailed a couple of grunts to keep an eye on the human and wandered away from the fire.

The snow might have been a little lighter. He didn't really notice. His mind was on weighing the stranger's words.

'Am I intruding?'

Stryke turned. 'No, Jup. I was just trying to make sense of what we heard. Starting with why we should believe this Serapheim.'

'Because there's a certain kind of logic to it?'

'Maybe.'

'Because we're desperate?'

'That's more like it.'

'Let's think this through, chief. *If* this human's speaking true, we assume the bounty hunters have Coilla because of the price on her head, yes?'

'If not, wouldn't they have killed her already?'

'That's what I figured. But why take her to Hecklowe?'

Stryke shrugged. 'Could be one of the places where the bounty's doled out. Let's work on believing him. That leaves us with a decision. Should we go after Coilla or keep the rendezvous with the rest of the band first?'

'We're nearer Hecklowe than Drogan.'

'True. But if Coilla has a value she's unlikely to be harmed.'

'You're not taking her nature into account. She'll be no passive hostage.'

'Let's trust to her good sense. In which case things are going to be hard for her but not life-threatening.'

'So that's an argument for meeting with Alfray first and going into Hecklowe with the whole band.'

'Yeah, better odds. The downside is that delay might mean Coilla being sent back to Jennesta. Then we really would have lost her.'

They glanced in the direction of the stranger. He was still by the fire. The grunts by him seemed a little more relaxed, and several were engaged in conversations.

'On the other hand,' Jup went on, 'there *is* an agreed time for rendezvousing with Alfray. Suppose he thinks the worst's happened to us and goes into Drogan to tangle with the centaurs?'

'I wouldn't put it past him.' Stryke sighed. 'It's on a blade's edge, Jup, and we need to be absolutely sure that—'

A chorus of shouts interrupted. Stryke and Jup spun around. The stranger had gone. So had his horse. They ran to the fire. Grunts were stumbling and yelling in the swirling whiteness. Stryke collared Gant. 'What the hell happened, trooper?'

'The human, Captain, he just . . . went.'

'Went? What do you mean, *went*?'

Talag intervened. 'That's right, sir. I took my eyes off him for a second and he was gone.'

'Who saw him go?' Stryke shouted.

None of the grunts owned to it.

'This is crazy,' Jup said, squinting into the snow. 'He couldn't have just disappeared.'

Sword in hand, Stryke stared too, and wondered.

13

Voices and laughter were all around him.

He was walking in a crowd of orcs. Orcs of both sexes and all ages. Orcs he had never seen before.

They sported tiny adornments of dress that told him they were from many different clans. Yet there was no obvious animosity. They seemed happy and he didn't feel in any way threatened. In fact there was an air of anticipation, a holiday mood.

He was on the sandy beach. The sun was at its highest point and beating down intensely. Shrieking white birds circled far overhead. The crowd was heading for the ocean.

Then he saw that a ship was anchored a little way offshore. It had three sails, now resting, and from the foremost mast a flag flew, decorated with a red emblem he didn't recognise. The carved effigy of a female orc, resplendent with raised sword, stood out from the prow. Battle shields lined the ship's side, each bearing a different design. It was the biggest vessel Stryke had ever seen, and certainly the most magnificent.

The leaders of the crowd were already wading out to it. They didn't need to swim, so the ship was either flat-bottomed or stood in a deeper strait edging the beach. He was taken along by the flow of orcs. None of them spoke to him, but in a strange way that made him feel accepted.

Over the hubbub he heard his name, or at least he thought he did. He looked around, taking in the torrent of faces. Then he saw her, moving against the crowd, coming his way.

'There you are!' she greeted him.

Despite his confusion, despite not knowing where he was or what was going on, he smiled.

She returned the smile and said, 'I knew you'd come.'

'You did?'

'Well, hoped,' she confessed. Her eyes sparkled.

Emotions welled up in him that he didn't understand, and certainly couldn't articulate. So he didn't try. He simply smiled again.

'Are you here to help?' she asked.

His reply was a baffled look.

She adopted the expression of good-natured pique that he was growing used to. 'Come on,' she said.

Stryke went with her to the ocean. They walked into the mild, chalky-flecked waves lapping the beach and waded, thigh-deep, to the ship. Orcs were using ropes and ladders to reach the deck. He watched admiringly as the female, moving with athletic suppleness, joined the climbers and scaled the side. Then he hauled himself aboard the gently swaying vessel.

A hold was open mid-deck. Crates, barrels and chests were being passed up. The orcs began carrying them to the rail and over the side, where another chain was forming back to the beach. Stryke and the female took places in the line, passing along the cargo. He admired the rippling of her arm and leg muscles as she hefted boxes and swung them to him.

'What are these things?' he asked.

She laughed. 'How do you make your way in the world knowing so little?'

He shrugged, abashed.

'Do they not import needed things where you come from?' she said.

'Orcs don't.'

'Oh, yes; you say your land is home to more than orcs. Those dwarves and gremlins and . . . what was it? Humans.'

His face darkened. 'Humans are not of my land. Though they would make it so.'

She handed him another piece of cargo. 'My point is that even where you come from, needful things must be brought in.'

'Where do these things come from?'

'From other orcs in other places that have things we don't.'

'I haven't heard of other such places.'

'You gall me.' Smiling, she waved a hand at the ocean. 'I mean those lands aross the ocean.'

'I didn't know there was anything across the ocean. Isn't the water all there is?'

'Obviously not. Where do you think all this came from?'

Suitably chided, he caught the next box she sent his way. Thrown with a little more force than before, he thought. He tossed it to the next orc in line, turned back to her and said, 'These are riches, then?'

'You could say that.' She moved out of the line, taking the crate she had with her. 'I'll show you.' He stepped aside too. The line closed up; there were more than enough orcs to help.

She put the crate on the deck. He knelt beside her. Producing a knife from her belt sheaf, she used it to lever open the box. It was full of a reddish, powdery material that looked like dried leaves. He obviously didn't know what it was.

'Turm,' she explained. 'A spice. It makes food better.'

'This has value?'

'If we want our food to taste good, yes! That's its value. Not all riches come as coins or gems. Your sword, for example.'

'My sword?' His hand went to it. 'It's a good blade, but nothing special.'

'In itself, perhaps not. But in skilful hands, in the hands of a warrior born, it becomes so much more.'

'I see. I really do see.'

'And so it is with orcs. With all living things.'

His craggy face creased. 'Now I'm not so—'

'They're like blades. As sharp or as dull.'

Now it was his turn to laugh.

'Yet all have value,' she emphasised.

'Even my enemies?'

'It is right that orcs have enemies. Even if they change, and today's enemy becomes tomorrow's friend.'

'That's not my situation,' he replied coolly. 'It won't happen.'

'Whether it comes to pass or not, even mortal enemies have their value.'

'How can they?'

'Because it's possible to respect, which is to say value, their fighting skills, their determination. Their courage, if they have it. Not least, they're precious in just being there for an orc to face. We need a foe. It's what we do. It's in our blood.'

'I'd never thought of it that way.'

'But although we fight that doesn't necessarily mean we have to hate.'

Stryke couldn't entirely accept that. Though it did set him thinking.

'But what we must value most of all,' she added, 'are those closest to us.'

'You make things seem so . . . straightforward.'

'That's because they are, my friend.'

'Here, perhaps. Where I come from, all hands are against us and there is much to be overcome.'

Her expression grew sombre. 'Then be a blade, Stryke. Be a blade.'

He woke with a racing pulse. His breathing was so rapid he almost panted.

Light, fetid rain was falling from a dismal sky, and most of the snow had been washed away. It was miserable and cold. The couple of hours' sleep hadn't refreshed him at all. There was a bad taste in his parched mouth and his head pounded.

He lay there, letting the rain bathe his face, and dwelt on what, for want of a better word, he termed the dream. Dreams, visions, messages from the gods; whatever they were, they had grown more vivid, more intense. The smell of ozone, the motes in his eyes from the glaring sun, the warm breeze that caressed his skin; all were slow to fade.

Again the thought that he was being betrayed by his own mind and going insane clutched his heart like an icy claw. Yet another, contrary, notion ran almost as strongly: the feeling that he'd come to expect the dreams, even welcome them.

That was something he didn't want to pursue, not now.

He sat up and looked around. All the others were awake and going about their chores. The horses were being tended, bedrolls shaken out, weapons sharpened.

The events of the night came back to him. Not those of his dream but what had occurred before that. They had kept their eyes peeled for the mysterious human for a long time, and even ventured out into the snow in small parties to search for him. There had been no sign and eventually they gave up. At some point Stryke must have drifted into sleep, although he couldn't remember doing it.

Serapheim, if that was the stranger's real name, was another mystery to add to the list. But it wasn't one Stryke was going to waste time pondering, mostly because he didn't want to consider the distinct possibility that the man was crazy. That would throw into doubt the only clue they had to Coilla's whereabouts. And at a time like this they needed something hopeful. Badly.

Stryke pushed all that from his mind. He had something more important to occupy his thoughts.

Jup stood by the horses, talking with a couple of the grunts. He strode over to them.

Without preamble he told the dwarf, 'I've decided.'

'We're going for Coilla, right?'

'Right.'

'It must have occurred to you that this Serapheim character was lying. Or just plain mad.'

'I've given some thought to both. If he was lying, why?'

'As bait for a trap?'

'Too fancy a way of doing it.'

'Not if it works.'

'Perhaps. I still don't think it's likely, though.'

'What about him being insane?'

'I grant that's more possible. Maybe he is. But . . . I don't know, I just didn't feel that. 'Course, human madness isn't something I've had too much experience with.'

'Really? Take a look around some time.'

Stryke smiled, thinly. 'You know what I mean. But what Serapheim said is the only clue we've had about Coilla.' He saw Jup's face and qualified that. 'All right, *possible* clue. I reckon Hecklowe's worth a try.'

'What about that delaying us meeting up with Alfray?'

'We'll have to let him know.'

'And what's your decision on him?' Jup nodded toward Haskeer, sitting to one side by himself.

'He's still part of this band. Only he's on probation. Object?'

'No. Just a little wary, that's all.'

'Don't think I'm not. But we'll keep an eye on him.'

'We've got time for that?'

'Believe me, Jup, if he causes any more trouble he's out. Or dead.'

The dwarf didn't doubt his captain meant it. 'We should tell him what's happening. He's an officer, after all. Isn't he?'

'For now. I hadn't planned on breaking him unless he gets out of hand again. Come on.'

They walked over to Haskeer. He looked up at them and nodded.

'How're you feeling?' Stryke asked.

'Better.' His tone and general demeanour indicated there was some truth in that. 'I just want the chance to prove I'm still worthy of being a Wolverine.'

'That's what I wanted to hear, Sergeant. But after what you did I'm going to have to put you on probation for a while.'

'But I don't *know* what I did!' Haskeer protested. 'That is, I know what you told me but I don't remember doing any of it.'

'That's why we're going to keep an eye on you until we find out what caused it, or until your behaviour's good enough for long enough.'

Jup put it less diplomatically. 'We don't want you going gaga on us again.'

Haskeer flared, *'Why don't you—'* then checked himself.

Stryke reflected that this might be a good sign, a flash of the old Haskeer. 'The point is that we don't need passengers and we certainly don't need a liability,' he said. 'Got it?'

'Got it,' Haskeer confirmed, more subdued again.

'See that you have. Now listen. That human who came here last night, Seapheim, said that Coilla was being taken to Hecklowe. We're going there. What I want from *you* is to obey orders and act like a member of this band again.'

'Right. Let's get on with it.'

Reasonably satisfied, Stryke gathered the others and explained the new plan. He gave them an opportunity to comment or protest. That drew a minor question or two, but nothing significant. He got the impression they were relieved to be doing something positive at last.

He finished by saying, 'I need two volunteers to take the message to Alfray. But be warned; it could be a dangerous mission.'

Every grunt stepped forward. He picked Jad and Hystykk, mindful that he was about to deplete numbers even more perilously.

'The message is simple,' he told them. 'Let Alfray know where we've gone, and that we'll get to Drogan as soon as we can.' He thought for a moment and added a rider, 'If from the time this message is delivered a week passes without sight of us, assume we're not coming. In which case Alfray and his band are free to act as they think best.'

He broke the sober mood that brought down by ordering them all to get ready to move.

As they hastened to obey, he reached into his belt pouch and brought out the three stars. He examined them thoughtfully, then looked up and saw Haskeer staring at him.

'That means you too, Wolverine,' he said.

Haskeer waved and jogged toward his horse. Stryke slipped the stars back into the pouch and climbed on to his own mount.

Then they were on the move again.

They called Hecklowe the city that never slept.

Certainly the normal rhythms of day and night meant little there, but it was not quite a city. Not in the way of great northern settlements like Urrarbython or Wreaye. Or even the human centres of the south like Bracebridge or Ripple, which were still growing at an alarming rate. But it was big enough to accommodate a constantly shifting population made up of all Maras–Dantia's elder races.

Some lived there permanently. They were mostly purveyors of vice, excess and usury. Not least among these were slavers and their agents, who found it convenient to be located in a place where a river of life constantly flowed. Although unrest was forbidden, all other kinds of crime had become common in Hecklowe. Many held this was another baleful effect of the incomers' influence, and there was truth in it.

These thoughts passed through Coilla's mind as the trio of bounty hunters hustled her out of the inn at dawn. They found the streets as crowded as they had been when they arrived the evening before.

After Lekmann warned her, again, about not trying to escape, Aulay had a question for him.

'You sure we're going to get more for her from a slaver than Jennesta?'

'Like I said, they pay good for orcs as bodyguards and such.'

'Crossing Jennesta's not a good plan,' Coilla put in.

'You shut up and leave the thinking to your betters.'

Coilla glanced at Blaan, vacant-eyed and slack-jawed. She looked at Aulay, with his patched eye, bandaged ear and splinted finger. 'Yeah,' she said.

'Suppose she's lying about the Wolverines being here,' Aulay said.

'Will you give that a rest?' Lekmann retorted. 'This is the logical place for them to be. If they're not, we'll still make a profit selling this bitch, then we can carry on searching somewhere else.'

'Where, Micah?' Blaan asked.

'Don't *you* start, Jabeez!' Lekmann snapped. 'I'll figure something out if it comes to that.'

They fell silent as a pair of Watchers lumbered by.

'Let's get on with it, Micah,' Aulay pleaded impatiently.

'Right. Like we agreed, you're going to search for orcs. They're trying to sell something, remember. So look in the bazaar, the gem traders' quarter, the information barterers' neighbourhood – anywhere they might find a buyer.'

Aulay nodded.

'Meanwhile, me and Jabeez are going to look for a new owner for her,' Lekmann went on, jabbing a thumb at Coilla. 'We'll see you back here no later than noon.'

'Where you going?'

'To the east side, to look up a name I heard. Now move your arse, we ain't got time to burn.'

They went their separate ways.

'What do you want me to do, Micah?' Blaan asked.

'Just keep an eye on the orc. If she gets smart, crack her.'

They made Coilla walk between them, even though that

irritated pedestrians in narrower streets. Coilla drew glances from passersby, many of them wary. She was, after all an orc, and it was well known that orcs were best dealt with respectfully.

'Question,' she said.

'Better be worth my breath answering,' Lekmann replied.

'Who's this slave buyer we're going to?'

'He's called Razatt-Kheage.'

'That's a goblin name.'

'Yeah, that's what he is.'

She sighed. 'A damn goblin . . .'

'Not much love between orcs and goblins, eh?'

'Not much between orcs and just about anybody, shit face.'

Blaan sniggered. Lekmann shot him a look that put a stop to it.

Lekmann transferred his glare to Coilla. 'You've got any more questions, just fucking forget 'em, all right?'

They turned a corner. A small crowd had gathered around a pair of fays having a loud argument.

Fays were said to be the offspring of unions between elves and fairies, and were generally regarded as cousins to those races. They were insubstantially built, with spiky, slightly upturned noses and black button eyes. Their small, delicate mouths had tiny rounded teeth. They weren't a naturally belligerent race and certainly weren't designed for combat.

These two were reeling drunkenly. They shouted at each other and aimed feeble blows. It was unlikely either was going to be hurt unless they fell over.

The bounty hunters laughed. 'Can't hold their liquor,' Lekmann mocked.

'It was *your* kind that brought this sort of behaviour to Maras-Dantia,' Coilla told him with withering scorn. 'You're destroying my world.'

'Ain't yours no more, savage. And it's called Centrasia now.'

'Like fuck it is.'

'You should be grateful. We're bringing you the benefits of civilisation.'

'Like slavery? That was almost unknown until your race came. Maras-Dantians didn't *own* each other.'

'What about you orcs? You're born into somebody or other's service, aren't you? That's serfdom, ain't it? We didn't start *that*.'

'It's *become* slavery. You tainted it with your ideas. It used to be a good arrangement; it let orcs do what they were born for. Fighting.'

'Talking of fighting . . .' He nodded to the other side of the cobbled street. The fays were brawling, sending ineffective punches at each other's heads.

Blaan laughed idiotically.

'See?' Lekmann taunted. 'You barbarians don't need lessons in violence from us. It's already there, just below the surface.'

Coilla had never been so in need of a sword.

One fay produced a hidden knife and began swinging it, though both combatants were obviously far too drunk to offer a really serious threat.

Then a pair of Watchers suddenly appeared; perhaps the ones they'd seen earlier, it was impossible to tell. Coilla was surprised at how fast they moved. It belied their cumbersome mien. Three or four more homunculi arrived, and all of them converged on the fighting fays. They were so drunk, so busy with each other and so taken by surprise by the Watchers' speed that they had no time to try running.

The fragile creatures were overwhelmed and held by powerful arms. They were lifted bodily, their tiny legs kicking in impotent anger. Little effort was required to disarm the one with the knife.

As the crowd looked on in silence, two Watchers stepped forward and took hold of the squealing fays' heads in their massive hands. Then, in a matter-of-fact, almost casual manner, the fays' slender necks were snapped. Even from where they were standing the bounty hunters and Coilla heard the crack of bones.

The Watchers trudged off, bearing the corpses of their victims like slack rag dolls. Wiser about Hecklowe's level of tolerance, the crowd began melting away.

Lekmann gave a low whistle. 'They take law 'n' order serious round here, don't they?'

'I don't like it,' Blaan complained. 'I've got a hidden weapon too, like that dead fay.'

'So keep it out of sight, then.'

Blaan continued grumbling and Lekmann carried on haranguing him. It diverted their attention from Coilla. She seized her chance.

Lekmann was blocking her path. She rammed her boot into his groin. He groaned loudly and doubled up. Coilla took the first step of a run.

An arm like an iron barrel band clamped around her neck. Blaan dragged her struggling into the mouth of an adjacent alley. Watery eyed and white faced, Lekmann limped in after them.

'You bitch,' he whispered.

He looked back towards the street. Nobody seemed to have noticed what was going on. Turning to Coilla he delivered a swingeing whack across her face. Then another.

The briny taste of blood filled her mouth.

'Pull something like that again and to hell with the money,' he snarled, 'I'll kill you.'

When he was satisfied she'd calmed, he told Blaan to let go of her. Coilla dabbed at trickles of blood from her mouth and nose. She said nothing.

'Now *move*,' he ordered.

They resumed their journey, the bounty hunters keeping close to her.

Nine or ten twists and turns later and they entered the eastern quarter. If anything the streets there were narrower and even more jammed. It was a maze, and difficult for outsiders to navigate.

As they stood on a corner waiting for Lekmann to get his bearings, Coilla's eye was caught by a tall figure moving through the crowd two or three blocks away. As on the day before, when she'd thought she'd seen a couple of orcs, it was a fleeting glimpse. But it looked like Serapheim, the human wordsmith they'd encountered on the plains. He'd told them he had just left Hecklowe, so why return? Coilla decided she was probably mistaken. Which was quite likely as all humans looked the same to her anyway.

Then they were off again. Lekmann took them to the heart of the quarter and an area of winding high-walled passageways. After a tortuous journey through these shadowy lanes, where crowds were very much thinner, they came to the mouth of an alley. At its end and to the side stood a building that had once been white and handsome. Now it was grimy and dilapidated. The few windows were shuttered, the sole door had been reinforced.

Lekmann got Blaan to rap on it, then nudged him aside. Having waited a full minute they were about to knock again when a viewing panel was slid aside. A pair of yellowy eyes scrutinised them, but nothing was said.

'We're here to see Razatt-Kheage,' Lekmann announced.

There was no response.

'The name's Micah Lekmann,' he added.

The disembodied eyes continued staring at them.

'A mutual friend cleared my path,' Lekmann went on, patience thinning. 'Said I'd be welcome.'

The silent inspection lasted another few seconds then the panel was slammed shut.

'Don't seem too friendly,' Blaan commented.

'They ain't exactly in a friendly line of business,' Lekmann reminded him.

There was the scrape of bolts being drawn inside and the door creaked open. Pushing Coilla in first, Lekmann and Blaan entered.

A goblin faced them. Another closed and re-bolted the door. Their frames were skeletal, with knobbly green flesh stretched tight and resembling parchment. They had prominent shoulder-blades that gave the impression they were slightly hunchbacked. But what they lacked in excess fat was made up with sinew; these were strong, agile creatures.

Their heads were oval-shaped and hairless. Their ears were small and flapped, their mouths rubbery-lipped gashes. They had squashed noses with punch-hole nostrils and large teardrop shaped eyes with black orbs and jaundice-yellow surrounds. Both were armed with long, thick clubs topped with studded maces.

In the spacious room that spread out beyond them there were seven or eight more of their granite-faced comrades.

A wooden platform, level with a human's chest, ran the length of the room's far wall. It was scattered with rugs and cushions. At its centre stood an ornately carved, high-backed chair like a throne. A guard was positioned on either side.

Seated in it was another goblin. But where the rest wore martial leathers and chain mail, he was dressed more grandly in silk, and he was bedecked with jewellery. One of his languid talons held the mouthpiece of a tube that ran to a hookah, from which thin tendrils of white smoke drifted.

'I am Razatt-Kheage,' the slaver said. His voice was sibilant. 'Your name has been made known to me.' He gave Coilla an appraising look. 'I understand you have merchandise to offer.'

'That we do,' Lekmann replied in a tone seeping false bonhomie. 'This is it.'

Razatt-Kheage made an imperious gesture with his hand. 'Come.'

Lekmann shoved Coilla and the trio walked to a small staircase at one end of the dais. A pair of henchlins accompanied them. When they approached the throne, Lekmann nodded at Blaan and he put an armlock on Coilla. She was kept a safe distance from the slaver.

Razatt-Kheage offered Lekmann the hookah pipe.

'What is it, crystal?'

'No, my friend. I prefer more intense pleasures. This is pure lassh.'

Lekmann blanched. 'Er, no, I won't thanks. I try to keep away from the more violent narcotics. And what with it being, uhm, habit forming and all . . .'

'Of course. It's a little indulgence I can afford, however.' He inhaled deeply from the pipe. His eyes took on a more glazed sheen as he expelled the heady cloud. 'To business. Let us examine the goods.' He waved lazily at one of his minions.

This goblin left his place by the throne and scuttled to Coilla. As Blaan held her firm, the goblin proceeded to paw her. He squeezed the muscles on her arms, patted her legs, stared into her eyes.

'You'll find she's fit as a flea,' Lekmann remarked, ladling the geniality some more.

The goblin roughly forced open Coilla's mouth and inspected her teeth.

'I'm not a damn horse!' she spat.

'She's a spunky one,' Lekmann said.

'Then she will be broken,' Razatt-Kheage replied. 'It has been done before.'

His henchlin finished with Coilla and nodded to him.

'It seems your wares are acceptable, Micah Lekmann,' the slaver hissed. 'Let us talk of payment.'

While they negotiated, Coilla took a good look around the

chamber. Its sole door, barred windows and profusion of guards, not to mention Blaan's hold on her, all quickly confirmed that she had no choice but to bide her time.

Lekmann and the slaver finally agreed a price. The amount was substantial. Coilla didn't know whether to be flattered by it.

'It is agreed, then,' Razatt-Kheage said. 'When will it be convenient for you to return for your money?'

That took Lekmann by surprise. 'Return? What do you mean, return?'

'Do you think I would keep such a sum here?'

'Well, how quickly can you get it?'

'Shall we say four hours?'

'*Four hours*? That's a hell of a—'

'Perhaps you would prefer dealing with another agent?'

The bounty hunter sighed. 'All right, Razatt-Kheage, four hours. Not a minute longer.'

'You have my word. Do you wish to wait or return?'

'I have to meet somebody. We'll come back.'

'It would make sense if you left the orc here in the meantime. She will be secure and you will not have the inconvenience of guarding her.'

Lekmann eyed him suspiciously. 'How do I know she's still going to be here when we get back?'

'Among my kind, Micah Lekmann, when a goblin gives his word it is a grievous insult to doubt it.'

'Yeah, you slavers are such an honourable bunch,' Coilla remarked sarcastically.

Blaan applied painful pressure to her arm. She gritted her teeth and didn't give them the satisfaction of crying out.

'As you say . . . *spunky*,' Razatt-Kheage muttered unpleasantly. 'What is your decision, human?'

'All right, she can stay. But my partner Blaan here stays with her. And if it ain't considered an insult to you and your race,

I'm telling him that if there's any . . . problems, he's to kill her. Got that, Jabeez?'

'Got it, Micah.' He tightened his hold on Coilla.

'I understand,' Razatt-Kheage said. 'In four hours, then.'

'Right.' He headed for the door accompanied by a henchlin.

'Don't hurry back,' Coilla called after him.

14

'It's just not *natural*, Stryke. Giving up their weapons isn't something orcs should be asked to do.'

It was the first definite thing Haskeer had said since being reunited with the band. He sounded almost like his old self.

'We don't get into Hecklowe otherwise,' Stryke explained again. 'Stop making a fuss.'

'Why don't we conceal a few blades?' Jup suggested.

'Bet *everybody* does that,' Haskeer said.

Stryke noted how Haskeer even seemed to be making an effort to be reasonable with Jup. Maybe he really had changed. 'They probably do. But stopping weapons going in isn't the point. It's using them in there that brings the death penalty. The Council knows that, everybody going in knows it. Even Unis and Manis know it, for the gods' sake. It's just that they don't search all visitors thoroughly. Otherwise the place would grind to a halt.'

Jup interjected, 'But get caught in a fight with weapons—'

'And they kill you, yes.'

'So we *don't* hide some weapons?'

'Are you mad? An orc without a blade? Of course we smuggle some in. What we don't do, *any* of us . . .' he gave

Haskeer a pointed look '. . . is use them without my direct order. Any orc should be able to improvise. We've got fists, feet and heads. Right?'

The band nodded and began slipping knives into boots, sleeves and helmets. Stryke chose a favourite two-edged blade. Jup did the same. Haskeer went one better. Having concealed a knife, he also wrapped a length of chain around his waist and covered it with his jerkin.

Hecklowe by day was as impressive and strange a sight as Hecklowe by night. This day, rain had given its incredibly varied architecture an oily sheen. The tops of towers, the roofs of buildings, the sloping sides of mini pyramids glistened wetly and gave off a rainbow sheen.

The band made its way to the freeport's main entrance. As usual, a multi-racial crowd was massed at the gates. Dismounting, the orcs got in line, leading their horses.

They had an interminable wait, during which Haskeer scowled menacingly at kobalds, dwarves, elves and any other species he had real or imagined grudges against. But eventually they reached the checkpoint and found themselves dealing with the silent Watchers.

Jup was first. An homunculus sentinel stood with arms outstretched waiting for his weapons. The dwarf handed over his sword, an axe, a hatchet, two daggers, a knife, a slingshot and ammo, a spiked knuckle-duster and four sharpened throwing stars.

'I'm travelling light,' he told the expressionless Watcher.

By the time the rest of the band had divested themselves of similar quantities of weapons the queue was much longer and shorter on patience.

Finally the band pocketed their wooden receipt tags and were waved in.

'The Watchers seem a lot more sluggish since I was last here,' Stryke observed.

Jup nodded. 'The bleeding of the magic is affecting everything. Though it probably isn't as bad here as further inland. I've noticed that the power's always stronger near water. But if humans keep carrying on the way they have been, even places like this are going to be in trouble.'

'You're right. Even so, I'd rather we didn't have to tackle the Watchers. They might be less powerful than they were but they're still designed to be killing machines.'

'I don't reckon they're so tough,' Haskeer boasted.

'Haskeer, *please*. Don't get into any fights unless there's no other way.'

'Right. You can rely on me, boss.'

Stryke wished he could believe that. 'Come on,' he said, 'let's get these horses stabled.'

They managed that without too much bother, and Stryke made sure the caches of pellucid weren't left in the saddlebags. Each member carried their portion about his person.

Then they walked the crowded streets, attracting a certain amount of attention and turned heads, which was no mean feat in a place like Hecklowe. Though it was noticeable that nobody lingered in their path. At length they found a small plaza where it was a little easier to talk without being jostled. There were trees in the square, but even here, with strong flows of magic, they looked frail and mean-leafed.

Stryke's troops bunched around him., 'Ten orcs and a dwarf hanging around together isn't tactful,' he told them. 'We're best splitting into two groups.'

'Makes sense,' Jup said.

'My group will be Haskeer, Toche, Reafdaw and Seafe. Jup, you'll take Talag, Gant, Calthmon, Breggin and Finje.'

'Why ain't I leading a group?' Haskeer complained.

'There are six in Jup's group, only five in mine,' Stryke explained. 'So of course I want you with me.'

It worked. Haskeer's chest swelled. Jup caught Stryke's eye, grinned and gave him an exaggerated wink. Stryke smiled thinly in return.

'We'll meet back here in . . . let's say three hours,' he decided. 'If either group comes across Coilla in a situation it can handle, we'll go for it. If that means not making the rendezvous here, we'll meet one mile west of Hecklowe's gates. If you find Coilla and the odds are too long, leave somebody watching and we'll go in with both groups.'

'Any ideas about where we should look in particular?' Jup asked.

'Anywhere buying and selling takes place.'

'That's the whole of Hecklowe, isn't it?'

'Right.'

'Should be a piece of piss, then.'

'Look, you cover the north and west sectors, we'll do south and east.' He addressed all of them. 'We know, or think we know, that Coilla's with three humans, probably bounty hunters. Don't undervalue them. Take no chances. And go steady on those concealed weapons. Like I said, we don't want the Watchers down on our necks. Now get going.'

Jup gave a thumbs-up and led off his group.

Watching them go, Haskeer said, 'We get smaller and smaller . . .'

Stryke's party searched fruitlessly for over two hours.

As they moved from the south to the east of the city, Stryke said, 'The trouble is we don't know *how* to look.'

'What?' Haskeer responded.

'We don't know anybody in Hecklowe, we've no contacts to help us, and slavers don't do business on the streets. The gods alone know what could be going on inside any of these buildings.'

'So what we going to do?'

'Just keep looking and hope we catch a glimpse of Coilla, I

suppose. It's not as though we can ask the Watchers where the local slavers live.'

'Well, what's the point, then? I mean, what the hell are we doing here if we haven't got a hope of finding her?'

'*Just a minute*,' Stryke seethed, barely containing his anger. 'We're here because of *you*! If you hadn't gone AWOL with the stars in the first place we wouldn't *be* here. And Coilla wouldn't be in the mess she's in.'

'That's not fair!' Haskeer protested. 'I didn't know what I was doing. You can't blame me for—'

'Captain!'

'What is it, Toche?' Stryke replied irritably.

The grunt pointed to the intersection they were approaching. 'There, sir!'

They all looked the way he indicated. A mass of beings swarmed where four streets met.

'What is it?' Stryke demanded. 'What are we supposed to be seeing?'

'That human!' Toche exclaimed. 'The one we saw in the snow. *There!*'

This time Stryke spotted him. Serapheim, the wordsmith who sent them to Hecklowe, and who disappeared so completely. Taller than most around him, he was an unmistakable figure with his flowing locks and long, blue cloak. He was walking away from them.

'Reckon he's one of the bounty hunters?' Haskeer wondered, the argument forgotten.

'No more than I did when we first saw him,' Stryke said. 'And why send us here if he was? Come to that, what's he doing here?'

'He's moving off.'

'It's too much of a coincidence that he should be here. Come on, we're going to follow. But take it easy, we don't want him seeing us.'

They pushed through the crowd, careful to keep a safe distance. Serapheim didn't appear to know he was being trailed and acted naturally, though he walked purposefully. The orcs followed him to the core of the eastern quarter, where the streets became winding alleys and every cloak seemed to hide a dagger.

In due course he turned a corner, and when they got to it and peered round they found themselves looking into an empty cul-de-sac. At the far end and to the side was a decaying, once white building. It had a single door. Indeed it was the only door in the street.

They made the obvious assumption that he must have gone through it and crept that way. The door was slightly ajar. The orcs flattened themselves against the wall on either side.

'We go in?' Haskeer whispered.

'What else?' Stryke said.

'Remember what you told Jup. If in doubt get help.'

Stryke thought that remarkably sensible coming from Haskeer. 'I don't know if this situation warrants it.' He glanced at the sky. 'Then again, the time we set for the rendezvous isn't that far off. Seafe, get back to that square and bring Jup's group here. If we're not waiting at the mouth of the alley we'll be inside. On the double.'

The grunt jogged away.

For the moment that left just Haskeer, Toche, Reafdaw and Stryke himself. But he reckoned that was enough to deal with a crazy human storyteller.

'We're going in,' he decided, discreetly slipping the knife from his boot. 'Draw weapons.'

He pushed the door and entered, the others close behind.

They were in a sizeable room with a long dais at one end supporting a massive chair. Other small items of furniture were scattered about the apartment. The place was deserted.

'What the hell happened to that Serapheim character?' Haskeer asked.

'There have to be other rooms, or another way out,' Stryke said. 'Let's—'

A sudden flurry of sound and movement cut him short. Wall hangings were torn aside. At the back of the dais a concealed door flew open. Ten or more armed goblins emerged and rushed to surround them. They held club maces, swords and short spears, weapons that outreached the Wolverines' knives. A goblin slammed and bolted the door to the street.

Spear tips and sword points were held to the orcs' throats and chests. Goblins snatched away the band's knives and searched their clothes for more. But they only seemed interested in weapons; the pellucid and stars were ignored. The blades, and Haskeer's chain, were tossed clanging into a pile on the floor.

Another goblin appeared on the platform. He was dressed in finery and gems. 'I am Razatt-Kheage,' he announced with more than a dash of melodrama.

'Slaver scum,' Haskeer rumbled.

One of the goblins delivered a hefty blow to his stomach with the shaft end of his mace. Haskeer doubled over and wheezed.

'Have a care with the new merchandise,' Razatt-Kheage cautioned.

'Bastard,' Stryke spat. 'Face me without these dolts and we'll settle this, orc to goblin.'

Razatt-Kheage gave a snorting laugh. 'How charmingly primitive. Put aside thoughts of violence, my friend, I have somebody for you to meet. Come!' he called.

Coilla appeared at the concealed door, Blaan holding her arms from behind. She reacted with surprise at seeing Stryke, Haskeer and the others.

'Corporal,' Stryke said.

'Captain,' she responded with admirable cool. 'Sorry you got involved.'

'We're a band, we stick together.'

She looked at Haskeer. 'We have a few things to work out, Sergeant.'

'This is all very touching,' Razatt-Kheage interrupted, 'but make the most of it. You'll be saying your goodbyes soon enough.'

'This one's cohorts are due back!' Coilla yelled, indicating Blaan.

'Is Serapheim one of them?' Stryke said.

'Serapheim? The storyteller?'

'*Be silent!*' the slaver hissed. 'Be still,' he said in a calmer voice, 'and we will wait for them together.' Then he snapped something to his guards in goblin language.

The henchlins moved forward to corral Stryke, Haskeer and the grunts in a corner. Almost as soon as it was done, there was a rap on the door. A goblin went to it, checked through the viewing hatch and opened up.

Lekmann and Aulay swaggered in.

'The rest of the rats,' Coilla said.

Blaan jerked her arm, hard. 'Stow it!' he growled. She winced.

Lekmann surveyed the scene. 'Now what have we got here? I heard you were a fixer, Razatt-Kheage, but this is something again. The rest of the bitch's band, yeah? Or some of them anyway.'

'Yes,' the slaver confirmed, 'and worth a tidy amount to me.'

'*To you?*' Aulay blurted. 'What is this, Micah?'

'Sharp practice, I reckon.'

'I hope you humans are not laying claim to my property,' Razatt-Kheage told them. 'That could be unfortunate.'

Lekmann's face darkened. 'Now look, these orcs are the ones my partners and me had a deal to bring in.'

'So what? Any agreement you have doesn't hold in Hecklowe. You didn't bring them here.'

'I brought *her*, and that brought them. Don't that stand for something?'

'Oi!' Haskeer roared. 'You're talking about us like we weren't here! We're not pieces of meat to be squabbled over!'

The goblin who hit him before did it again. Once more, Haskeer doubled up.

'Meat's just what you are, orc,' Lekmann sneered.

When Haskeer straightened he aimed a cold, level stare at the goblin that struck him. 'That's twice, scumpouch. I'll be paying you back with interest.'

The impassive-faced creature pulled back his club for another blow. Razatt-Kheage barked a curt order and the minion stayed his hand. In words all understood, he added, 'I'm sure we can come to a mutually profitable arrangement, human.'

'That's more like it,' Lekmann replied, brightening a little. 'Though from what I've heard of these renegades, you ain't gonna have an easy time turning them into something fancy like bodyguards.'

The slaver looked at the orcs. He studied their muscular, combat-hardened physiques, saw the scars they bore, regarded their murderous, steely-eyed expressions.

'Perhaps they would be somewhat more of a challenge than the female,' he conceded.

Stryke glanced at Coilla and thought how little the slaver knew.

'We're promised gold for their heads,' Aulay interjected. 'From Queen Jennesta.'

Razatt-Kheage thought about it. 'That may prove a less bothersome option.'

Jup's group spent its time in a futile search. When his allotted three hours were almost spent, he took the grunts back to the square.

They found Seafe waiting for them. He conveyed Stryke's message.

'Let's hope it's not fool's gold,' the dwarf said. 'Come on.'

If the passersby thought there was anything odd in a dwarf leading half a dozen orcs at double time through the streets of Hecklowe, they knew better than to show it. Fortunately no Watchers were encountered.

There was a sticky moment when they reached the eastern quarter and Seafe was unsure of which passage to take. But he chose right and five minutes later they got to the alley with the white house. Nobody was about.

Jup didn't like the look of it. 'Stryke said they'd be waiting for us here, right?'

'Yes,' Seafe confirmed. 'If there was no trouble.'

'Then we assume there has been.' To the whole group he added, 'We'll have to expect hostility in there. I reckon this is a time when weapons can be used, and to hell with Hecklowe law.'

Keeping an eye on the street behind them, they pulled out their knives.

Jup stretched a hand to the door and pushed. It didn't shift. He signalled for the others to join him. At his word they shouldered the door *en masse* three times with all the force they could muster. It cracked, splintered and gave. They tumbled in.

And froze.

Ahead of them were two humans armed with knives. To their right, Stryke, Haskeer and the other orcs lined a wall. Seven or eight goblins with maces, swords and short pikes guarded them. On a raised platform at the far end of the room stood a goblin in silken robes. To his left a mountainous human had Coilla in a neck lock.

A goblin stepped from a corner and stood among the broken shards of the doorway, barring it with a spear, its barbed tip glinting.

'Ah,' Jup said.

Lekmann grinned. 'This just gets better and better.'

Leering, Aulay chimed in with, 'A regular little reunion.'

'Drop your weapons,' Razatt-Kheage hissed.

Nobody moved.

'Give it up,' Lekmann said. 'You're outnumbered and under-armed.'

'I don't take orders from goblins, and certainly not from a stinking human.'

'Do as you're told, freak!' Lekmann snarled.

Jup looked to Stryke. 'Well, Captain?'

'Do what you have to, Sergeant.'

There was no mistaking Stryke's meaning.

Jup swallowed. Sounding as casual as he could manage, he said, 'Fuck it, what's life without a bit of excitement?'

15

Jup flung his knife at the nearest guard, striking him hard just above the collarbone. It broke the stand-off, and the goblin's neck.

Then all hell was let loose.

One of the grunts quickly snatched up the fallen guard's spear and turned it on another goblin. Simultaneously, Stryke and Haskeer leapt forward and grappled with their captors. A desperate struggle for the weapons began.

Jup's group rushed towards Lekmann and Aulay. They drew their blades and launched into a knife fight.

The dwarf himself was blocked from joining it. Waving a sword, a henchlin barred his way. Dropping to avoid the swinging blade, Jup drove himself at the creature's legs and brought him down. They rolled on the floor, fighting for possession.

Clutching the wrist of the goblin's sword arm, Jup repeatedly hammered it against the flagstones. But he wouldn't let go. Then a screaming guard collapsed beside them, its face ribboned by an orc dagger. Jup reached out and grabbed its sword. Still holding his opponent's wrist, he plunged the blade into its chest.

He leapt to his feet, tossed one sword to a comrade and used the other to rejoin the fray.

On the dais, Coilla was fighting like a wildcat to free herself of Blaan's hold. Nearby, Razatt-Kheage was yelling orders, interspersed with curses.

Stryke had managed to get his foe in a bear hug with the goblin's arms pinned to his sides. Wriggling, unable to lift his sword, he was trying to rake the orc's legs with it. Stryke cooled him with a couple of head butts to the brow. Eyes rolling, he went down. Prising the sword from his hand, Stryke slashed his throat.

He turned and saw Haskeer vying for a spear. It belonged to the guard who had hit him. As he passed, Stryke swiped at the goblin, slicing him in the side. The minor wound was distraction enough to throw the henchlin's poise. Stryke bowled off through the mêlée, making for the bounty hunters.

Haskeer wasn't slow exploiting the upset. He managed to seize the spear's shaft. They tussled for it. Using all his strength, he twisted the spear and got its lethally barbed point under the goblin's chin. Then he pushed upward with all his might. The howling creature was skewered. Haskeer ripped loose the spear in a burst of gore and looked for a fresh victim.

Still struggling in Blaan's arms, Coilla shouted something. The words were lost, but she seemed to be indicating a large chest on the dais.

Lekmann and Aulay slashed wildly with their knives, trying to keep the orcs clear. The arrival of Jup and Breggin with swords had them backing off.

Coilla's attempts to break loose of Blaan went on. She called out again. He began applying pressure to her neck and looked set to snap it.

Haskeer rushed at the platform. A henchlin stepped out to stop him. The orc levelled his spear and impaled the goblin, the shaft piercing his stomach, and tossed him back into the scrum. Abandoning the spear, Haskeer hurtled on and leapt up to the dais. He landed a couple of feet away from Coilla and Blaan. Razatt-Kheage was near the other end of the platform, shrieking at his bodyguards. Haskeer ignored him.

At a run, he landed a massive roundhouse blow to the side of Blaan's meaty head. The hulking human cried out in rage. Haskeer hit him again on the same spot, just as heavily. Bellowing, Blaan let go of Coilla and turned on the orc. They commenced swinging at each other in earnest.

Coilla dived across the platform and collided with the wooden chest. She wrenched open its lid. It was filled with cutlasses, rapiers and scimitars. She seized a broadsword then overturned the chest, toppling it from the dais. It crashed to the floor, its weaponry spilling out.

She hadn't noticed in her haste that it would land at Aulay's and Lekmann's backs. They spun and fell upon the weapons, scrabbling for swords. They weren't alone. Four or five orcs piled in too, anxious to swap daggers for lengthier blades. Twenty seconds of kicking and punching saw all of them re-armed.

What had been a series of hand-to-hand brawls transformed into swordplay.

'*Bounty hunter!*' Stryke yelled, skidding to a halt in front of Lekmann. 'Defend yourself!'

'Come and get it, freak!'

Jup and the grunts disengaged and quickly found other foes. Stryke and Lekmann squared off.

The human went for a quick kill. He powered in, his sword a blur as he carved air with shocking rapidity. Stryke stood his ground and parried everything coming at him. Deflecting a half-dozen passes cleared the way for advancing a step or two. He went into offensive mode. Lekmann countered with equal fluidity, reclaiming the gained space.

They fenced with total focus, oblivious to everything else, beating a steel rhythm with their blades.

Jup had Aulay to himself. The human was a lesser swordsman than his partner, which was to say he was merely good. But he was fuelled with anger and desperation. That fed him fury while clouding his skill.

The dwarf got off a weighty swing aimed at decapitation. Aulay ducked and returned a scything horizontal sweep meant for disembowelment. Jup sprang back and avoided it. Then he was in again and battering.

All across the room orcs and goblins went at the business of murder with a will. Blades hacked spears, knives slashed at mail, swords met in a ringing din. A grunt hefted a table and smashed it across the back of a henchlin, allowing another trooper to dart in and deliver a stabbing. An orc slammed against a wall, impelled by a flesh wound to the arm from a goblin mace. He dodged the follow-up and brought his sword into play.

On the platform, Haskeer and Blaan slugged it out in a furious bare-knuckle contest. Each sponged up the other's blows and dealt their own. Neither would give.

Blaan landed a piledriver punch to Haskeer's chin. 'Go down!' he hollered.

The impact rocked Haskeer but didn't fell him. He responded with a crazed howl and a counterblow that sank his fist in the human's belly. Blaan staggered back a bit but otherwise seemed unaffected. Both of them were unused to anybody staying upright once they hit them. It stoked their wrath.

Arms outstretched, moving surprisingly fast for his bulk, Blaan shot forward and encircled Haskeer with his powerful arms. They set to wrestling, faces strained, muscles bulging.

Coilla thought about going for the slaver, but had a more longed-for target. She jumped down from the platform. A goblin came out of the mêlée and engaged her. They crossed swords, the goblin making up for subtlety by powering in with savage swipes. She countered every swing, batting aside the blade with ease. Then she wrong-footed him, shifted her centre of balance and sent her blade point into his eye. The shrieking henchlin dropped.

She headed for the humans.

Lekmann and Stryke were still matching knock for knock. That didn't interest Coilla. She wanted Aulay.

He and Jup battled on, toe to toe, sweat flecking their brows.

'Mine!' she yelled.

Jup understood. He pulled back, spun, and connected with a goblin sword. That duel moved him clear.

Coilla took his place and glared at Aulay. 'I've dreamed of this, you *fucker*!' she spat.

'And I owe *you*, bitch!' He absently touched bandaged ear with wrapped finger.

The jarring impact of their clashing blades rang out. Coilla dodged and weaved, looking for any chance to plant cold steel in his flesh. Aulay fought back with a bravado bordering on panic. The homicidal expression she wore was enough to sustain the energy of his defence. It made his passes wild and not entirely accurate; it also added an element of unpredictability to his style.

For her part, Coilla poured all her resentment and hatred of the bounty hunters into her onslaught. Only blood would assuage the injury they'd done her. She pounded at the one-eyed human's sword with such frenzy it was a wonder it didn't snap. He was hard put to fend off the assault. His attacking stance began dissolving into pure self-preservation.

Stryke had found that despite looking dissolute, Lekmann fenced like a demon. Theirs was a duel that demanded every ounce of concentration and strength.

It was an old orc adage that the way an enemy fought

betrayed the way they thought. So it befitted his nature that the bounty hunter used feignts and deceitful moves as key techniques. Stryke was equally adept at duplicity and replied in kind. Though he would have far preferred the honesty of straightforward homicide.

They circled, alert for any flaw in each other's guard, ready to kill. Lekmann vaulted in, whipping his blade at Stryke's head. Stryke swatted it aside and paid him back with a swipe to the chest. It was short. They kept up their lethal dance.

Razatt-Kheage's outpourings of rage, frustration and orders continued, spouted in both his native tongue and universal. It stopped when a grunt on the floor below lashed out at his legs. The slaver jumped clear. In lieu of a weapon, he snatched up a bulky cloth sack and swung it down at the orc's head. He missed and nearly lost his balance. The grunt slashed the sack. A torrent of silver coins, the bounty hunters' payment, gushed out and bounced in all directions. Orcs and goblins slipped on them as they scattered.

Dozens of coins rolled the way of Stryke and Lekmann. Crunching underfoot, they slowed but didn't stop their combat. Both were tiring now and the fight was near the point where stamina could be the deciding element. Not that either allowed it to lessen the blows they dealt.

For all their strength, Haskeer and Blaan were hitting the same barrier. Haskeer knew he had to finish their bout quickly while he still had enough in reserve. He and the human were locked in a wrestling hold, Blaan's clasped hands in the small of Haskeer's back, one of Haskeer's arms trapped immovably. Drawing deep from his depleted well of energy, the orc slowly raised his free arm and repeatedly fisted the bounty hunter's head. Simultaneously he applied outward pressure with his snared arm.

The strain showed on Blaan's contorted face. He was struggling to contain his foe. Haskeer needed just one more bit of leverage. He found it. With all his might he stamped his boot down on Blaan's foot, heel first. The human cried out. Haskeer stomped repeatedly. With a great out-rush of breath, Blaan lost control and the hold was shattered.

He half staggered, half limped backwards. Haskeer lurched the few paces separating them and delivered a solid kick to Blaan's crotch. The human gave an anguished high-pitched scream. Without pause, and giving it all he'd got, Haskeer landed a swift combination of punches – to the chin, to the stomach, then to the chin again. Blaan went down like a felled oak. The wooden platform trembled.

Haskeer moved in and conferred a kicking on him, right foot, left foot, targeting any vulnerable spot that presented itself. Blaan's hand flashed out, grabbed one of Haskeer's legs, tugged and downed him. There was a scramble to be the first one up. They made it at the same time. Blaan closed the gap, his enormous face demonic with frenzy, and raised his ham fists. Bloodied and bruised, they were back to sparring.

Coilla was making headway with Aulay. She sent in blows high and low, forcing him to skip and swerve to avoid them. But his movements were leaden-footed, his vigour ebbing. She sensed a kill was close.

Jup and the grunts, working shoulder to shoulder, had thinned out the ranks of goblins. Just three or four were left, and they were retreating to the dais end of the room. When their backs were to the platform they put up a frenzied last stand. Two tried to break through the semicircle of approaching orcs. One swung his studded mace in a wide arc. A pair of orcs ducked under the flying weapon and shredded the henchlin's chest. Jup took care of the other. He dashed the sword from its grip and hacked into the creature's neck.

But that had given the two remaining goblins their chance. They sprang on to the dais and rained blows down on the Wolverines' heads, preventing them from following.

Razatt-Kheage sheltered behind them, raving encouragement.

Lekmann and Aulay, likewise being forced back by their implacable orc opponents, knew the game was up.

'*Get out!*' Lekmann bawled.

His partner needed no further encouragement. He swiftly backed off from Coilla, turned and ran. With a last flash of his blade in Stryke's direction, Lekmann did the same. The orc captain and corporal went after them.

Aulay tripped and fell. As he got up, Lekmann raced past him. He made the dais, arriving at a point between Haskeer's and Blaan's fight to the left and the battling orcs and goblins to the right. Unimpeded, he scrambled up.

Swerving to evade a lone orc trying to stop him, Aulay got there too. Lekmann stretched a hand and hoisted him up. They turned to fend off Stryke and Coilla, who swept in a second later. All the humans and remaining goblins were on the platform. All the Wolverines battled to climb it.

All save Haskeer. Trading punches with Blaan at their end of the platform, he was oblivious. The human was more conscious of the need to withdraw. Still sparring, he began edging towards his comrades.

Alone among the Wolverines, Coilla managed to ascend the dais. She fetched up nearest Aulay and went for him.

'What does it take to stop you, bitch?' he snarled.

'Just die,' she said.

He attacked. Coilla deflected the blows. Aulay turned his sword and started to advance again.

She held fast. Giving way to rage, he came at her recklessly with wild, ill-judged slashes. His guard was careless. A thrust missed her head by a good three inches. Seeing a chance, Coilla quickly spun to one side and chopped downward with all her strength.

Her blade sliced cleanly through the flesh and bone of his left wrist. The hand fell away and slapped wetly on the boards. A fountain of blood gushed from the stump. Agony and disbelief stamped on his face, Aulay began screaming.

Coilla drew back her sword to finish him.

From behind, a pair of massive arms encircled her waist. As though she weighed nothing, Blaan tossed her from the dais. She landed heavily on the floor below.

Lekmann pulled Aulay away. He was wailing. Copious quantities of his blood drenched the platform.

Haskeer caught up with Blaan. The human elbowed him in the stomach. Gasping, Haskeer doubled over. Blaan thundered in the direction of his fellow bounty hunters and the goblins. He stopped short of them and took hold of Razatt-Kheage's ponderous wooden throne. Haskeer was on his feet again and charging. Hoisting the chair like a toy, Blaan swung round and struck Haskeer with it. The force knocked the orc across the platform and slammed him into the wall.

Then Blaan hefted his load to the edge and hurled it down on the orcs. They scattered as it smashed to the floor.

Taking advantage of the confusion, the slaver led his henchlins and the bounty hunters to the door at the back of the dais. They were going through it before Stryke shouted out and everybody rushed the platform.

Too late. The door slammed in their faces. They heard bolts being thrown on the other side. Stryke and a couple of grunts shouldered it several times. Haskeer joined them and added his strength. But it wouldn't give.

'Forget it,' Stryke panted.

Haskeer pounded his fist against the door in frustration. *'Damn!'*

Recovering from her fall, stretching her aching limbs, Coilla walked across the platform towards them. 'I'm going to kill those bastards if it's the last thing I do,' she vowed.

'Look out!' Jup yelled, pushing her aside.

A spear winged past and embedded itself in the wall.

It had been thrown by a goblin in the body of the room, wounded and bleeding but on his feet. Now he had a sword in his hand.

That was too much for Haskeer. He leapt from the platform and ran at the creature. The goblin took one ineffective swipe at him. Then Haskeer dashed away the sword with his bare hands and battered the henchlin senseless. Not content with that, he took the goblin by the scruff of its neck and hammered its head against the wall, again and again and again.

The others came over and watched the limp and lifeless body being reduced to pulp.

Jup said, 'I think he's dead.'

'I know that, short arse!' Haskeer snapped. He unceremoniously dumped the goblin's body.

Stryke smiled. 'Good to have you back, Sergeant.'

From their rear came the splintering crash of wood. They turned.

A Watcher, grim faced and unstoppable, was beating its way through what was left of the door to the street. There were others beyond it.

Coilla sighed. 'Fuck, what a day.'

16

'Don't try taking on the things,' Stryke warned. 'Let's just get away from them.'

'Easier said than done,' Jup reckoned, staring at the lumbering homunculus.

They backed off as the Watcher moved into the room. The vast head slowly turned, its gem eyes, animated by synthetic life, surveying the scene. Two of its fellows filed through the door behind it.

The foremost Watcher lifted its hands, palms up. There was a loud click. Shiny metallic blades sprang from slots in the heels of the hands. They were half a foot long and wickedly keen. As though on signal, the other Watchers snapped out similar weapons.

'Uh-oh,' Jup said.

'Minimum engagement then,' Stryke amended. 'Just what it takes to get out of here.'

'That could turn out to be *whatever* it takes to get out of here,' Coilla remarked, eyeing the Watchers. 'I've seen them in action. They're faster than they look, and mercy's not their strong point.'

'You do realise they've seen the weapons and that means they're in execution mode?' Jup asked.

'Yes,' Stryke replied. 'But remember the bleeding of the magic's made them less effective.'

'There's a comfort.'

The Watchers were on the move again. Their way.

'Can we *do* something?' Haskeer growled impatiently.

'All right,' Stryke said. 'Simple mission. All of us through that door.'

'Now?' Coilla prompted.

He studied the advancing Watchers. 'Now.'

The band rushed forward, flowing to either side of the lead Watcher, intending to go around it. Dazzlingly fast, its arms shot out horizontally, barring the way. The other two did the same. Light glinted from their extended blades. Everybody stopped.

'Any more bright ideas?' Haskeer wondered, flirting with insubordination.

The homunculi kept coming, arms outstretched as though shepherding cattle. The band backtracked.

'Maybe we shouldn't go at this as a group,' Stryke suggested. 'They might find individual action harder to deal with.'

'If you mean every Wolverine for themselves,' Haskeer grumbled, 'I wish you'd say so.'

'You and me are going to have to have a little talk, Sergeant.'

'Let's try getting out of here alive first,' Coilla reminded them.

Jup had a notion. 'Why don't we attack this one all at once? I mean, how invulnerable can they be?'

'I'm game,' Haskeer rumbled, hefting a goblin's mace.

'We'll go for it,' Stryke decided. 'But if it doesn't work, don't linger. Ready? *Now!*'

They charged again, and set about the first Watcher. They

slashed at it with swords, stabbed at it with daggers, pounded it with maces, crashed spears against it. Haskeer tried kicking it.

The Watcher stood impassive, stock still and completely unaffected.

The band moved back and regrouped. The Watchers resumed their inexorable advance.

'We're running out of room,' Jup said, glancing behind them. 'One more time?'

Stryke nodded. 'And give it all you've got.'

They thoroughly assaulted the creature. To the extent that spears snapped, blades broke and knives were blunted. None of it had any greater effect than before.

'Retreat!' Stryke yelled.

Coilla jerked her head at the dais. 'Up there, Stryke. It's all we've got left.'

Haskeer grinned. 'Yeah, I bet they can't climb!'

They made for the platform and swarmed on to it. The Watchers turned and followed.

'Now what?' Coilla wanted to know.

'Let's try that door again.'

Battering it with maces made no difference.

'Inlaid with steel, I'd say,' Stryke judged.

'We have to get out of this building fast,' Coilla said, 'before more of those damn things get here.'

The three already in the room reached the platform and stopped.

'See?' Haskeer announced smugly. 'Can't climb.'

As one, the trio of Watchers retracted their blades. Their hands curled into fists. They lifted them above their heads. Then they brought them down on the dais with the force of a small earthquake. The platform shook mightily. They did it again. Wood cracked and splintered. The platform lurched at an angle. Wolverines fought to keep their footing. A final triple blow did it.

The dais collapsed with a roar.

Planks, struts and Wolverines crashed to the ground in a cloud of dust and chaos.

'They don't *need* to climb, bonehead!' Jup yelled.

'I think it's back to every orc for themselves,' Coilla spluttered, extricating herself from a tangle of timber.

'I've had enough of these fucking pests!' Haskeer bellowed. He seized a large joist and made for a Watcher.

'*No!*' Get back here!' Stryke ordered.

Haskeer ignored him. Muttering, he strode to the nearest Watcher and smashed the beam across its chest. The joist snapped in two. Nothing changed for the Watcher.

Suddenly it brought up an arm and delivered a weighty back-hander that sent Haskeer flying. He collided with the remains of the platform. A couple of grunts ran to help him up. Haskeer cursed and waved them away.

Stryke spotted something that gave him an idea. 'Calthmon, Breggin, Finje. Come with me, I want to try something.'

As the rest of the band played cat and mouse with the Watchers, he led them to the other side of the room. The chain Haskeer had brought with him was lying on the floor. Stryke explained the plan.

'The chain's a little short for our purposes,' he added, 'but let's give it a go.'

Finje and Calthmon took hold of one end, Breggin and Stryke the other. He decided there weren't enough of them, and beckoned over Toche and Gant.

Three orcs at each end of the chain, they positioned themselves behind a Watcher. It was busy having chunks of wood thrown at it by the others. The missiles bounced off uselessly. At Stryke's word his group got a good grip on the chain, then they ran.

The taut chain hit the back of the Watcher's legs. The orcs kept going, pulling on the chain like two tug-of-war teams. At first nothing happened. They strained on the chain. The Watcher swayed a little. It took a step forward. They kept tugging, muscles standing out, breath laboured. The homunculus started swaying again, more pronounced this time. They pulled harder.

Suddenly the Watcher toppled. It hit the floor with a deafening crash.

Almost immediately its arms and legs began working frenziedly. It thrashed and wriggled in an attempt to right itself, making a metallic scraping noise on the flagstones.

'That'll give the bastard something to think about,' Stryke said.

They were targeting another Watcher when the sound of Haskeer whooping distracted them.

Launching himself from the platform debris, he landed on the back of a Watcher. The creature twisted and shook, in a stiff kind of way, trying to dislodge him. Its arms were too rigid to reach the orc, so it snapped out its blades to poke at its unseen assailant. That made it even more dangerous for Haskeer, who had to dodge the probing steel.

He got his arms around the Watcher's neck and his feet in the small of its back. Pulling with the former and pushing with the latter, he rocked back and forth. The Watcher was soon rocking with him. Its efforts to skewer the tormentor on its back grew more urgent. Haskeer was hard put to avoid a hit, but he kept on pushing and pulling with all his strength. The fact that the Watcher was already moving and had its arms up helped Haskeer's scheme. It reeled like a drunk. Then its balance deserted it.

As it fell backwards, Haskeer swiftly disentangled himself and leapt clear. The Watcher smacked on to the floor with a resonant clang.

Stryke and the others, watching this, ran in and showered the downed creature with blows from their weapons. They needed a little fancy footwork to evade its flailing blades, but its accuracy was out of whack. Haskeer joined them, snatched a mace from a grunt and set to on the Watcher's face. He struck one of the gem-like eyes and it cracked. Encouraged, he hammered at it again. It smashed.

A high-pressure plume of green smoke spurted from the fissure. Almost reaching the ceiling, it formed a small cloud that shed verdant-coloured droplets. The smell it gave off was foul and some of the orcs clamped hands over their noses and mouths.

Following Haskeer's example, Stryke leaned in and hacked at the other eye with his sword. That shattered too, releasing another gassy spout. The Watcher shuddered, its legs and arms hammering the floor. Gagging at the odour, the band backed off.

'I don't think we could have done that in the old days,' Stryke told them.

The remaining Watcher was nowhere near the door now and engaged with the rest of the band.

'*Get out!*' Stryke shouted at them.

'Orcs don't retreat!' Haskeer exclaimed.

Jup and Coilla arrived in time to hear that.

'We do this time, dummy!' Jup said.

'The way your kind does, eh?'

'For fuck's sake, *move*, you two!' Coilla urged. 'Argue later!'

Everybody ran for the door.

Four more Watchers were coming along the alley from its open end. Enough to block that as an escape route. The Watcher in the house was moving to the doorway.

'Don't give up, do they?' Jup remarked.

Stryke realised the only chance was to try getting over the wall that blocked their end of the alley. It was tall and plaster smooth. He got two of the band's beefier members, Haskeer and Breggin, to give leg-ups.

Two grunts went straight up and balanced on the wall's

narrow top. They reported another alley on the other side, then started reaching down to help the next in line. Troopers began scrambling up and dropping down the other side. Because of his shortness, Jup needed an extra boost from a grumbling Haskeer, and the grunts above had to stretch lower for his hand.

Only Coilla, Stryke, Breggin and Haskeer were still to go when the Watcher came out of the house. Stryke and Coilla got to the top of the wall.

'Hurry!' Haskeer called out.

He and Breggin stood, arms above their heads. Eager hands clasped theirs and began pulling. The Watcher made a grab for Haskeer's foot. He shook free and scrambled frantically. The four other Watchers were near now.

Haskeer and Breggin made the top. Everybody lowered themselves into the next thoroughfare.

Jup made a face. 'Phew, that was close!'

A section of the wall they'd just climbed exploded. Masonry fell, powdery dust billowed. Tearing aside the obstruction like paper, a Watcher appeared, white plaster coating its metal body. A little further along, the fist of another blasted through.

'Get out of here!' Stryke ordered. 'And conceal your weapons! We don't want to attract even more attention.'

Swords were awkwardly hidden. Larger weapons like spears and maces were reluctantly discarded. The Wolverines ran.

They got themselves into the main thoroughfares of the quarter and slowed down a bit. Stryke had them break up into three groups rather than attract attention as a mob. He led with Coilla, Jup, Haskeer and a couple of grunts.

'I don't know if the Watchers have a way of communicating with each other,' he told them in an undertone. 'But sooner or later they're all going to know and be after us.'

'So it's the horses, the weapons and out of here, right?' Jup said.

'Right, only we forget the weapons. It'd be too risky hanging around at the entrance checkpoint. Anyway, we've got some weapons.'

'Getting the horses is a risk too,' Coilla said.

'It's one we've got to take.'

'I need one myself,' she remembered. 'We'll be short.'

'We'll buy another.'

'With what?'

'Pellucid's all we've got. Fortunately it's as good as any currency. I'll dig out a little before we go into the stables. Don't want to flaunt the stuff.'

'Pity about those weapons,' Haskeer complained. 'I had a couple of favourites there.'

'Me too,' Jup agreed. 'But it's worth it to get you and Coilla back.'

Haskeer couldn't work out if the dwarf was being sarcastic, so he didn't reply.

All the way to the stables, near the main entrance, they were nervous of what might happen. At one point a pair of Watchers appeared ahead of them. Stryke signalled everybody to be calm and they walked past them without incident. It seemed the homunculi didn't have any way of communicating over distances. Stryke speculated that perhaps that was another consequence of the fading magic.

They got to the stables. Their horses were collected, and another bought, without too much delay or attracting suspicion.

Back on the street, Jup said, 'Why don't we stay in three groups while we make our way out? Less attention.'

'Hang on,' Coilla put in. 'Won't it look suspicious when the first group leaves without collecting any weapons? Could go bad on groups two and three.'

'Perhaps they'll just assume we didn't bring any.'

'Orcs without weapons? Who's going to believe that?'

'Coilla's right,' Stryke decided. 'What we're going to do is stay together. We get as near the main entrance as we can on foot then mount up and make a run for it.'

'You're the boss,' Jup conceded.

They were in sight of Hecklowe's main gate when a number of Watchers, perhaps a dozen or more, appeared a way behind them. They were marching purposefully in the same direction. A crowd was gathering and walking with them, aware that such a large number of the homunculi meant some kind of drama was about to unfold.

'For us, you think, Stryke?' Jup asked.

'I don't think they're out for a ramble, Sergeant.' The band was further from the exit than he would have liked. But there was no choice now. 'Right, let's go for it! Mount up!'

They hurriedly obeyed as passersby stared and pointed.

'Now move out!'

They spurred their horses and galloped for the open gates. Elves, gremlins and dwarves scattered, shaking fists and bawling insults.

The gallop became a charge. Up ahead, Stryke saw a Watcher starting to close the gate. It was heavy work, even for a creature of such prodigious strength, and went slowly.

Jup and Stryke got there first. Stryke took a chance and pulled up his horse. He sidled as close to the Watcher as he dared and booted it in the head. Coming in high, and with the added strength of a horse behind it, the blow toppled the creature. The Watchers tending the queue turned and made for Stryke. One came out of the guardhouse. Blades zinged from their palms.

Jup had stopped too. 'Get going!' Stryke told him.

The dwarf rode off, dispersing the crowd waiting to get in. There were outraged shouts.

Then the rest of the band tore through the gates. Stryke prodded his mount and went after them.

They left Hecklowe behind.

They didn't slow until they'd put a good five miles between themselves and the freeport. Getting a bearing on the trail to Drogan, they fell to exchanging stories of what had befallen them since they were parted. Only Haskeer had nothing to contribute.

Recounting her experiences with the bounty hunters, Coilla still burned with resentment at the way she'd been treated.

'I'm not going to forget it, Stryke. I vow I'll make them pay, the human scum. The worst thing was the feeling of . . . well, helplessness. I'd rather kill myself than let that happen again. And you know what kept going through my head?'

'No, tell me?'

'I kept thinking how it was just like our lives. Like the lives of all orcs. Born into somebody else's service, having to be loyal to a cause you haven't chosen, risking your life.'

They all saw her point.

'We're changing that,' Stryke said. 'Or at least trying to.'

'Even if it means dying I'll never go back to it,' she promised. He wasn't alone in nodding agreement.

Coilla turned her attention to Haskeer. 'You haven't explained your behaviour yet.' Her tone was curt.

'It's not easy . . .' he began and trailed off.

Stryke spoke for him. 'Haskeer's not entirely sure what did happen. None of us is. I'll fill you in as we ride.'

'It's true,' Haskeer told her. 'And I'm . . . sorry.'

It wasn't a word he was accustomed to using, and Coilla was a little taken aback. But as she couldn't decide to accept his apology until she knew more, she didn't answer.

Stryke changed the subject. He told her about their encounter with Serapheim. She recounted hers.

'Something didn't ring true about that human,' she reckoned.

'I know what you mean.'

'Do we count him as an enemy or a friend? Not that I'm used to thinking of humans in friendly terms.'

'Well, we can't deny that he helped us find you by sending us to Hecklowe.'

'But what about the trap at the house?'

'Might not have been his fault. After all, he got us to the right place, didn't he?'

'The biggest mystery,' Jup said, 'is how he seemed to disappear each time. Particularly back there at the slaver's house. I don't understand it.'

'He didn't come in,' Coilla supplied.

'It's obvious,' Stryke volunteered. 'He went over the wall, same as us.' He didn't entirely convince himself, let alone any of the others.

'And how does he *survive*?' Coilla added. 'If he really does wander the country unarmed, that is. These are times when even an armed orc does that at their peril.'

'Maybe he *is* mad,' Jup offered. 'Many of the insane seem to have the luck of the gods.'

Stryke sighed. 'Probably no sense in worrying about it. Whoever he is, chances are we'll never see him again.'

The strategy meeting was held in the usual cavernous chamber. It was a place that looked more organic than fashioned, and water freely flowed through it.

Adpar's military commanders and her Council of Elders were present. She was contemptuous of both, particularly the latter, whom she regarded as senile fools. But she had to concede to herself that even an absolute ruler needed help administering her subjects. She saw no reason to hide her disdain, however.

They fell silent as she addressed them. 'We are close to defeating the merz entirely,' she announced. 'Only two or three nests of the vermin remain to be cleared. It is my command . . .' She paused and corrected herself for the sake of tiresome nyadd politics. 'It is my wish that this be achieved before summer is out. Or what passes for the season these days. I don't have to tell you that the *real* cold of winter will mean another year's delay. That isn't tolerable. It gives the enemy a chance to regroup, to . . . *breed*.' An expression of disgust passed across her face. 'Do any of you see a problem with that?' Her tone didn't exactly invite dissent.

She scanned their sombre, and in most cases compliant, faces. Then a bolder than normal swarm commander raised a webbed hand.

'Yes?' she asked imperiously.

'If it pleases your Majesty,' the officer replied, his voice edged with timorousness, 'there are logistic difficulties. The remaining merz colonies are the hardest to get to, and they're bound to be better defended now that our intentions are clear.'

'Your point?'

'There are bound to be casualties, Majesty.'

'I repeat: your point?'

'Majesty, we—'

'You think I'm concerned with the fact that a few lives may be lost? Even *many* lives? The realm is more important than any individual, as the swarm is more important than a single member. You, Commander, would do well to—'

Adpar stopped abruptly. A hand went to her head. She swayed.

'Majesty?' a nearby minion inquired.

Pain was coursing through her. It felt as though her heart was pumping fire and searing her veins.

'Majesty, are you all right?' the official asked again.

Agony clasped her chest. She thought she might faint. The thought of such a display of weakness gave her a little strength.

Her eyes had been closed. She hadn't realised. Several

officials and a clutch of commanders were hovering around her.

'Would you like us to summon the healers, Majesty?' one of them asked anxiously.

'Healers? Healers? What need have *I* of their kind? You think me in need of their attentions?'

'Er, no, Majesty,' the awed speaker replied. 'Not if you say so, Majesty.'

'I *say* so! Your impertinence in bringing up the subject means this meeting is at an end.' She had to get away from them, and could only hope they didn't see through her flimsy excuses and haste. 'I'm retiring to my private chambers. We'll discuss military matters again later.'

All bowed as she left. None dared offer to help her. They exchanged alarmed looks as she slithered into the tunnel leading to her quarters.

Once she was out of sight, Adpar began gulping air. She leaned over, cupped her hands in water and splashed her face with it. The pain was worse. It rushed from her stomach to her throat. She retched blood.

For the first time in her life she felt afraid.

17

Alfray and his group were near enough to Drogan that they could see the trees fringing Calyparr Inlet. They were no more than a couple of hours away.

The weather grew ever more unpredictable. As opposed to yesterday, for instance, today had been sunny and noticeably warmer. Many suspected that the varying strength of magic created pockets of good and bad weather. Alfray was sure this was true. But one drawback of more clement weather was that it brought the fairies out. They mostly irritated the band, and lead to much slapping of flesh, though some preferred snacking on them.

Alfray and Kestix were discussing the relative merits of other warbands and their place in the league table every orc kept in his head. The conversation was interrupted by the sighting of two riders coming in from the east. They were dots at first, but riding all-out. Soon they were near enough to be seen properly.

'They're orcs, Corporal,' Kestix said.

Nearer still, they were identified as Jad and Hystykk.

By the time they drew up, Alfray was alarmed. 'What's happened?' he asked. 'Where are the others?'

'Take it easy, Corporal, everything's OK,' Hystykk assured him. 'The others are following. We've got news.'

As it was an agreeable day, Jennesta decided to intimidate her general in the open air.

They were in a palace courtyard, with one of the citadel's massive walls towering over them. There was nothing as frivolous as a seat. All that broke the drab aspect was a large open-topped water butt. Its prosaic function was to feed horse troughs.

Mersadion stood in the wall's shadow. The queen faced him ten paces away. All things considered, he thought it incongruous that she should be the one in sunlight.

Jennesta was in full flow, berating him for his perceived shortcomings.

'. . . and still no word from those wretched bounty hunters or any of the many other agents you've sent out at the expense of my coffers.'

'No, ma'am. I'm sorry, ma'am.'

'And now, when I tell you I want to take a hand in events myself and ask you to muster a modest army, what do you do? You give me excuses.'

'Not so much excuses, my lady, with all due respect. But ten thousand is hardly *modest*, and—'

'Are you telling me I don't have even that trifling number of followers and bonded orcs?' She fixed him with a withering stare. 'Are you saying that my popularity among the lower orders is insufficient to raise a meagre ten thousand willing to die for my cause?'

'Of *course* not, Majesty! It isn't a question of loyalty but logistics. We can build the army you need, only not as quickly as you've decreed. We are, after all, stretched on several fronts at the moment and . . .'

His defence trailed off when he saw what she was doing.

Jennesta was silently mouthing something, and weaving an intricate conjuration with her hands. Eventually she cupped them, three or four inches apart. As he watched, spellbound, a small swirling cloud formed between her palms. It looked like a miniature cyclone. She stared at it intently. Tiny streaks of yellow and white began rippling through the darkening mist, like diminutive lightning bolts. The little cloud, still twisting and flashing, slowly moulded itself into a perfectly round form, about the size of an apple.

It started to glow. Soon it shined brighter than any lamp, giving off a brilliance it was difficult to look at. Yet it was so beautiful that Mersadion couldn't tear his eyes away. Then he remembered the spell she had cast on a battlefield not long ago. It began in a similar way to this and ended with countless numbers of the enemy rendered sightless for the slaughter. A cold chill tickled his spine. He sent a silent prayer to the gods, begging their grace.

She removed one hand and laid flat the palm of the other, so that the radiant ball balanced on it just above the skin. Mersadion's fear didn't lessen, but he remained transfixed.

Jennesta slowly raised her hand until the radiant sphere was level with her face. Then, looking almost coquettish, she puffed her cheeks and blew at it. Very gently, like a maiden with a dandelion clock.

The little ball, dazzling as a minute sun, sailed from her palm. It drifted in Mersadion's direction. His muscles tensed. When the sphere had almost reached him, and apparently following the Queen's hand movements, it veered to one side and headed for the wall. Mersadion's gaze followed as it floated into the brickwork.

There was a blinding flash of light and a detonation like a thunderclap. The force of displaced air buffeted Mersadion and breezed Jennesta's gown.

He cried out.

A black scorch mark scarred the wall. A sulphurous odour hung in the air.

Mersadion looked at her, slack-jawed. She held another glowing ball.

'You were saying?' she asked, as though she really expected a recap. 'Something about not being willing to carry out a straightforward order, wasn't it?'

'I am more than *willing* to carry out your orders, ma'am,' he babbled. 'This is simply a case of numbers, of—'

This time she seemed to flick the ball, and it moved with greater speed.

It struck the wall a couple of feet above his head with another deafening bang. He flinched. Small bits of stone and flakes of masonry showered his quivering head.

'You're offering me excuses again, General,' she chided, 'when what I want are solutions.'

As though having started the process made it easier for her, yet another ball appeared on her palm, fully formed and pulsing. With a girlish laugh she tossed it like a child's toy.

It flew his way, looking as though it would hit him this time. But the trajectory was finely judged, and as he pressed his back to the wall the sphere went past.

The ball collided with the water butt. Though it wasn't really a collision. The orb touched the wood of the barrel and was *absorbed* by it. Instantly, the water bubbled and boiled. Steam rose from the butt's open top and sprayed from between its higher metal hasps.

Badly shaken, Mersadion looked back at Jennesta. She hadn't produced another sphere so he started talking, fast. 'Of course, Majesty, anything you will is possible and can be undertaken immediately. I'm sure we can overcome any minor obstacles in the path of gathering an army.'

'Good, General. I knew you'd see sense.' Her point made, she dusted her hands by slapping them lightly together, as though giving him a round of slow applause. 'One other thing,' she added.

All the tension seeped back into Mersadion's body. 'Ma'am?'

'A question of discipline. You must be aware that this Stryke and his warband are taking on the mantle of heroes for certain sections of the army.'

'Unfortunately that's true, Majesty. Though it's by no means widespread.'

'Be sure it doesn't become so. If a thing like that takes hold it can fester. What are you doing to counter it?'

'We're making widely known your version . . . er, the *truth*, that is, of how the Wolverines went renegade. Members of the lower ranks heard defending the actions of the outlaws are subject to a flogging.'

'Make that all ranks, and punish them for *any* mention of Stryke and his band. I want their names stamped out. As to flogging, it's too lenient. Execution should be the price. Burn a few troublemakers as an example and you'll soon see an end to sedition.'

'Yes, ma'am.' Whatever doubts he might have had about the effectiveness of a strategy like that he kept to himself.

'Attention to detail, Mersadion. It's what keeps the realm functioning.'

Eager to ingratiate himself, he replied, 'Ah, the secret of your success, my lady.'

'No, General. The secret of my success is brutality.'

For the better part of two days, Stryke, Coilla, Haskeer, Jup and the grunts travelled uneventfully. They stopped as infrequently as possible and made the best time they could.

By the afternoon of the second day they were bone tired. But they could see a line of trees that marked the inlet, and far to the right, the edge of Drogan Forest.

As shadows were lengthening, the rear lookouts saw four

horsemen coming at them from the east. There was no cover for miles and it seemed reasonable to assume they weren't part of a larger group.

'Trouble, you think?' Jup wondered.

'If it is I reckon we can handle four, don't you?' Stryke told him. He slowed the column to a trot.

A few minutes passed and Haskeer said, 'They're orcs.'

Stryke took a look for himself. 'You're right.'

'Doesn't mean to say they're friendly,' Coilla reminded them.

'No. But like I said, they're only four.'

In due course the quartet of riders arrived. The foremost threw up his arm in greeting. 'Well met!'

'Well met,' Stryke replied cautiously. 'What's your business?'

The leading orc stared. 'You're him, aren't you?'

'What?'

'Stryke. We've never met, Captain, but I've seen you once or twice.' He scanned the others. 'And these are Wolverines?'

'Yes, I'm Stryke. Who are you and what do you want?'

'Corporal Trispeer, sir.' He nodded at his companions. 'Troopers Pravod, Kaed and Rellep.'

'You with a warband?'

'No. We were infantry in Queen Jennesta's horde.'

'Were?' Jup picked up.

'We've . . . left.'

'Nobody leaves Jennesta's service unless it's feet first,' Coilla said. 'Or has she started a retirement scheme?'

'We've gone AWOL, Corporal. Same as your band.'

'Why?' Stryke wanted to know.

'I'm surprised at you asking, Captain. We've had enough of Jennesta, pure and simple. Her injustice, her cruelty. Orcs'll fight, you know that, and we'll do it without grumbling. But she's pushing us too far.'

The trooper called Kaed added, 'Lot of us don't feel comfortable fighting for humans neither, begging your pardon, sir.'

'And we're not the only ones to vote with our feet,' Trispeer went on. 'Granted it's just a few so far, but we reckon it'll grow.'

'You were looking for us?' Jup said.

'No, Sergeant. Well, not exactly. Once we deserted we had hoped to find you but didn't know where to look. Fact is we've just come from Hecklowe. Heard about the uproar there and figured it sounded like your band. Somebody told us you'd been seen riding west, so . . .'

'Why do you say you'd hoped to find us?' Stryke asked.

'Your band's been officially named renegades. There's a bounty on your heads. Big one.'

'We know that.'

'You're being slandered by everybody from Jennesta down. They say you're common outlaws, that you kill your own kind, and that you've stolen some kind of treasure belonging to the queen.'

Stryke's face clouded. 'I'm not surprised. What's your point?'

'Well, some of us reckon we're not being told the truth. You've always had a good reputation, Captain, and we know the way the queen and her lackeys lie about those who've fallen out of favour.'

'For what it's worth,' Coilla informed him, 'they are lying about us.'

'I knew it.' He turned and nodded at his companions. They nodded and smiled back. He went on, 'So we reckoned you might be able to use us.'

That puzzled Stryke. 'What do you mean? Use you for what?'

'We figured that you've got to be mustering an army, a force of disenchanted orcs, like us. Maybe to fight Jennesta. Maybe to found a homeland. We want to join.'

Stryke contemplated their hopeful faces for a moment. He sighed. 'I'm not running a crusade, Corporal, and I'm certainly not looking for recruits. We didn't mean to set out on the path we're following and now we're having to make the best of it.'

Trispeer's face fell. 'But, Captain—'

'It's hard enough being responsible for the lives and fortunes of my band members. I don't want the burden of taking on more.' Softening his tone, he added, 'You'll have to find your own way.'

The corporal looked disappointed. They all did. 'You mean you're not making a stand? You don't want to strike a blow for all us orcs in bondage?'

'We're making a stand of sorts, but in our own way. It's going to take somebody else to strike that blow. You're looking in the wrong place. I'm sorry.'

Trispeer decided to be philosophical. 'Oh, well, perhaps I knew it was too good to be true. But you and your band's starting to be celebrated in the ranks. There'll be others thinking what we thought and wanting to join with you.'

'I'll tell them what I've just told you.'

'I guess we'll have to do something else then.'

Haskeer entered the conversation. 'Like what?'

'Get ourselves to Black Rock forest maybe.'

'To take up a life of banditry?' Coilla guessed.

'What else can we do?' Trispeer replied shamefacedly. 'Apart from mercenary work, and none of us fancy that.'

'That it should come to this for our kind,' she brooded. 'Fucking humans.'

The corporal smiled. 'It's them we'll concentrate on. An orc's got to eat.'

'If that's what you decide, don't go too near Black Rock

itself,' Stryke advised. 'There's kobolds there that aren't too fond of orcs after we had a recent run-in with them.'

'We'll remember that. Anyway, maybe it won't be Black Rock, perhaps we'll just go freelance and fight humans for the hell of it. We'll see.'

'Need anything?' Haskeer asked. 'Not that we got much food or water, but—'

'No, thanks, Sergeant. We're fine for now.'

'Maybe you could use a little of this,' Stryke said. He dug out his pouch of pellucid. With his other hand he patted his jerkin, then drew the proclamation of the Wolverines' renegade status from a pocket. It was all he had that was suitable. Somehow it seemed apt. He folded it to make a rudimentary bag and poured in an ample quantity of the drug. This he handed to the corporal.

'Thanks, Captain, that's generous. Appreciate it.' He beamed. 'You know the old saying: "Crystal gets you through times of no coin better than coin gets you through times of no crystal."'

'Enjoy. Only use it wisely. It's been a mixed blessing for us.'

Trispeer looked mystified by the comment but said nothing.

Stryke stretched out and offered the corporal a warrior's handshake. 'We've got to be moving on to Drogan. Good luck.'

'And to you. The gods be with you in whatever it is you're doing. Watch your backs.'

He and his troopers saluted them, turned their horses and started galloping back more or less the way they had come.

As they watched them go, Coilla said, 'They seemed like decent orcs.'

'I thought so too,' Jup agreed. 'It's a pity we couldn't let them join us. You know, maybe we could use a few more swords.'

Stryke firmly crushed that. 'No. Like I said, I'm carrying enough of a load as it is.'

'If what he said about you is true, Stryke,' Coilla mused, 'you could be a rallying point for—'

'I don't want to be no rallying point.'

Jup grinned and announced melodramatically, 'Stryke messiah!'

His commander just glared at him.

It was night when they arrived for the rendezvous.

Stryke wished he could have been more specific about where they were going to meet. He couldn't, because none of them knew the area well enough. So they had to ride along the treeline bordering the inlet, in the dark, looking for their comrades.

Haskeer, as of old, was the first to complain. 'I think we're wasting our time. Why don't we wait 'til morning?'

This time Coilla was inclined to agree with him. 'There might be something in that. We need light.'

'We were late getting here,' Stryke said. 'Least we can do is try looking for them. We'll give it another hour. But I reckon we're best dismounting.'

That gave Haskeer the opportunity for a bit more grumbling.

Leading their horses, they walked by the undergrowth that spread from the trees. They could hear the flow of water in the inlet, perhaps a hundred feet away.

'Maybe they didn't get here,' Haskeer offered.

'What do you mean by that?' Jup asked.

'They were only half a band. Anything could have happened.'

'*We're* only half a band,' Stryke reminded him, 'and we got here.'

'Could be they went into Drogan to parley with the centaurs,' Coilla suggested.

'We'll see. Now pipe down, all of you. There could be foes as well as friends about.'

They'd trudged in silence for another ten minutes when there was a rustle in the undergrowth. Swords were quietly drawn. A pair of shadowy figures emerged from the bushes.

'Eldo! Noskaa!' Coilla exclaimed.

Greetings were exchanged, weapons resheathed. Then the grunts led them into the thicket and to their camp.

Alfray came forward, beaming, and clasped Coilla's arm. 'Good to see you, Corporal! And Stryke, Jup!'

'I'm here too, you know,' Haskeer rumbled.

Alfray frowned at him. 'Yes, well, you've got some explaining to do.'

'And it'll be done,' Stryke promised. 'Don't be too hard on him. How was your journey here? What's happening? Any developments?'

'Whoa!' Alfray grinned. 'Journey more or less uneventful. Nothing much happening. No developments.'

'Well, we've got a lot to tell *you*,' Jup said.

'Come and eat, and rest. You look like you could use it.'

The band reunited. Grunts hailed each other. There was back-slapping, warriors' grips, laughter and chatter. Food and drink were issued, and they allowed themselves a fire to temper the cold. Sitting round it, they bartered news.

At length they discussed the centaurs.

'We've seen nothing of them,' Alfray reported. 'Mind you, we haven't ventured far into the forest. Thought it best to stick to your advice and just observe.'

'You did right,' Stryke confirmed.

'So how best to handle it?'

'Peaceable approach. We've no argument with centaurs. Anyway, they're going to outnumber us and it's their home ground.'

'Makes sense. Only don't forget that though they're slow to rouse, they can be unforgiving enemies.'

'That's why we'll go in under a flag of truce and offer a trade.'

'And if they won't treat, what then?' Haskeer said.

'Then we'll think about other ways. If that means hostile action, well, it's what we're trained for. But diplomacy first.' He gave his sergeant a pointed look. 'And I won't tolerate anybody in this band not toeing that line. We only fight if I say so, or if we're attacked out of hand.'

With the exception of Haskeer, who said nothing, there was general agreement with that.

Alfray stretched his hands to the modest fire. Like everybody else, his breath was visibly misting. 'This damn cold isn't getting any less,' he complained.

Stryke pulled closer his jerkin and nodded. 'We could be better kitted out than this standard issue.'

'We saw a small herd of lembarrs this morning. I was thinking of bagging a few for furs. They're still quite plentiful in these parts, so we could cull a few without doing too much harm.'

'Good idea. Fresh meat too. Going into the forest at this hour isn't wise; it could look like a raid. Let's rise early, do some hunting, then get ourselves to Drogan.'

They were up at first light.

Stryke decided to lead the hunting party himself. Jup and Haskeer volunteered to go along. They picked Zoda, Hystykk, Gleadeg, Vobe, Bhose and Orbon to join them. It was a good number; split into two stalking groups it wasn't too many to spook the prey, but enough to carry back the carcasses they'd need.

What they couldn't take were horses. Lembarrs had both an uncanny ability to detect their approach and an aversion to the animals. The best way to put a lembarr to flight was to go anywhere near it on horseback. They had to be hunted on foot.

As they were about to set off, Alfray took Stryke aside. 'I think you should leave the stars with me,' he said.

Stryke was taken aback. 'Why?'

'The more we get, the more precious they are. What if something happens to you on the hunt and they're lost? Matter of fact, maybe we should do something similar to the crystal, like dividing them amongst the officers. Haskeer excepted, of course.'

'Well . . .'

'You think I'm going to do the same as Haskeer and run off with them? With two thirds of the band around me?'

'It's not that I don't trust you, old friend, you know that. But I've been thinking about what might have happened to Haskeer. Thinking about it a lot. Suppose it was an enchantment that made him act that way?'

'Cast by Jennesta, you mean?'

'She's the most likely suspect.'

'Then what's to stop her doing the same to you? If it *was* one of her spells, that's an argument for leaving them here, isn't it? 'Cause the first thing I'd do is issue an order for the others to keep an eye on me, and if I started acting strange they'd hog-tie me. That or cut me down.'

Stryke knew he meant it. 'All right,' he agreed reluctantly. He unclipped the pouch and gave it to him. 'But we're going to have to give some thought to security for the future.'

'Right. Trust me. Now go and get us some winter outfits.'

18

In under an hour they were out on the plain and had sighted their first herd of lembarrs. They resembled small deer, and the males had antlers, but their build was much more robust. Their shaggy, abundant pelts, which were brown in colour and streaked with grey and white, were like bear fur, and almost as prized.

As the animals grazed unawares, the hunters split into two groups. Haskeer led four of the grunts. Their job was to act as beaters and drive the animals toward the second group for the kill. This group consisted of Stryke, Jup and the two remaining troopers.

The hunt started well. With the element of surprise on their side, they swiftly downed three lembarr. After that, the quarry grew more wary and required some determined chasing. They were not exceptionally fleet beasts, and an orc could match their speed on the flat. It was when they got themselves into less certain terrain that the lembarrs' agility gave them an edge.

Stryke found himself working as a backstop, well to the rear of his group, as Haskeer's party stampeded half a dozen of the prey in their direction. Three took off at angles and were lost. Two bowled into Jup and the grunts, who proceeded to lay into them with spears and swords. The last slipped through and came Stryke's way, running fit to burst.

Raising his sword, he made ready to block the animal and finish it. The lembarr wasn't to be caught that easily. When only a couple of feet away it veered and shot past him. Stryke's blade cut air.

'*Mine!*' he yelled and dashed after it.

He wasn't sure if the others heard him, absorbed as they were in slaughter.

The fleeing creature ran into a copse. He crashed in after it, ducking low and swatting branches away. A minute later they were out the other side and on level sward. Stryke began to gain. The lembarr swerved and headed for a series of hillocks. It climbed the first one like a goat, Stryke twenty paces behind. Then it was down into a dip and up the next incline.

It was hard work but Stryke was enjoying it.

He reached the next small plateau just a couple of feet behind his target. The creature went down the other, steeper side half running, half skidding, into a gully below. Stryke slid after it. The lembarr reached the bottom, spun to its right and flashed into some trees. Panting now, Stryke followed. He caught a glimpse of the white streaky fur a spear cast distant. Putting on a burst of speed, he dashed for it.

Then the world fell in on his head.

He went down, a searing pain hammering his temple, and rolled across the mushy leaf carpet. On his back, dizzy and hurting, he started to come out of the black maw that had nearly swallowed him.

Somebody was standing over him. He made that several somebodies as his vision cleared. One of them snatched away the sword he was still holding. They conversed with each other in a clipped, guttural and all too familiar tongue.

The goblins hauled him rudely to his feet. He groaned. They tore at his clothes, searching for other weapons. Satisfied he had none, they brandished maces at him, and one waved the club that had undoubtedly been used to bushwhack him with. They had swords too, and their points jabbed and goaded him into motion. He lifted a hand to his head as he walked. One of the goblins roughly pulled it away and jabbered something he didn't understand. But the threatening tone was unmistakable.

They marched him to the end of the gully and up yet another hillock. His bones ached and he limped a little, yet they allowed no slowing of pace. At the top he looked down the far side and saw a sizeable longhouse. As they urged him to descend he thought that they couldn't have been too far from the rest of the hunting party. Trouble was, the chase had taken some unlikely twists and turns, and they might just as well have been half the land away. He couldn't count on help from that source.

Breathing heavily, he arrived at the building, surrounded by his posse of belligerent captors.

The longhouse could have been built by any one of a dozen races; it had the all-purpose look of a lot of Maras–Dantia's architecture. Simply but sturdily constructed from wood, with a thatched roof, it had a single door at one end. There had been a couple of windows at one time which were now boarded over. The place had obviously been abandoned. It was decrepit. The thatch was badly weathered and wet rot had taken hold on some of the outer facing.

They bundled him through the door.

Razatt-Kheage was waiting for him.

The slaver grimaced hideously in what passed for a smile with goblins. His expression was redolent with triumph and vengeance. 'Greetings, orc,' he hissed.

'Greetings, yourself.' Stryke fought to regain his senses and rid his head of muddle. He defied the pain, pushing it away. 'Couldn't wait to say goodbye properly, eh?'

'We trailed you.'

'You don't say. Not to thank me, I'd guess.'

'Oh, we want to . . . *thank* all of your band, personally. A plan that has the added advantage of money on your heads from Jennesta. And I've now seen a certain proclamation that indicates you have a relic of hers. I expect there'll be a reward for that too.'

Stryke was glad he didn't have the stars on him. He looked to the six or seven goblins present. 'You're going after my warband with this strength? Got a death wish or something?'

'I'm not doing it. I'll send word to Jennesta.'

That sobered Stryke further. 'And you think the band will stick around waiting for her army to get here?'

'As a matter of fact I was thinking of holding you hostage to make sure they do.'

'They won't buy it, slaver. Not my band. You don't know much about orcs, do you?'

'Perhaps it would be amusing to learn something now,' Razatt-Kheage replied mockingly. 'Do feel free.'

It suited Stryke to buy a little time and try to think of a stratagem. 'All orcs know that the cost of war is death. We grow up with the creed that you do your best to save a comrade in danger, but if that fails you don't go on risking everybody else's life for one individual. That's why using me as a hostage won't work. They'll walk away.'

'Yet you did the exact opposite when you rescued your female comrade.' He leered unpleasantly. 'Perhaps some individuals are worth more than others. By which marker, the commander should be worth most of all. We shall see.'

To keep him talking, Stryke changed the subject. 'I don't see your human friends around.'

'Business associates. They have gone their own way. It was a disagreeable parting. They seemed to blame me for being in some way responsible for you orcs escaping. I believe it might have come to *blows* if one of them hadn't been in need of a healer's assistance. Fortunately I was able to sell them a name.'

'I bet they were grateful.' He scanned the lengthy room. 'So what now?'

'You'll be our guest while I draft a message for the Queen's agents.' The slaver nodded at his henchlins.

They herded Stryke to the far end of the room. Like the rest of the hut there wasn't much there, save a brazier of glowing coals that took some of the chill out of the air. He was left near it while the guards conversed in their own tongue. Razatt-Kheage stayed near the door, standing at a rickety table. He had parchment and a quill.

Stryke glanced at the brazier. An insane idea formed. Something that would affect him as well as them, but he'd have the advantage of knowing it. Checking that nobody was watching, he slipped his hand into his belt pouch and scooped out a fistful of pellucid. He tossed it on to the fire. Then he dipped for some more and did it again. The massive quantity of pinkish crystals began discharging plumes of creamy white smoke.

No one noticed anything for a good half-minute as the smoke grew more copious. Stryke tried holding his breath. Then one of the goblins left his comrades and came over. He gawped at the smoking brazier. Stryke sneaked a quick look at the others. They hadn't realised anything was wrong yet. Time to act.

He didn't know very much about goblin biology. But he figured they shared one thing in common with most of the elder races. When he directed a sturdy kick at the goblin's crotch he found he was right. The henchlin emitted a keening squeak of pure agony and began to double up. So Stryke did it again.

The others were moving in. Stryke grasped the wheezing goblin's sword arm and brought it down hard on his upraised knee. The weapon was dislodged. Taking it and flipping his wrist, he drove the blade into the henchlin's back.

He made ready to face the others. They moved in warily, a semicircle of five heavily armed, determined assassins.

'You really do make a habit of this kind of thing, don't you?' Razatt-Kheage raged from behind them. 'Every time you kill one of my servants you cost me coin! I think you'd be safer dead.'

The henchlins levelled their weapons and kept coming. Stryke was still holding his breath.

More and more smoke billowed from the brazier. It began filling the enclosed longhouse. Milky tendrils started drifting across the floor. A thickening cloud formed in the rafters above.

One of the goblins moved in, hefting his mace.

Unable to hold his breath any longer, Stryke expelled it. By instinct he took another. He felt a familiar light-headedness and battled to hang on to his concentration.

Swinging his mace, the goblin charged.

Stryke side-stepped and slashed at him. *The rolling waves of an immense ocean.* He shook his head to clear it of the image. His swing had missed. He aimed another. That was avoided too. The henchlin sent in a blow of his own that came near to connecting with Stryke's shoulder. *A faultlessly blue sky.* Stryke backed off, desperately trying to focus on reality.

What worried him was that the goblin he was fighting didn't seem affected by the crystal. He couldn't tell if the others were or not.

Stryke went on the attack.

When he swung his blade it appeared to him to be many blades, each one birthing the next; a blade for every degree of space it passed through. So that at the end of its arc a shimmering multi-coloured fan hung in the air. The goblin's mace shattered it, imploding the chimera like a soap bubble.

That made Stryke mad. He powered forward, swiping at the henchlin, driving him back under a deluge of blows. As he did so, he thought he saw, through the kaleidoscopic pageant flashing in his mind's eye, that the goblin swayed unsteadily and wore a glassy expression.

Stryke took hold of his sword two-handed, as much to have something to hang on to as anything else, and dashed the mace from his opponent's hands. Then he lunged forward and skewered his chest.

It had never occurred to him before what a fetching colour blood was.

He snapped out of it, taking deep breaths to steady himself. Then realised that was a mistake.

A pair of goblins sleepwalked into view, moving in ponderous slow motion.

Crystalline droplets of rain on the petals of a yellow flower. He squared off with the nearest and engaged his sword. They fenced, though it felt more like wading through the depths of a peat bog. One of Stryke's passes opened his foe's arm, drawing fascinating, luminous crimson. He followed that with a gash to the goblin's stomach that exposed another palate of colours. As the dying henchlin fell for ever, Stryke spun, casually, to face his comrade.

The second goblin had a spear he could have better employed as a walking stick. His legs seemed fit to fold under him as he poked the weapon feebly in Stryke's direction. He struck out at the spear like *a searing bolt of lightning against a velvet blue sky* and succeeded in severing it. The goblin stood stupidly with half a spear in each hand, his pinprick eyes blinking at the wonder of it.

Stryke pierced his heart and revelled in the beautiful scarlet spray.

Riding on horseback through a forest of towering trees. No, that wasn't what he was doing. He focused blearily on the two remaining guards. They wanted to play a strange game with lives as wagers. He'd half forgotten the rules. All he could remember was that the object was to stop them moving. So he set about it.

The first of them, eyes dilated, was practically staggering. He had a sword in his hand and he swung it repeatedly. But mostly not in Stryke's direction. For his part, Stryke returned the swings, though he had to advance a step or two before their blades connected. *Moonlight on a river with trailing weeping willows.* That wasn't it either. He had to keep his mind on the game.

Something dazzling passed in front of his face. Turning, he realised it was the second guard's flailing sword. He thought that was unfriendly. To pay him back, he flashed his own sword towards the goblin's face. It struck deep and soft, inspiring a surprisingly musical wail that faded as the vanquished unhurriedly fell from sight.

That left one henchlin and Razatt-Kheage. The slaver still held back, his mouth twisted and working, disgorging silent words. *A ruined cliff top fortress, white in the sun.* Stryke shook that one off and went for the guard. He took some finding in the pellucid fog.

Once located he bartered blows almost politely. For his part, Stryke stepped up the force and quantity of passes, doing his best to break the other's guard. Though in truth it was a guard that took little breaking. *A waterfall plunging down a granite precipice.* Pushing that back from him, he leapt forward, floating like a feather, and tried carving his initial on the henchlin's chest. Half an S and he was deprived of his canvas. *Verdant meadows, dotted with herds of grazing game.*

Stryke was finding it hard to stay on his feet. But he had to, the game wasn't over yet. There was one more player. He looked around for him. Razatt-Kheage was near the door but making no attempt to leave. Stryke swam toward him through a long, long tunnel filled with honey.

When he finally got there, the goblin hadn't moved. He

couldn't, he was petrified. As Stryke faced him, the slaver went down on his knees, as though curtseying. The mouth was still working and Stryke still couldn't make out the words, or indeed hear a sound except a kind of faint sibilant whining. He supposed the goblin was pleading. That was something players did sometimes. *The sun blazing on an endless beach.* Only this creature wasn't playing. He was refusing to, and it had to be against the rules. Stryke didn't like that.

He drew back his sword. *Walking along an endless beach.* Razatt-Kheage, dirty little rule-breaker, carried on opening and closing his mouth. *Rolling green hills and exalted frosty clouds.*

Stryke's sword travelled home. The slaver's mouth stayed open, wide, in a silent scream. *The smiling face of the female orc of his dreams.*

The sword cleaved Razatt-Kheage's neck. His head leapt from his shoulders, flew upward and back. The body gushed and slumped. Stryke's gaze followed the spiralling head, a dumpy bird without wings, and fancied he saw it laugh.

Then it hit the floor a dozen feet away with a noise like a dropped ripe melon, bounced twice and was still.

Stryke leaned against the wall, exhausted. But elated too. He had done a *good* thing. He moved himself. Coughing and heaving, head full of sights and sounds and smells and music, he tottered to the door. A few seconds' fumbling with the bolts got it open.

He reeled out, wreathed in heady white smoke, and stumbled off into the dazzling landscape.

19

'Drink this,' Alfray said, offering Stryke another cup of steaming green potion.

Head in hands, Stryke groaned, 'Gods, not more.'

'You took in a massive dose of crystal. If you want to clear your system of it, you need this, food, and plenty of water, to make you piss it out.'

Stryke lifted his head and sighed. His eyes were puffy and red. 'All right, give it here.' He accepted the cup, downed the noisome brew in one draft and pulled a face.

'Good.' Alfray took back the cup. Bending to the cauldron over the fire he scooped another ration. 'This one you can sip until the food's ready.' He pushed it into Stryke's hand. 'I'm going to check on the preparations.' He walked off to supervise the grunts loading their horses.

When he was sure Alfray wasn't looking, Stryke turned and poured the cup's contents into the grass.

It had been a couple of hours since he came out of the longhouse. He'd wandered for a while, uncertain of his bearings, before running into the hunting party. They were dragging half a dozen dead lembarrs. Lurching erratically and mouthing gibberish, he had to be practically carried back to camp, where his faltering account of what had happened proved a jaw-dropper.

Now lembarr carcasses roasted on spits, giving off a delicious smell. Appetite sharpened by the pellucid, Stryke's mouth watered in anticipation.

Coilla arrived with two platters of meat and sat beside him. He wolfed his as if starving.

'I'm really grateful, you know,' she said. 'For killing Razatt-Kheage that is. Though I would have preferred doing it myself.'

'My pleasure,' he replied, mouth full.

She stared at him intently. 'Are you *sure* he didn't say anything about where Lekmann and the others might have gone?'

Stryke was still coming down from the crystal. Right now, he didn't want to be nagged. 'I've told you all I know. They've gone.' He was a little testy.

Dissatisfied, Coilla frowned.

'I reckon you won't see them bounty hunters again,' he added placatingly. 'Cowards like that wouldn't tangle with a warband.'

'They owe me a debt, Stryke,' she said. 'I'm going to collect it.'

'I know, and we're going to help any way we can. But we can't go looking for them, not now. If our paths ever cross again—'

'Fuck that. It's time somebody hunted *them*.'

'Don't you think this is getting to be a bit of an obsession?' He chewed as he talked.

'I *want* it to be an obsession! You'd feel the same way if you'd been humiliated and offered for sale like cattle.'

'Yes, I would. Only there's nothing we can do about it at the moment. Let's talk about this later, shall we? My head, you know?'

She nodded, dropped her plate by the fire and walked off.

In the background, several grunts were stitching fur jerkins. There had been just enough pelts to go round.

Stryke was finishing his food when Alfray reported back.

'Well, we're ready for Drogan. Any time you are.'

'I'm fine. Or I will be soon. I wouldn't say my head was exactly *clear*, but the ride will fix it.'

Haskeer came over holding a pile of the fur jackets. Jup drifted after him.

'They ain't exactly refined,' Haskeer opined as he sorted sizes.

'Wouldn't have thought that would have bothered you,' the dwarf remarked.

Haskeer ignored him and started handing out the garments. 'Let's see. Captain.' He tossed a fur. 'Alfray. And here's yours, Jup.' He held it up for them to see. 'Look at the size of that. Like a hatchling's. Wouldn't cover my arse!'

Jup snatched it. 'You should use your head for that. It'd be an improvement.'

Simmering, Haskeer strode off.

Stryke stood, ever so slightly unsteady on his feet, put on the fur jacket and wandered over to Alfray.

'How you feeling?' the corporal asked.

'Not too bad. Don't want to see any more crystal for a while, though.'

Alfray smiled.

'You were right about the stars,' Stryke went on. 'If I'd had them on me—'

'I know. Lucky.'

'I'll take them back now.'

'Given any thought to dividing them?'

'I know it makes sense, but I reckon I'll hang on to them. If I'm going to be parted from the band again, I'll give them to you for safekeeping.'

'You know best, Stryke.' His tone indicated that he didn't agree, but perhaps he thought now wasn't the time to argue. He dug into a pocket and produced the three stars, but didn't return them immediately. He held them in his cupped palm and studied them. 'You know, despite what I said about keeping these, I'm glad to be handing them back. Having them feels like an awesome responsibility.'

Stryke accepted the stars and they were returned to his belt pouch. 'I know what you mean.'

'Strange, isn't it? We feel that way about them yet we still haven't got a clue what they're for. What we going to do, Stryke? I mean, whether we got another star from the centaurs or not?'

'It was always my idea to use them to barter a pardon from Jennesta. But the more I think about it, the more I reckon that's what we *shouldn't* do.'

'Why not?'

'Well, for a start, can you see her honouring her end of any bargain? I can't. More important than that, though, is the power these things seem to have.'

'But we don't know what kind of power it is. That's the point.'

'No. But we've heard enough hints along the way. What Tannar had to say, for instance. And the fact that Jennesta, a sorceress, wants them.'

'So what *do* we do with them?'

'I was thinking along the lines of finding somebody who could help us use them. But for good, not evil. To help orcs and the other elder races. Perhaps to strike a blow against humans, and our own despots.'

'Where would we find somebody like that?'

'We found Mobbs, and he told us about the instrumentalities in the first place.'

'Don't you sometimes wish he hadn't?'

'Things had to change. They *were* changing. Mobbs didn't make us do what we did. He just gave us a reason, albeit a pretty cloudy one. All I'm saying is that maybe we could find someone even more knowledgeable. A magician, an alchemist, whatever.'

'So that's what you think we ought to do? Rather than trading them for our lives with Jennesta?'

'It's an idea, that's all. Think on this, Alfray. Even if we did get Jennesta to deal, and she stuck to it, what kind of a life would we have? Do you honestly think we could just go back to being what we were? Carrying on as if nothing's happened? No, that's over. Those days are gone. In any event, the whole land's going down in flames. Something bigger's needed.' He slapped the pouch. 'Maybe these things are the key to that.'

'Maybe.'

'Let's get to Drogan.'

He gave the order to break camp.

The forest was only two or three hours away, and the route couldn't have been simpler. All they had to do was follow the inlet.

As he hoped, the ride, which they took steadily, helped clear Stryke's still-pounding head. But his mouth seemed permanently dry and he drank copious amounts of water on the way.

He offered the canteen to Coilla, riding next to him at the head of the column. She shook her head. 'I've been talking to Haskeer,' she said, 'or trying to, about what happened when he went off with the stars.'

'And?'

'In most ways he seems like his old self again. Except when it comes to explaining what happened then.'

'I believe him when he says he really doesn't know.'

'I think I do too. Despite the whack over the head he gave

me. But I'm not sure I can ever trust him again, Stryke. Even though he did help rescue me.'

'Can't blame you for that. But I think what happened to him was somehow beyond his control. Hell, we have to believe that about a comrade, and whatever else you can say about Haskeer, he's no traitor.'

'Just about the only thing he said was that the stars sang to him. Then he clammed up, embarrassed. That singing stuff sounds crazy.'

'I don't think he's crazy.'

'Neither do I. So, any idea what he means?'

'No. They're just dead objects far as I'm concerned.'

'Still no idea what they're for?'

He grinned. 'If I did, believe me, I'd have told you. Yelled it. I was talking to Alfray about this earlier. What I didn't say to him was that even if the stars are a blind, useless pieces of wood or something, I'd still have us go after them.'

Coilla gave him a quizzical look.

'No, I'm not crazy either,' he told her, pushing his doubts about the dreams to arm's length. 'I see it like this. If we need anything, we need a purpose. Without one, this band would fall apart quicker than you can spit. It's our military upbringing, I suppose. Even though we're not part of the horde any more we're still orcs and we're still part of the orc nation, scattered and reviled as that might be. I figure we hang together or get hanged apart.'

'I understand. Maybe there's something in the orc nature that craves comradeship. I don't think we're really meant to be lone beings. Anyway, whatever happens, whatever we might or might not have thrown away, you've given us that purpose, Stryke. Even if it all goes murderously wrong any minute, we still had that. We tried.'

Stryke smiled at her. 'Yes, right. We tried.'

They had reached the edge of the forest. It was mature, enormous, dark.

Stryke halted the column. He waved forward Alfray, Jup and Haskeer.

'What's the plan, chief?' Jup asked.

'Like I said before; simple and straightforward. We raise a flag of truce and try to make contact with Keppatawn's clan.'

Alfray began preparing the flag, using the Wolverines' banner spar. 'Suppose there's more than one clan in the forest, Stryke?' he said.

'We'll have to hope they're all friendly with each other and pass us on. Let's go.'

With some apprehension they entered the trees. Alfray held aloft the flag. He was aware, as they all were, that it was universally recognised but not always universally respected.

The interior of the forest was cool and smelt earthy. It wasn't as dark inside as it appeared from without. The silence was near absolute, and that made all of them edgy.

After riding for ten minutes they entered a small clearing.

'Why do I feel I have to whisper?' Coilla whispered.

Alfray looked up at the forest's ceiling far above, where sunlight shafted. 'This place seems almost holy, that's why.'

Jup agreed. 'I reckon the magic's strong here. The water from the inlet, the covering of trees; they both help hold it. This might be one of Maras-Dantia's few remaining untouched oases. Something like the way it once was.'

Haskeer seemed oblivious to all that. 'What do we do, just keep wandering about in here until we find a centaur?'

All around, scores of centaurs appeared from behind trees and crashed out of bushes. Some held long, slim spears. Most had short horn bows, notched and pointing the band's way.

'No,' Coilla replied.

'Take it easy!' Stryke told the band. 'Steady now.'

A centaur came forward. He was young and proud. The hair on the lower, equine, portion of his body was silken brown. He had a fine tail and sturdy hoofs. Above, where his body somewhat resembled that of a human, he had muscular arms and abundant chest hair. He was straight-backed. A curly beard adorned his face.

Several of the band's horses shied.

'You're in clan territory,' the centaur announced. 'What's your business here?'

'Peaceable business,' Stryke assured him.

'Peaceable? You're orcs.'

'And we have a reputation, yes. It tends to go before us. As does yours. But like you, we fight in just cause, and we don't betray a flag of truce.'

'Well said. I am Gelorak.'

'I'm Stryke. This is my warband, the Wolverines.'

The centaur raised an eyebrow. 'Your name's known here. Have you come on your own account or do you act for others?'

'We're here for ourselves.'

The other centaurs still had their bows levelled at the band.

'You're gaining a reputation as an orc who brings trouble with him, Stryke. I ask again, what business have you here?'

'Nothing that brings you trouble. We seek a centaur called Keppatawn.'

'Our chief? You require armaments?'

'No. We want to talk with him on another matter.'

Gelorak studied them thoughtfully. 'It's for him to decide whether he wishes to treat with you. I'll take you to him.' He glanced at Stryke's sword. 'I would not demean you by asking that you surrender your weapons during your stay here. That's not something one should lightly ask of an orc, I think. But you are on your honour not to draw them in anger.'

'Thank you. We appreciate the consideration. Our weapons will not be drawn unless any draw theirs against us. You have my word.'

'Very well. Come.'

He waved a hand. The bows were lowered.

Gelorak led the band deeper into the great forest, the other centaurs close to hand. Eventually they came to a much larger clearing.

There were buildings that resembled stables, along with more conventional thatched, round huts. The largest structure by far looked like an open-fronted barn. It housed an enormous forge. In blasting heat and clouds of smoke, sweating centaurs hammered on anvils and worked bellows. Others used tongs to remove glowing pieces of metal from braziers. They plunged them, hissing and steaming, into barrels of water.

Fowl and pigs ran free. There was a distinct odour of dung in the air, and it wasn't all from the livestock.

Dozens of centaurs, young and old, were going about their chores. Most of them stopped and stared when the Wolverines arrived. Stryke took some comfort from the fact that their reaction seemed born more of curiosity than ill will.

'Wait here,' Gelorak instructed. He cantered off towards the armoury.

'What do you think?' Coilla asked.

'They seem friendly enough,' Stryke judged. 'And they let us keep our weapons. That's a good sign.'

Gelorak re-emerged accompanied by another centaur. He was of middle years and his beard was greying. The powerful, muscular physique that must have marked him out in youth was still in evidence, but it was tempered by a deformity. He was lame. Withered and spindly, his right foreleg dragged as he walked.

'Well met,' Stryke greeted.

'Well met. I am Keppatawn. I'm also a centaur of direct impulses and busy. So you'll forgive me if I'm blunt. What do you want?'

'We have business to discuss with you. A trade that could prove to your advantage.'

'That remains to be seen.' He assessed them, eyes shrewd. His tone lightened. 'But if it's business, that's always best discussed over a meal. Join us for food and drink.'

'Thank you.' Stryke dreaded the idea of anything else to eat, but knew protocol demanded acceptance.

The band was ushered to heavy oak tables placed near the clearing's centre. There were benches on just one side for the orcs' benefit; centaurs stood to eat.

Meat and fish were brought. There was freshly baked bread, dishes of fruit, and baskets brimming with nuts, as befitted forest dwellers. Ale was provided too, along with jugs of heady red wine.

Once they were into the meal, which in Stryke's case meant eating just enough to avoid offence, he toasted their hosts. 'A generous repast.' He raised a flagon. 'We thank you.'

'I've often thought there are few disputes that can't be put right by a good meal and some fine wine,' Keppatawn replied. He drained his own flagon, then belched. It was a demonstration of the centaurs' well-known liking for life's more sensual pleasures, which not uncommonly veered into excess. 'Though I guess it's a little different with you orcs, eh?' he added. 'We tend to ask questions first, preferably while feasting, then fight. It's the other way round with you, isn't it?'

'Not always, Keppatawn. We are capable of reason.'

'Of course you are,' he replied good-naturedly. 'So what is it you want to be reasonable about today?'

'You have an item we'd like to trade for.'

'If you're talking of weapons, you won't find better anywhere in Maras-Dantia.'

'No, not weapons, though in truth yours are renowned.' He lifted his cup and took a drink. 'I'm talking about a relic. We call it a star. You may know it better as an instrumentality.'

The remark silenced the table. Stryke hoped it hadn't put a permanent damper on things.

After a pause, Keppatawn smiled, signalling a resumption of chatter. Though it was at a lower level as all strained to hear. 'We do have the artifact you refer to,' he admitted. 'And you're not the first to travel here hoping for it.'

'There have been others?'

'Over the years, yes.'

'Can I ask who?'

'Oh, a motley bunch. Scholars, soldiers of fortune, those claiming mastery of black sorcery and white, dreamers . . .'

'What was their fate?'

'We killed them.'

The band stiffened a little at hearing that.

'But not us?' Stryke persisted.

'You've come asking, not trying to take. I'm talking about the ones who arrived with ill intent.'

'There were those who didn't?'

'Some. We usually let them live, and of course they left disappointed.'

'Why?'

'Because they couldn't, or wouldn't, meet my terms for bartering what you call the star.'

'What might those terms be?'

'We'll get to that. I have somebody for you to meet.' He turned to Gelorak, standing next to him. 'Bring Hedgestus, and tell him to fetch the relic.' Gelorak downed the last of his wine and trotted off. 'Our shaman,' Keppatawn explained to Stryke. 'He's the instrumentality's keeper.'

In due course, Gelorak came out of a small lodge on the fringe of the clearing with an ancient centaur of unsteady mien. Unlike any of the other clan members the band had seen, he wore several necklaces threaded with what looked like pebbles, or possibly nut shells. For his part, Gelorak carried a small wooden box. Both walked slowly.

After introductions, to which Hedgestus responded

solemnly, Keppatawn ordered the star produced. The ornately carved box was placed on the table and opened.

It held a star that again differed from the others Stryke had. This one was grey, with just two spikes projecting from the central ball.

'Doesn't look like much, does it?' Keppatawn commented.

'No,' Stryke agreed. 'May I?'

The centaur chieftain nodded.

Stryke gently lifted the star from its box. It had occurred to him that it might be a fake. He tried applying some subtle pressure. The thing was absolutely solid, like the others.

Apparently Keppatawn realised what Stryke was doing, but didn't seem to mind. 'It's more than tough, it's indestructible. I've never seen anything like it, and I've worked with every material there is. I tried it in the furnace once. Didn't even scorch it.'

Stryke put the star back.

'Why do you want it?' Keppatawn said.

It was a question Stryke had hoped to avoid. He decided on an outdated answer, figuring that counted as partial truth. 'We're out of Queen Jennesta's horde. We figured we might be able to use this to bargain our way back in.' He added, 'She has a passion for old religious artifacts.'

'Given her reputation as a ruler, that seems a strange ambition.'

'We're orcs and we need a horde. Hers is the only one we fit into.'

Stryke had the distinct impression that Keppatawn didn't believe a word of it. And he feared he might have put a foot wrong by mentioning Jennesta. Everybody knew her character. The centaur could think she was an unsuitable custodian of the star.

So he was surprised when Keppatawn said, 'I don't really care what you want it for. I'd be glad to get rid of the damn thing. It's brought us nothing but ill-luck.' He nodded at the box. 'What do you know of this and its rumoured fellows?'

Stryke latched on to the word rumoured. The centaurs didn't know for a fact that others existed. He made up his mind not to tell them he had any. 'Very little, to be honest,' he replied truthfully.

'That's going to disappoint Hedgestus here. All we know is that they're supposed to have magical powers. But he's been trying to squeeze something out of this one for twenty seasons now without success. I think it's all lembarr shit.'

Keppatawn wasn't offering information, he was asking for it. Stryke was relieved. A little knowledge could have complicated the situation. 'You said you had some kind of terms laid down for trading the star,' he reminded him, 'and nobody's taken them up.'

'Yes. None has even tried.'

'Is it a question of trade? We can offer a large quantity of prime pellucid for—'

'No. What I require in exchange for the star is a deed, not riches. But I doubt you'll be willing to undertake it.'

'What do you want done?'

'Bear with me while I explain. Have you not wondered *where* I got the star from?'

'It had crossed my mind.'

'The star and my lameness I got from Adpar, Queen of the nyadd realm.'

Stryke wasn't alone in being surprised by that. 'We always thought her a myth.'

'Perhaps you were encouraged in that belief by her sister, Jennesta. Adpar's no myth.' His hand went to his spoilt leg. 'She's all too real, as I discovered. She just doesn't leave her domain. And few who enter it uninvited come out again.'

'Would you mind telling us what happened?' Coilla said.

'It's a simple story. Like your race, mine has certain rites of passage. When I was a youth I was vain. I wanted to achieve adulthood with a task no other centaur had dreamed of. So I took myself off to Adpar's palace in search of the star. By sheer blind luck I secured the thing, but I paid for it. I escaped with the star and my life, but barely. Adpar employed a spell that left me as you see me. Now instead of using weapons in the field I'm reduced to making them.'

'I'm sorry for your trouble,' Coilla told him. 'But I for one don't understand what you want us to do.'

'Restoring the full use of my body means more to me than any amount of gems or coin. Or even crystal. It's the only thing I would barter for the star.'

'We're not healers,' Jup reminded him. 'How can we achieve that? Our comrade Alfray here has some curative powers, but—'

'Mending such an injury would be beyond my meagre abilities, I'm afraid,' Alfray put in.

'You misread me,' Keppatawn said. 'I *know* how my condition can be righted.'

Stryke swapped puzzled looks with his officers. 'Then how can we be of help?'

'My hurt was magically inflicted. The only cure is itself magical.'

'We aren't wizards either, Keppatawn.'

'No, my friend; had it been that simple I would have engaged the services of a wizard long since. The only thing that will make me whole again is the application of one of Adpar's tears.'

'What?'

There were general murmurs of disbelief from the orcs.

'You're taking the piss,' Haskeer reckoned.

Stryke glared at him.

Fortunately, Keppatawn didn't take umbrage. 'I wish I was,

Sergeant. But I speak the truth. Adpar herself let it be known that such was the sole remedy.'

The ensuing silence was broken by Coilla. 'I suppose you've thought of offering her a trade? The star for the return of your health.'

'Of course. Her treachery bars that. She would see it as a way of having both the star back and my life. I was only maimed in the first place because she couldn't kill me. Nyadds are a malicious and vengeful race. As we know too well from the raiding parties that occasionally swim up the inlet to the forest.'

'Let's get this straight,' Stryke said. 'We get you one of Adpar's tears and you'll give us the star?'

'On my word.'

'What would it involve, exactly?'

'A journey to her realm, which lies at the point where Scarrock Marsh blends into Mallowtor Islands. That's only a day's ride from here. But there's trouble there. Adpar makes war on her merz neighbours.'

'They're peace loving, aren't they?' Haskeer asked. He used the word peace like a curse.

'With Adpar so close they've had to learn not to be. And there are disputes over food. The ocean is not immune from the disruption wrought on the supply of magic by humans. We have problems with nature's balance ourselves.'

'Where does Adpar's palace lie precisely?' Stryke wanted to know. 'Can you show us on a map?'

'Yes. Though I fear getting there is by far the easiest part of the task. My father once mounted an expedition with the aim of seizing Adpar. He and all his companions were lost. It was a grievous blow to the clans in its time.'

'No disrespect to your father's spirit, but we're used to fighting. We've handled determined opposition before.'

'I don't doubt it. But that wasn't what I meant about the

hardest part. I was wondering how you could induce a stony-hearted bitch like Adpar to produce a tear.'

'The subject's a bit of a mystery to us,' Coilla confessed.

'How so?'

'Orcs don't cry.'

Keppatawn was taken aback. 'I didn't know that. I'm sorry.'

'Because our eyes don't leak?'

'We'll have to think on that aspect of it,' Stryke interrupted. 'But subject to talking this over with my band, we'll give it a go.'

'You *will*?'

'I make no promises, Keppatawn. We'll spy out the land, and if it looks an impossible task we won't go on. Either way, we'd be back to tell you.'

'Possibly,' the centaur remarked in an undertone. 'No slight intended, my friend.'

'None taken. You've made the dangers clear.'

'I suggest you rest here tonight and set out on the morrow. And I couldn't help but notice that your weapons are somewhat less than adequate. We'll re-equip you with the best we have.'

'That's music to an orc's ears,' Stryke replied.

'One more thing.' Keppatawn slipped a hand into a pocket of his leather apron. He brought out a small ceramic phial and handed it to Stryke.

Alfray studied its exquisite decoration. 'Do you mind if I ask where you got this?'

An expression came to Keppatawn's face that could almost be called bashful. 'Another youthful prank,' he admitted.

20

Every time he ventured into what he persisted in thinking of as *out there*, he paid a price. His powers diminished by a small but discernible degree. The ability to properly co-ordinate his thoughts grew poorer.

He hastened his own death.

As he couldn't spend enough time here regenerating between visits, the problem was likely to escalate. Indeed his actions were endangering even here itself.

He dwelt on the very real likelihood that he made no difference by going out. He might even have made things worse, for all that his interventions were light and as limited as he could manage.

On the last occasion he almost brought disaster down on their heads. In trying to do the right thing he came near doing wrong again.

But there was no choice. Events were too advanced. And now even the vessels of his own blood were turning on each other. Only unpredictable fate prevented catastrophe, and what little he might be able to do. Weary as he felt, he had to prepare to go forth once more, in the guise.

He could have wished for death to remove the burden, but for the guilt engendered by knowing he was responsible for so much suffering. And for worse to come.

★

The sombreness of the gathering was only outweighed by its rising sense of panic.

Adpar lay in a dimly lit coral chamber. She had been placed on a seaweed bed, whose healing properties were thought beneficial, through which water was allowed to ebb in the hope that it too might prove rejuvenating. For good measure her body was covered in plump leeches that gorged on her blood in the belief it would thereby be purified.

She was in a delirium. Her lips trembled, and the silent words she mouthed could be made sense of by nobody. When semi-delirious she raged against the gods and, more vehemently, her sibling.

A select group was present, drawn from higher elders, the military's upper ranks and her personal healers.

The chief of all the elders took aside the Head Physician for a whispered conversation.

'Are you any nearer finding the cause of this malady?' he asked.

'No,' the elderly physic admitted. 'All the tests we have tried give no clue. She responds to none of our remedies.' He moved closer, conspiratorially. 'I suspect a magical influence. If it didn't go against all of her Majesty's expressed wishes, when she was able to make them, I would have called in a sorcerer.'

'Dare we disobey and do so anyway? Given that she seems beyond ken of what's happening?'

The healer drew an appraising breath through his scabrous nyadd teeth. 'I know of no manipulator of the magic anywhere near competent enough to deal with this. Not least because she disposed of all the best ones herself. You know how much she dislikes the thought of rivalry.'

'Then can we not summon one from outside the realm?'

'Even if you could find anyone willing to come, there's the question of time.'

'Are you saying she might not survive?'

'I wouldn't care to pronounce on that, to be honest. But we have brought back patients with ailments as grave, though granted we knew what *they* were. I can only—'

'No procrastination, please, healer. The future of the realm is at stake. Will she live?'

He sighed, wetly. 'At the moment she is more likely to pass than stay.' Hurriedly he added, 'Though we are of course making every possible effort to save her.'

The elder looked at the queen's dreadfully pale, sweat-drenched face. 'Can she hear us?'

'I'm not sure.'

They moved back to the bedside. Lesser minions gave them room.

Stooping, the chief elder whispered gently, 'Majesty?' There was no response. He repeated himself in a louder tone. This time she stirred slightly.

The physician delicately applied a damp sponge to her brow. Her colouring took on a paltry improvement.

'Your Majesty,' the elder said again.

Her lips moved and her eyes flickered.

'*Majesty*,' he repeated insistently. 'Majesty, you must try to listen to me.'

She managed a faint groan.

'There is no provision for the succesison, Majesty. It is vital the issue be settled.'

Adpar mumbled weakly.

'There are factions who will vie for the throne. That means chaos unless an heir is appointed.' In truth he knew she had made sure there were no obvious contenders by the simple expedients of murder and exile. 'You must speak, ma'am, and give a name.'

She was definitely trying to speak now, but it didn't carry.

'A name, Majesty. Of who is to rule.'

Her lips moved more tenaciously. He bowed and put his ear close to her face. Whatever she was saying was still unclear. He strained to understand.

Then it became clear. She was repeating a single word, over and over again.

'. . . *me* . . . *me* . . . *me* . . . *me* . . .'

He knew it was hopeless then. Perhaps she wanted to leave chaos. Or perhaps she couldn't believe in her own mortality. Either way the result would be the same.

The elder looked to the others in the chamber. He knew they could see what was coming too.

This was the time when the inexorable process began. They would abandon confidence in the realm and start to think of themselves. As he had.

Stryke was aware that the centaurs didn't think the orcs would come back. He couldn't avoid knowing; they made no secret of it.

They had armed the band with excellent new weapons everybody approved of. Coilla was particularly happy with the set of perfectly balanced throwing knives they'd given her. Among other things, Jup had a handsome battle axe, Alfray a fine sword. Stryke possessed the keenest blade he'd ever known.

Now the band was on its way and out of the centaurs' earshot, doubts had begun to surface.

Haskeer, not surprisingly, was the most forthright with criticisms. 'What crazy scheme have you got us into now?' he grumbled.

'I've told you before, Sergeant, watch your mouth,' Stryke warned. 'If you want nothing to do with it, that's fine. You can head out somewhere else. But I thought you said something about wanting to prove you're worthy to be a member of this band.'

'I meant it. But what good's that if the band's off on a suicide mission?'

'You're pitching it too high, as usual,' Jup told him. 'But what *are* we letting ourselves in for, Stryke?'

'A reconnaissance. And if we see anything we can't handle, we'll go back to Drogan and tell Keppatawn it isn't possible.'

'Then what?' Alfray said.

'We'll try trading again. Maybe offer to undertake some other task. Like finding him a good healer.'

'You know he ain't going to buy it, Captain,' Haskeer reckoned, accurately. 'If we want that damn star so badly we should go back and take it. We're going to end up fighting for it anyway, probably, so why not make use of the surprise element?'

'Because that's not honourable,' Coilla informed him indignantly. 'We said we'd try. That doesn't mean sneaking back and cutting their throats.'

Alfray reinforced the sentiment. 'We gave our word. I hope never to see the day when an orc goes back on an oath.'

'All right, all right,' Haskeer sighed.

They rode by a hill, its grass sickly and yellowing. An orc called out and pointed. They all turned and looked to its summit.

They caught a glimpse of a human on a white horse. He had a long blue cloak.

'Serapheim!' Stryke exclaimed.

'That's him?' Alfray asked.

'Shit, would you believe it?' Jup said.

Coilla was already spurring her horse. 'I want a word with that human!'

They followed her headlong gallop up the hill. Meantime the human went down the other side and out of sight.

When the band got to the top there was no sign of him. Yet there was nowhere near by he could have concealed himself. The terrain was more or less even and they had good visibility in every direction.

'What in the name of the Square is going on?' Coilla wondered.

Haskeer twisted his head from side to side, a palm shading his eyes. 'But how? Where? It's impossible.'

'Can't be impossible, he did it,' Jup told him.

'He's got to be down there somewhere,' Coilla reasoned.

'Leave it,' Stryke ordered. 'I have a feeling we'd just be wasting our time.'

'He's good at running, I'll say that for him,' Haskeer remarked, getting in a last shot.

The start of Scarrock Marsh could be seen from their new vantage point. And beyond it, further west, the ocean with its broken necklace of brooding islands.

It had been too long since Jennesta rode at the head of an army and took personal control of a campaign.

Well, mission really, she conceded, and perhaps not even that, as she had no firm aim beyond a little pillaging and harassment of enemies. And maybe she harboured the hope that her travels might glean some clue as to the whereabouts of the hated Wolverines. Having acted at last in the matter of her too ambitious sister, it had also given her a little more zest for life and the taking of it.

But mostly it was just important to give herself an airing, and it was doing her a power of good.

No more than half a day out from Cairnbarrow, they had good fortune. Forward scouts reported a Uni settlement too new for the maps. It was unknown even to her spies. That was an oversight she would mete out punishments for when she got back. Meanwhile she led her army of orcs and dwarves, ten thousand strong, against the enclave.

If ever the cliché about using a battleaxe to crack a pixie's skull had any truth it was here. The settlement was a flimsy, poorly defended collection of half-built shacks and barns. Its inhabitants, numbering perhaps fifty, counting the children, hadn't even finished building the defensive wall.

She regarded the humans who chose to settle in that particular spot as fools; ignorant farmers and ranchers so lacking in sense that they knew no better than to encroach on her domain.

They compounded their error by trying to surrender. She wished all Unis were as easily defeated.

What followed made for a welcome addition to her magical resources – the hearts of near two score sacrifices, plucked from those she spared in the slaughter. She had only been able to consume a fraction of them, of course, but the abundance gave her the opportunity to test something she had found referred to in the writings of the ancients.

Before setting out on this adventure she had despatched agents to the north, deep into the Hojanger wastelands, to bring back wagonloads of ice and compacted snow. Suitably insulated in barrels swathed with hessian and furs, the cargo survived without melting. She had the organs packed into the barrels with the intention of thawing them as needed on the journey. Naturally there was no substitute for the fresh variety, but they would serve at a pinch.

If it worked, she was thinking of using it as a way of preserving food for her horde in its campaigns.

Jennesta came out of one of the huts, sated for now with torture and other indulgences, and dabbed her bloodied lips with a delicate lace handkerchief. She had surprised even herself with the energy she put into the scenes just enacted. Perhaps the open air had increased her already healthy appetites.

Mersadion didn't seem so content with the situation. He awaited her astride his mount, stiff and sour faced.

'You look less than pleased, General,' she said, wiping gore from her hands. 'Is the victory not to your liking?'

'Of course it is, Majesty,' he hurriedly replied, adopting a smile of patent falseness.

'Then what ails you?'

'My officers report more dissatisfaction in the ranks, ma'am. Not much, but enough to be of concern.'

'I thought you were on top of that, Mersadion,' she told him, her displeasure undisguised. 'Did you not have troublemakers executed, as I ordered?'

'I did, ma'am, several from each regiment. It seems to have fomented further unrest.'

'Then kill some more. What is the nature of today's complaints?'

'It seems some are questioning . . . well, questioning your order to raze this settlement, my lady.'

'*What?*'

He blanched but carried on. 'The feeling, among a very small minority you understand, is that these buildings could be used to house the widows and orphans of orcs who have fallen in your service. Dependants who would otherwise be destitute, ma'am.'

'I *want* them to be destitute! As a warning to the males. A warrior who knows his mate and hatchlings face such a fate should he fail is a better warrior.'

'Yes, ma'am,' Mersadion replied in a subdued tone.

'I'm starting to worry about your ability to keep order, General.' He shrank in his saddle. 'And I think the first thing we're going to have to do once back in Cairnbarrow is purge the ranks of these radicals once and for all.'

'Ma'am.'

'Now get me a brand.'

'Ma'am?'

'A *brand*, for the gods' sake! Do I have to draw you a picture in the dirt?'

'No, Majesty. Right away.' He dropped from his horse and ran towards the jumble of buildings.

As she waited impatiently for his return, she watched a

squadron of her battle dragons soaring overhead, far up near the cloud cover.

Mersadion jogged back holding a wooden torch, its head wrapped in cloth and dipped with tar. He offered it to her.

'*Light* it,' she intoned with dangerous deliberateness.

He fumbled with flints while she silently fumed. At last he got the brand alight.

'Give it here!' she barked, snatching it away. She stood near the door of the building she had so recently defiled. 'This settlement is a hive of Uni pestilence. To do anything less than destroy it sends a weak message. And I'm not in the habit of displaying weakness, General.' She tossed the brand into the hut. Flames immediately began to spread. Screams sounded inside from the few humans she had left alive.

She went to her horse and mounted. He did the same.

'Get the army moving,' she ordererd. 'We'll look for the next nest.'

As they came away she glanced at the settlement. The fire had a hold that wouldn't be broken.

'If you want something done properly, do it yourself,' she informed the general cheerily. 'As my esteemed mother Vermegram used to say.'

21

Scarrock Marsh appeared to have its own weather.

It wasn't that the conditions were different from those on the plains the band had recently left, there just seemed to be *more* of it. The clouds were more lowering, the rain more incessant, the winds more biting. And it was colder. Perhaps that was because the squalls blowing down from the advancing ice sheet in the north were unimpeded. There were no mountains or forests to temper them, and once they arrived they combined with the frigid air generated by the great Norantellia Ocean.

Grateful for their recently acquired furs, the band stood on the edge of the marsh and took in its foreboding countenance.

What stretched before them was a vast, flat quagmire of black mud and sand. Ditches and even small lakes of dark gelatinous water littered the terrain. Here and there, dead, skeletal trees poked out of the barren landscape, indicating that the blight was spreading. The place stank of rotting fish and other, less wholesome, things. There was no sign of life, not even a bird.

From their vantage point, on a slightly higher elevation than the marsh proper, they could see the beginnings of the ocean. It was sluggish and grey. The inky outlines of the Mallowtor islands lay beyond, mist shrouded and desolate. Somewhere out there, beneath the waves, the merz clung on to their precarious existence.

It was a forlorn scene, and one Stryke couldn't help but compare with the glorious seascape of his dreams.

'Right,' Haskeer said, 'we've seen it, I don't like it, let's go back.

'Hold your horses,' Stryke told him. 'We said we'd do a recce.'

'I've seen all I need to know. It's a bloody wasteland.'

'What did you expect?' Jup wondered. 'Dancing maidens throwing rose petals?'

Coilla cut off their impending squabble by asking, 'How are we going to go about this, Stryke?'

'According to Keppatawn, the nyadd realm lies on the far edge of the marsh, fringing the ocean. So a lot of it's submerged.'

'Great,' Haskeer muttered. 'Now we're fish.'

Stryke ignored him. 'But Adpar's palace has access from both land and water sides, apparently. The way I see this mission is going in with the full strength, less whoever we leave with the horses.'

'I hope you're not thinking of assigning me that detail,' Alfray said. His manner was prickly.

It was the age thing again, Stryke guessed. He seemed to be getting more touchy about it. 'Of course not. We need you with us. But like I said, we can't take the horses. Talag, Liffin, that's your job. Sorry, but it's important.'

They nodded glumly. No orc liked being left on a routine duty when there was the prospect of combat.

Jup steered the conversation back to the matter at hand. 'Straight in, you said. No scouting?'

'No. We'll cross the marsh and if conditions look right, we'll go for it. I don't want to spend any more time here than we have to.'

'Now you've said something I agree with,' Haskeer remarked.

'Remember, Keppatawn said there was trouble in Adpar's realm,' Stryke went on. 'That might help us, it might not. But if it looks too hot in there we're coming out without engaging. I figure the existence of this band is more important than a bit of local strife.'

Jup nodded. 'Suits me.'

Stryke looked at the sky. 'Let's go before we get some real rain.' To Talag and Liffin he added, 'Like I said, we don't intend hanging around in there. But to be safe give us until this time tomorrow. If we're not back by then consider yourself free of any obligation to the band. You can sell the horses. That should keep you for a while.'

On that sobering note, they set off.

'Stick together, keep your eyes peeled,' Stryke instructed. 'If anything moves, drop it.'

'Usual procedure, then,' Jup commented.

'Remember, they'll be in their element,' Stryke added. 'They can live in air *and* water. We're strictly air. Got it, Haskeer?'

'Yeah.' A thought hit him. 'Why you telling *me*?'

They moved into the marsh. Like Drogan forest, it was quiet. But it was a different kind of silence. That had been peaceful. This was uneasy, somehow malevolent. Where Drogan promised, this threatened. Again like Drogan, they felt the need to converse in whispers. Though they all knew it was unnecessary; there was nowhere for an enemy to hide.

The going shifted from spongy to oozing. Stryke looked around and saw that Haskeer was walking a little apart from the others. 'Stay together,' he called out. 'Don't get separated. We don't know what this place holds in the way of surprises.'

'Don't worry, chief,' Haskeer replied dismissively, 'I know what I'm doing.'

There was a loud sucking noise. He instantly sank waist deep in a mire.

They rushed over to him. He was still sinking.

'Don't struggle, you'll only make it worse,' Alfray advised.

'Get me out of here!' He went down some more. 'Don't just stand there, *do* something!'

Stryke folded his arms. 'I'm thinking about whether to let it get to your mouth. Might be the only thing to shut it.'

'Come on, Captain!' his sergeant pleaded. 'It's fucking *cold* in here!'

'All right, get him out.'

With some difficulty they hauled him clear. He came out cursing. His kit was filthy. Black tenacious ooze clung to him.

'Phew, I stink!' Haskeer complained, creasing his face.

'Don't worry,' Jup said, 'nobody'll notice.'

'Thank the Square you didn't fall in yourself, shortshanks! Two foot and it would have been over your head!'

Coilla lifted her hand to cover a grin.

'This time let's stick together, shall we?' Stryke suggested.

They resumed the trek with Haskeer grumbling under his breath and his boots squelching.

After an hour of careful footwork they saw a line of irregularly shaped rocks dead ahead. Stryke ordered the band to spread out and watch their step.

On arriving they found the rocks towered over them. Several had cave mouths. In one or two cases, large round holes bored straight through the rocks and the ocean could be seen.

Coilla frowned. 'If this is the beginning of the nyadd realm, shouldn't there be guards?'

'You'd think so,' Stryke agreed. 'Maybe they're further on.'

'So where to?' Alfray said.

'Keppatawn said at least one of these entrances leads where we want to go. Pity he couldn't remember which. Pick a cave.'

Alfray thought about it and pointed. 'That one.'

They approached stealthily and went in. It was just a cave.

'Good thing you didn't have a wager on that, Alfray,' Haskeer ribbed. 'Now what, Styrke?'

'We keep picking them until we get in.'

They had three more tries and drew three more blanks.

'I'm getting sick of caves,' Haskeer told them. 'I feel like a bat.'

Then Coilla chose one that turned out more promising. It went back a long way, and the light from its entrance was barely enough to guide them. But at its end there was a natural archway. They crept to it. The arch opened on to a sloping tunnel, like a slide. There was a green glow at the bottom.

Weapons drawn, they went down fast, ready for trouble.

Instead of waiting nyadds, they found themselves in a grotto. It was damp and echoing. The emerald illumination came from hundreds of pieces of coral–like material that seemed to be growing out of the walls and ceiling.

Alfray studied the slithers of radiant green. 'I don't know what this stuff is, but it's damn useful,' he whispered.

'Right,' Haskeer said. He snapped off a chunk resembling a stalactite and handed it to him.

'Take some more,' Stryke ordered.

Several of the grunts set to dislodging pieces.

There was only one way to go – a narrow tunnel in the far wall. Unlike the grotto, it was unlit, so the makeshift torches came in handy. The band filed into it. Stryke leading.

It turned out to be quite short, and led into a round cave. This had high walls but its top was open to the air. Three more dark tunnels ran from it. Everywhere, water flowed freely, ankle deep.

'Time to play choose again,' Coilla said.

'*Ssshh!*' Alfray had a finger to his lips.

The band froze. They heard a sloshing sound. Something

was approaching along one of the tunnels. They couldn't tell which.

Stryke ushered them back into the shaft they came out of. The glowing brands were concealed. As they watched, two nyadds came out of the centre tunnel. They moved in their race's characteristic undulating fashion, impelled by immensely powerful lower muscles. These were creatures that may well have been more at home, and certainly more graceful, in water, but there was no doubt they had command of land too. On an evolutionary scale they were at equipoise, though whether they were heading for a future of exclusively air or water dwelling was a moot point.

They were armed with their traditional jagged half sword, half spears, fashioned from hardened shale mined in the ocean's depths. Coral daggers were strapped to their shiny carapaces.

Alfray whispered, 'Just the two?'

'I think so. Try to keep one alive. Jup, make sure our rear's guarded.'

At his signal, Alfray, Haskeer and Coilla rushed out with him to engage the nyadds. Three or four grunts backed them.

Taken by surprise, overwhelmed by numbers, the creatures had no realistic chance. Alfray and Haskeer hacked one of them about the head and neck until it fell. Stryke and Coilla took the other, and inflicted wounds that downed it but weren't immediately fatal. It lay heaving like a crushed armoured slug, its blood mingling with the running water.

Stryke knelt. 'The queen,' he demanded. 'Which way to the palace?'

The nyadd took shuddering, rapid breaths and made no reply.

'Where's the queen?' Stryke repeated, his tone more threatening. He used the tip of his sword to back his words.

With an effort, the nyadd lifted an arm and pointed a shaking webbed hand. It indicated the right-hand tunnel.

'The palace?' Stryke persisted. 'That way?'

The nyadd managed to weakly nod its massive head. Then it slumped to a prone position.

'You better not be lying,' Haskeer warned.

'Save it,' Coilla said. 'He's dead.'

Jup and the rest of the band splashed out of their hiding place.

The bodies were left where they fell. Cautiously, the band entered the indicated tunnel, producing the sticks that glowed to light their way.

It proved a longer tunnel than the previous one. But eventually it took them to another area open to the sky. The difference this time was that they were on a ledge. Sweeping down before them was a series of uneven rocky tiers, like piled slabs, that led to a jumble of further passageways and tunnels.

Ahead, and looming high above, was a huge contorted confection of a structure. A bizarre fusion of nature and nyadd handiwork, it featured no straight line or untwisted tower. Rock and shell and ocean weeds combined to give the whole a wetly glistening organic aspect.

'Well, we've found it,' Stryke declared.

Jup tugged his sleeve and pointed downward. A dozen tiers below, and far to the left, a commotion was spilling into view. Two groups of nyadds were fighting each other. It was a vicious, no-holds-barred blood match, and even as the band watched several combatants went down.

'Keppatawn was right about there being trouble here,' Coilla said.

'If they've fallen into chaos it's the perfect cover,' Jup added. 'Seems we timed our visit well.'

'But if they've fallen into civil war,' Stryke reasoned, 'maybe Adpar's already dead.'

'If she governed wisely this shouldn't be happening,' Coilla reckoned. 'What kind of a ruler is it who's selfish enough to let her realm die with her?'

'The usual kind, from what I've seen,' Jup told her. 'And she's Jennesta's sister, remember. Maybe it runs in the family.'

Stryke indicated a wide carved passageway, directly ahead and below, that seemed to approach the palace. 'Right, let's go.'

Keeping low, lest they be seen by the fighting parties, the band quickly moved down the rocky tiers to the passage. They got to it, and into it, without incident. Once inside it was a different story.

About twenty paces in the tunnel took a sharp turn. Before they reached it, five nyadds came around the corner. Four were armed, and they seemed to be escorting the fifth, who bore no weapons. But he didn't look like a prisoner.

Mutual surprise was soon overcome. The nyadds levelled their weapons and moved in.

Coilla put one out of the picture instantly with a well-aimed knife lob. Conscious of the creatures' tough shells, she aimed for the head. Her blade penetrated its eye.

The rest were tackled at close quarters, and again the orcs' superiority of numbers swayed it.

Haskeer, hefting his sword two-handed, simply bludgeoned his hapless foe into oblivion. Alfray and Jup, working together, slashed at their opponent with determined efficiency. He went down with a multiplicity of wounds. Several grunts overwhelmed and killed the remaining warrior.

Coilla made sure she retrieved her knife. It was the best blade she'd ever owned.

That left just the unarmed nyadd. He cowered. 'I'm an elder! Non-military! Spare me! *Spare me!*' he pleaded.

'Where's Adpar?' Stryke demanded.

'What?'

'You want to live, take us to her.'

'I don't—'

Haskeer put a blade to his throat.

'All right, all right,' the elder blurted. 'I'll take you.'

'No tricks,' Jup warned him.

He took them through a maze of stony, lichen-covered passages. Like everywhere else they'd seen in the nyadds' land, they waded through inches of water all the way.

At length they arrived at a broad corridor illuminated by slivers of the glowing rock. A pair of great doors stood at its end, guarded by two warriors. The band gave them little time to react, piling into them as a mob and cutting them to pieces. One ended the encounter with his head near completely severed.

Several grunts dragged the corpses out of sight. The terrified nyadd elder was brought forward.

'Is there anybody in there apart from her?' Stryke asked.

'I don't know. A healer, perhaps. Our realm is in confusion. Rival factions are at each other's throats. For all I know the queen may already be dead.'

'Damn!' Jup exclaimed.

The elder looked puzzled. 'You mean that you're not here to kill her?'

'What we're here for is too complicated to explain,' Alfray told him. 'But your queen still being alive is pretty important to it.'

Stryke nodded and with caution they tried the doors. They weren't locked. Throwing them open, the band tumbled in.

There was no one in the private chamber except the queen herself, spread out on her bed of swaying green tendrils. Everybody splashed over to her.

'Gods,' Coilla murmured on seeing the queen's face. 'The resemblance to Jennesta's uncanny.'

'Yes,' Alfray agreed. 'A bit sobering, eh?'

'And they left her alone at the end,' Jup said.

'Says a lot about what they thought of her, doesn't it?' Coilla replied.

'The point is, is she still alive?' Stryke wanted to know.

Alfray checked. 'Just.'

The elder, forgotten, sneaked to the door. He got through it and sped along the corridor yelling, '*Guards! Guards!*'

'Shit,' Stryke said.

'Leave it to me,' Coilla snapped.

She flew to the doorway, plucking a knife. Back went her arm. The missile struck the fleeing elder in the back of the neck. He twisted and fell, displacing gouts of water.

'Said they were good blades,' Coilla remarked.

Stryke assigned a couple of grunts to watch the door and they returned their attention to Adpar.

'We've been lucky so far,' he told them. 'It won't last. Do you reckon she can hear us, Alfray?'

'Difficult to say. She's pretty far gone.'

Stryke leaned into her. 'Adpar. *Adpar!* Hear me. You are dying.'

Her head moved slightly on its emerald pillow.

'Hear me, Adpar. You are dying, and your sister, Jennesta, is responsible.'

The queen's lips began to move. She grew more agitated, albeit weakly.

'Hear me, nyadd queen. Your own sister did this to you. Jennesta was the one. *Jennesta.*'

There was some fluttering of eyelids and quivering of lips. Her gills pulsated a little. Otherwise there was no reaction.

'It's hopeless,' Coilla sighed.

Haskeer weighed in with, 'Yeah, face it, Stryke, it ain't going to work. There's no use just standing here repeating Jennesta, Jennesta, Jennesta.'

Stryke was crestfallen. He began to turn away from the deathbed. 'I just thought—'

'Wait' Jup exclaimed. 'Look!'

Adpar's eyelids were flickering, blinking almost.

'It started when Haskeer repeated Jennesta's name,' Jup reported.

As they watched, the lashes of Adpar's eyes moistened. Then a single tear appeared and ran a little way down her cheek.

'Quickly!' Alfray urged. 'The phial!'

Stryke got out the tiny container and tried laying it against Adpar's flesh. His hands were clumsy.

'Here,' Coilla said, taking the phial. 'This needs a female's touch.'

Very carefully, she got the neck of the little bottle under the tear and gently compressed the cheek. The tear rolled and was caught. Coilla replaced the stopper and handed it to Stryke.

'Ironic, isn't it?' she said. 'I'll bet she never shed a single tear in her whole life for the suffering she inflicted on others. It took self-pity to do it.'

Stryke studied the phial. 'You know, I never thought we'd do this.'

'*Now* he tells us,' Haskeer grumbled.

'And the gods were with us,' Alfray announced, lowering Adpar's wrist. 'She's dead.'

'Fitting that her last act should be the healing of one of her victims,' Stryke judged.

'All we have to do now is get out of here,' Jup said.

22

Jennesta was in the middle of a strategy meeting with Mersadion when it happened.

Reality reconfigured itself, became pliant. Changed. She had something like a vision, only it wasn't precisely that. It was more an overwhelming impression of *knowing*, a certainty that an event of great importance had taken place. And parallel with the knowledge came another thing, a distinct and vivid message, for want of a better word, that she found equally exciting.

Jennesta had never before experienced anything like the sensation that possessed her. She supposed it resulted from the intimate telepathic link she involuntarily shared with her sibling. *Had* shared, she corrected herself. Adpar was dead. Jennesta knew that without a doubt. And it wasn't all she now knew.

She hadn't realised that her eyes were closed, nor that she had reached out for the back of a chair to steady herself. Her head began to clear. She straightened and took some deep breaths.

Mersadion was staring at her, a look of alarm on his face. 'Are you . . . all right, Majesty?' he ventured.

She blinked at him, uncomprehending for a moment, then gathered herself. 'All right? Yes, I'm all right. In fact I've rarely felt better. I've had some news.'

He couldn't see how she could have. She had simply stopped mid flow and looked set to faint. No messenger had arrived, no notes had been passed into the tent. He snapped out of gaping at her and said, 'Good news, I trust.'

'Indeed. A cause for rejoicing. In more ways than one.' Her somewhat dreamy, detached manner melted away. In a determined tone nearer the style he was used to, she snapped, 'Bring me a map of the western region.'

'Ma'am.' He hurried to comply.

They laid the map on the table and she circled one of her bizarrely long fingernails around an area embracing Drogan and Scarrock Marsh. 'There,' she announced.

He was puzzled, again. 'There . . . *what*, Majesty?'

'The Wolverines. They're to be found in this vicinity.'

'Begging your pardon, ma'am, but how do you know that?'

She smiled. It was triumphant and cold. 'You'll just have to take my word for it, General. But that's where they are. Or at least one of them – their leader, Stryke. We're moving as soon as you can organise the army. Which is to say in no more than two hours.'

'Two hours is very tight, Majesty, for a force of this size.'

'Don't *argue* with me, Mersadion,' she seethed. 'Timing is vital. This is the first solid lead we've had to that damned warband's whereabouts. I'm not throwing it away because of your sloth. Now get out there and set things in train!'

'Majesty!' He made for the tent flap.

'And send Glozellan in right away,' she added.

The Dragon Dam appeared a few minutes later. Without preamble, Jennesta beckoned her to the map. 'I have intelligence that the Wolverines are here somewhere. You'll take a squadron of dragons and go ahead of the army. Scan the area for them. But *don't* attack unless you absolutely have to. Corner them if you must, but I want them intact when we get there.'

'Yes, your Majesty.'

'Well don't just stand there! Move yourself!'

The haughty brownie gave a tiny bow and slipped from the tent.

Jennesta began gathering what she needed for the journey. For the first time in weeks she felt positive about the turn of events. And she was rid of Adpar, which came like a great weight lifted.

Then it seemed to her that the air in the tent grew somehow more . . . pliable. And the light was dimming, despite the lamps. She thought it must be the return of what she had undergone earlier, and wondered what else the cosmos might have to convey.

But she was wrong. In almost total and unaccountable darkness now, she saw a pinprick of light wink into existence a couple of feet away. It was quickly joined by scores of others. They swirled and took on a more robust form. Jennesta made ready to defend herself against an attack of sorcery.

A blotch of pulsing light hovered in the air. It coalesced and became something she could recognise. A face.

'Sanara!' she exclaimed. 'How the hell did you do that?'

'It seems my abilities have grown stronger,' her surviving sibling explained. *'But that isn't the point.'*

'What is?'

'Your wickedness.'

'Oh. You too, eh?'

'How could you do it, Jennesta? How could you subject our sister to such a fate?'

'You always thought her as . . .' she struggled for a word '. . . as *reprehensible* as me! Why change your tune now?'

'I never thought her beyond redemption. I didn't wish her death.'

'Of course, you're assuming I had anything to do with it.'

'Oh, come on, Jennesta.'

'Well, what if I did?' she replied defensively. 'She deserved it.'

'What you've done is not only evil, it adds complexity to a situation already fraught with uncertainty.'

'What the hell does that mean?'

'This game you're playing, with the relics. The bid for even greater destructive power. There are other players now, sister, and their abilities may well outstrip your own.'

'Who? What are you talking about?'

'Repent. While there is still time.'

'Answer me, Sanara! Don't palm me off with platitudes! Who have I to fear?'

'In the end, only yourself.'

'Tell me!'

'They say that when the barbarians are at the gate, civilisation is as good as dead. Don't be a barbarian, Jennesta. Make good your ways, redeem your life.'

'You're so *bloody* strait-laced!' Jennesta raged. 'Not to mention obscure! Explain yourself!'

'I think you know what I mean, in your heart. Don't think what you have done to Adpar will go unrecorded, or unpunished.'

The likeness of her face faded and disappeared, despite Jennesta's ravings.

In another tent, not too far away in Maras-Dentian terms, a father and daughter conversed.

'You promised me, Daddy,' Mercy Hobrow whined. 'You said I'd have the benefit.'

'And you will, poppet, you will. I said I'd get back the heritage for you and I meant it. We're working on where those savages might be right now.'

She pouted grotesquely. 'Will it be long?'

'No, not long now. And soon I'll make you a queen. You'll

be a handmaiden of our Lord, and together we'll cleanse this land of the sub-humans.' He stood. 'Now dry your tears. I need to attend to this very business.' He planted a kiss on her cheek and went out of the tent.

Kimball Hobrow walked a couple of yards to the fire and the group of custodians. The bodies of three orcs had been laid to one side. The fourth, still alive but only just, had now been finished with.

Hobrow nodded to the Inquisitor. 'Well?'

'They're tough. But this one broke at the last, praise the Lord.'

'And?'

'They've gone to Drogan.'

The death rattle sounded in Corporal Trispeer's throat and he died.

The growing chaos aided the band in getting out of Adpar's palace. They took some wrong turns in the labyrinth of passages, and had a skirmish or two with warriors encountered, but generally the populace were too busy fighting their own battles.

But the exit they found was nowhere near the way they came in.

'Looks like we've come out further north,' Stryke reckoned.

'What do we do, go back in and try again?' Jup said.

'No, it's too much of a risk.' He pointed. 'If we can cross that stretch of water yonder, then veer east, we should reach the marsh near where we left the horses.'

Coilla frowned. 'Hell of a diversion, isn't it?'

'I reckon going back into the palace is more chancy. One of those factions is going to come out on top any time soon. Then they'll notice interlopers.'

'Let's get started, shall we?' Alfray suggested. 'We're too exposed here.'

They traversed a spread of jagged rocks at double time, reached a flat and faced the water. It was covered in green scum.

'Smells about as pleasant as everything else here,' Haskeer observed. 'How deep do you think it is, Stryke?'

'Only one way to find out.' He eased himself in. It was cold, but his feet touched the bottom at waist-height. 'Going's a bit soft, but it seems all right otherwise. Come on.'

They followed him, weapons held high, and began wading.

'We should get extra pay for this,' Haskeer moaned.

'*Extra?*' Jup said. 'Hell, Sergeant, we don't get *any* at the moment.'

'Yeah! I'd forgotten that!'

They carried on for another ten minutes. It looked as if they were going to make it. The marshy shore was in sight.

Then there was turbulence in the water a few yards ahead. Bubbles reached the surface and burst. The band stopped.

More mini whirlpools appeared in other places. More bubbles drifted up.

'Maybe this wasn't such a good idea after all,' Jup muttered.

A plume of water erupted. Dead ahead, a nyadd appeared.

In short order more emerged from the fetid liquid clutching their saw-toothed weapons.

'Remember what you said about fighting them in their own element, Stryke?' Coilla reminded him.

'It's too late to turn back now, Corporal.'

Splashes from behind had them turning. More nyadds were coming up. They began moving in, front and behind.

'Let's carve some flesh,' Stryke growled.

The back half of the band took up a rearguard action, led by Jup and Haskeer. Stryke, Coilla and Alfray were in the vanguard of the coming fight. As it stood, the band out-numbered the nyadds they faced. But Stryke reckoned fighting in water at least evened the odds.

He augmented his swords with a knife and lashed out at the foremost creature. His sword struck the creature's crusty shell and did some damage. Blood trickled. But the wound wasn't sufficient to put the warrior out of the fight. Stryke gritted his teeth and went in again, this time aided by a couple of grunts harrying the nyadd from either side. They succeeded in battering it into a dive.

Coilla proceeded to toss throwing knives at the enemy's heads. But every shot meant a lost blade and her supply was limited. She spent two knives to no good effect, then her next shot connected with the side of her target's head. The nyadd bellowed and disappeared beneath the water, leaving a widening cloud of red.

A triumphant roar from behind marked their first confirmed kill.

'We're thinning their ranks,' Stryke yelled, 'but not fast enough. If more come—!'

He broke off as a nyadd propelled itself towards him waving its jagged spear. The warrior swiped at him. Stryke ducked, and in doing so took himself below the surface. The cold, foul water covered his head. He counted to three, hoping that meant the swing had passed, and resurfaced.

The nyadd was practically on top of him. Stryke rammed his sword into its belly with all his might. The carapace crunched and shattered. Blood flowed. Another great gout issued from the creature's mouth and it disappeared beneath the water. Stryke coughed up a lungful of the putrid stuff.

Haskeer and Jup were hacking at a foe from both sides. They'd already torn open one of its arms, and it was fighting to keep them off.

Wading in, Haskeer aimed a heavy blow at the creature's neck. The nyadd moved down, instinctively seeking the protection of water. It would have done better going in any other direction. The blade cleaved its head, spilling brains.

That left just four nyadds, and though they looked no less murderous, Stryke was confident they could be overcome. The whole band went for three of them.

Except Coilla, who splashed forward to engage the remaining one, which lurked apart. She didn't see another emerge from the water on her blind side, moving with remarkable speed. She spun at the last minute, two nyadds to deal with. One raised its sword.

Kestix had noticed. '*Look out, Corporal!*' he yelled, propelling himself in her direction.

He got between her and the second nyadd's swinging blade. If he hoped to deflect it with his own sword, he miscalculated.

The nyadd's wickedly sharp weapon cut into his chest as if into butter. There was an explosion of gore. Kestix cried out in agony.

'*No!*' Coilla screamed. Then she had to pay heed to the other raider, bringing up her own sword to block his.

Kestix, still alive but grievously wounded, had been grabbed by his assailant. He struggled feebly. His cries had been heard by the others. Several, including Stryke, answered the call.

They got there just in time to see him dragged under water by the submerging nyadd. Only a bloody stain was left behind.

A couple of grunts splashed around, ducking their heads under trying to save their comrade.

'Leave it!' Stryke ordered. 'It's too late for him.'

They turned their grief-driven fury on the remaining nyadds.

Near defeating them, they noticed fresh turbulence and bubbles breaking out all around.

'Shit, chief,' Jup panted, 'we can't take much more of this!'

The band braced themselves for a last stand.

More heads began appearing.

But they weren't nyadds. They were Merz. Dozens of them, armed with trident spears and daggers.

'Gods!' Alfray exclaimed. 'Are they out for us too?'

'I don't think so,' Stryke replied.

His judgement proved true. The merz set about the few nyadds still present, tearing into them with savagery born of injustice.

One of the merz turned and raised a dripping hand to the orcs. It was a salute.

Stryke wasn't alone in returning it.

'We owe them one,' he told his comrades. 'Now let's get out of here.'

They left the slaughter and made their way to the bank, mourning Kestix.

23

The journey back to Liffin and Talag was a sombre affair. Things were no less dismal on the return journey to Drogan, despite their victory.

'Is any of this worth one orc's life?' Alfray wondered. 'Let alone one as valiant as Kestix?'

'Risking our lives is what we do,' Stryke reminded him. 'And orcs have died for less good causes.'

'You're really sure this *is* a good cause? Gathering together a bunch of objects we don't know the purpose of for some end we can't see?'

'We have to believe that, Alfray. And I'm sure the day will come when we'll toast Kestix, and the others who have fallen, as heroes of a new order. But don't ask me what that might be. I just feel it has to be better.' Stryke wished he entirely believed that himself. As it was he was trying not to show the crushing sense of responsibility he felt at their comrade's death.

For his part, Alfray fell silent and stared up at the band's war banner he was clutching. He seemed to draw some kind of comfort from it, perhaps musing on the unity it represented. Or that which it once did.

They were almost within sight of Drogan Forest when Jup called out, 'Eyes west!'

A large party of riders was heading their way, and they weren't far off.

'I think they're Hobrow's men,' the dwarf reported.

'Don't we ever get any peace?' Coilla complained.

'Not today, by the looks of it,' Stryke replied. 'Burn leather.'

They broke into a gallop.

'They've seen us!' Haskeer yelled. 'And they're putting on a hell of a spurt!'

A chase began in earnest. The band rode at breakneck speed for the sanctuary of the forest. But the custodians were determined and gaining.

Urging the Wolverines onward, Stryke found himself at the back of their onward rush. Then disaster struck. As the rest of the band rounded a bend and disappeared from sight, his horse caught its hoof in a rabbit hole and went down. Stryke was thrown clear. As he scrambled to his feet the horse rose and bolted.

The thunder of other hoofs had him spinning around.

A charging mob of custodians was bearing down on him. Stryke looked around desperately for cover. None presented itself. He drew his sword.

A great shadow covered him.

Just above, a dragon hovered, the beat of its mighty wings throwing up dust and leaves. The custodians, terrified, pulled up to a skidding halt. Several of them tumbled from their saddles at the violence of their halt.

For his part, Stryke was sure he was finished. It was one of Jennesta's war dragons, he was sure of that, and he expected nothing but incineration.

The dragon sank down between him and the human posse. When it was near level he saw that the handler was Glozellan herself.

She extended a hand. 'Get on, Stryke,' she urged. 'Come on! What have you to lose?'

He climbed the beast's scaly hide and sat behind her.

'Hold tight!' she shouted and they were away.

The climb was fast and dizzying. Stryke looked down. He saw silvery snaking rivers, green pastures, burgeoning forests. From up here it didn't look like a land raped.

He tried shouting questions at Glozellan over the wind's rush, but she either couldn't hear or ignored him. They flew north.

Perhaps an hour elapsed. They approached a mountain. Unerringly, the dragon made for its plateau. Minutes later they touched down.

'Get off,' the brownie ordered.

He slid to the ground.

'What's happening, Glozellan?' he asked. 'Am I a prisoner?'

'I can't explain now. You'll be safe here.'

She stuck her heels into the dragon's flanks. It began rising again.

'Wait!' he cried. 'Don't leave me here!'

'I'll be back!' she called. 'Have courage.'

He watched until the dragon became a dot, then disappeared altogether.

He sat for hours on his involuntary mountaintop retreat, brooding over events, regretting lives lost.

Having established that there was no possible way down, he took out the stars and contemplated them.

'Well met.'

He leapt up at the sound of the voice.

Serapheim stood before him.

Stryke was confounded. 'How did you get here? Were you another of Glozellan's passengers?'

'No, my friend. How I got here isn't important. But I

wanted to apologise for leading you into that trap set by the goblin slavers. It was not my intention.'

'It turned out right in the end. I have no hard feelings towards you.'

'I'm glad.'

Stryke sighed. 'Not that any of it matters much. Things seem to be falling apart faster than I can cope with. And now I've lost my band.'

'Not lost, merely mislaid.' He smiled. 'The important thing is that you do not despair. There is still much for you to do. Now is not the time to surrender to defeatism. Have you ever heard the story of the boy and the sabre leopards?'

Now it was Stryke's turn to smile, albeit a little cynically. 'A story. Well, I suppose it's as good a way of passing the time as any.'

'There was once a boy walking in the forest,' Serapheim began, 'when he came across a savage sabre leopard. The leopard saw the boy. The boy ran with the leopard in hot pursuit. Then the boy came to the edge of a cliff. There were vines trailing over the edge, so he lowered himself down them, leaving the beast growling impotently above. But then the boy looked down and saw another, equally hungry leopard below, waiting for him. He could neither go up nor go down. Next thing, the boy heard a scratching sound. He glanced up and saw two small mice, one white and one black, chewing through the vine he was holding on to. But he saw something else. Off to one side, almost out of reach, a wild strawberry was growing. Stretching as far as he could, the boy plucked the stawberry and popped it into his mouth. And do you know something, Stryke? It was the sweetest, most delicious thing he'd ever tasted.'

'You know, I think I almost understand that. It reminds me of the sort of thing someone I know might have said . . . in a dream.'

'Dreams are good. You should pay heed to them. You know, the magic energy flows a bit stronger in these parts. It could have some effect on those.' He nodded at the stars in Stryke's hand.

'There's a connection?'

'Oh, yes.' Serapheim paused. 'Will you give them to me?'

Stryke was shocked. 'Like hell I will.'

'There was a time when I could have taken them from you, with ease. And when I would have been inclined to do so. But now it seems the gods want you to have them.'

Stryke glanced down at them. When he looked up again the human had gone. Impossibly.

He would have wondered at it, but now something else had claimed his awe.

The stars were singing to him.